THE COMPLETE CASES OF
JOHN WADE, VOLUME 1

THE COMPLETE CASES OF

JOHN WADE™

VOLUME 1

WILLIAM R. COX

ILLUSTRATIONS BY

JOHN FLEMING GOULD

POPULAR PUBLICATIONS • 2024

TABLE OF CONTENTS

A BOOM IN BLOOD

JOHN WADE WAS THE MOST POWERFUL, RESOURCEFUL CON-MAN IN THE BUSINESS, AND RICKEY BOLES, HIS BOWER, WAS THE ONLY HONEST KILLER IN CRIMEDOM. IT WAS INEVITABLE THAT THE STATE'S CHIEF EXECUTIVE SHOULD DEAL WITH JOHN—IN BLOOD.... A STORY YOU WILL NEVER FORGET!

CHAPTER ONE
EXPENSIVE HEAT

JOHN WADE sat in the rear room of the gin-mill known as Pete's Place. It was a small room with a back door. He sat where he could watch both the entrance into the bar and that portal of retreat which led to alleys and fences.

He was a tall man, slim and too well-dressed for fence-hopping. His creases were impeccable. He was a man of creases, in a manner of speaking.

He had a creased face. It was crisscrossed with lines; laughing lines, squinting lines, lines that had been etched by the vicissitudes of thirty-seven years of living.

There was no speck of dust upon his dark double-breasted jacket and the lines of his English-draped trousers were smart. His carefully arranged cravat was in excellent taste. Even his Homburg hat was carelessly dented in perfect style.

His eyes were narrow and wide-spaced and intelligent. About him, blending with his air of quiet elegance was an aura of confidence.

Yet he had no right in Pete's Place. He had no right being abroad in Midburg. He was hot. The police were supposed at that moment to be searching high and low for him.

Pete, who had one eye, sported a handle-bar moustache and seemed to be carrying a small watermelon under his apron, came into the back room and said, "That man's here."

"I suppose he would be," said John Wade. "Okay, Pete."

The man came in. He was a short, stout man with a carnation in his button-hole and a red, bulbous nose to match. His pig eyes were avid, buttony. He had loose lips and a big mouth. His name was Aloysius P. Perryman, He bore a bottle of Scotch and glasses.

He said loudly, "Hiya, Wade? Shouldn't be here. Should be up in Attersbee's place. Wouldn't cost you much. Attersbee's a pal of mine. Have a drink, Wade?"

John had no choice in his method of
procedure. He aimed the revolver and
squeezed carefully on the trigger.

He plumped into a chair across the deal table and
poured two big drinks. Wade swirled his in the glass without touching it. The stout man tossed his off and gulped
noisily at his chaser. He went on, "However, the heat is
practically off. You gimme five grand and that ends it, pal."

Wade said slowly, "Five gees, huh? That's a hell of a lot
of money, Perryman."

The stout man took another drink and smacked his lips.
He said sententiously, "You oughta be more careful, Wade.
That Simon, that guy you shook down, is a cousin. He is
Yarnell's wife's cousin. You can't con the relative of the
prosecutor, Wade. That ain't kosher."

Wade shrugged. He said, "I can't keep track of the suckers' families. Simon went in for wire-tappin'. He's a crook himself. They all are. I've never fleeced an honest man yet. I don't believe there is an honest man."

Perryman said reprovingly, "Now, Wade! You shouldn't talk like that. You know there are honest men. They dig ditches and drive trucks and clerk in banks." The fat man roared with laughter. He said, "Five grand, Wade. That's nothin' to a big time con guy like you. Five gees to little Al and you're free as the air." He took another drink.

Wade waited until it was well distributed in his ample innards and sipped his own glass. Then he said, "Perryman, you got a swell in. You fix this and you fix that. Since you've been disbarred you never missed a meal. How do you do it?"

The stout man closed one small eye. He said, "Wouldn't you like to know? Mebbe I know where the bodies are hidden, huh, pal? Mebbe I got a closet full of skeletons."

"And you live?" asked Wade quietly. "You walk around and shoot off your mouth and stay alive?"

Perryman leaned forward. The liquor, Wade saw, was getting him. Of late the liquor had been getting Perryman pretty often.

"Lissen, pal," said Perryman, "they ain't bumpin' Al Perryman, see? Here's one guy too big to bump. I know too much, see? I handled things you wouldn't believe, pal. When I was—before they framed me outa the law business I did jobs for biggies, get it? And if they ever make a break, there's stuff in my safe deposit box with the right address on it. The Feds'll get my evidence if they bump me. No local hot shot's gonna cover it up. Al Perryman is smart and they know it. Don't you forget that, pal."

He took another big slug of the Scotch. He said. "Howz-about that oughday, pal? You gonna lay it on the line? Or you gonna take a rap?"

Wade said musingly, "I take a crook. I take him plenty, I admit it. If it's the right guy, I don't have trouble because I pay off a certain party. It's the wrong man, I got heat on me. So, where the hell does honesty stop and crookedness begin?"

PERRYMAN MADE an expansive gesture. He said, "What the hell diff does it make? A buck is a buck, ain't it? You take what you can get. You're a grifter, a con guy. The law says you can't operate. Me, Al Perryman, I say you can operate in Midburg. But that costs dough. You don't think I get all your five grand, do you, pal?"

He was dejected at the thought. He went on, "Wade, when I was on top I did business direct. I'd have taken three grand from you and been satisfied. But I got—framed. The guys that are in now won't do business direct. I have to split it too many ways."

Wade was suddenly impatient. The new restlessness which had lately kept him sleepless, uneasy, rode him again. He took a packet of green money from his pocket and said, "Here it is. Perryman. Five thousand dollars. Take that heat off me. And do it quick."

The fat man fumbled with the money, not counting it. He put it in his coat pocket and said, "Have a drink on me, pal. The heat is off."

"Not until you phone me the money has passed," said Wade sharply, getting to his feet. His features were keen, satanic, staring down at the pig-eyed man. "I'll expect a call tomorrow morning. Here, on Pete's phone. And don't miss, Perryman."

The fat lawyer said, "Miss? Me? Don't be a sap, pal."

Wade said coldly, "I'm not your pal, Perryman. I wouldn't be a pal to a guy that belches his guts like you've been doing lately. I'd lay off that stuff and go home if I were you. When I came in here I saw Bones Magill, Itzy Schloff and a couple of others outside."

"Those gunsels," scoffed the fat man. "You think I'm afraid of hoods? Me? Al Perryman? They eat outa my hand, pal. They...."

Wade turned impatiently and went out the back door. He put one hand on the five foot fence and vaulted. He came down on the other side in perfect gymnasium form, landing on the balls of his feet. He went out the alley to the street in back of Pete's Place.

A car cruised along the curb and a horn mooed softly. The door swung open. Wade caught it in motion, leaped into the front seat, pulling the heavy door shut behind him.

The man at the wheel said succinctly, "You catch?"

"He came," said Wade shortly.

The man at the wheel sighed gustily. He was a giant of a man. He bulged in his clothes. He had a hooked, crooked nose and scarred eyebrows. He looked like an ex-prize-fighter.

But Rickey Boles wasn't an ex-ringman. He had gained the scars in street fights. He had been a muscle man for this racketeer and that crooked labor leader for years. At twenty-eight he was at the top of his profession. He was the best bodyguard in the underworld. He was, to John Wade's earnest belief, the only thoroughly honest man in Midvale.

For Rickey Boles would not steal a dime. Neither would he connive in the stealing of other people's pelf. Rickey would guard you with his life if you hired him and paid him and then stole other people's money. But Rickey had his own peculiar code. It forbade him to steal.

He said, "He's a wrongo, that shyster. But he can fix."

"Yes," said Wade disgustedly, "he can fix. In this town anything can be fixed."

"Lucky for guys like you," said Rickey cheerfully. "You birds on the make have gotta have an in. If you didn't where would you be? In stir half the time."

"I suppose you'd be running free," said Wade amusedly. It tickled him always that Rickey Boles could blandly assume his own innocence while alleging the crookedness of his employer and close confidante.

"I'd be drivin' a truck," said Rickey bluntly. "Mebbe I'd be better off, huh, John?"

WADE STARTED and cast a startled glance at the big man. The car turned into a street called Avery Place, a small, neat suburban street with a row of identical cottages. It was a neighborhood of almost deadly respectability. Vines grew over the front of the well-kept houses, tiny lawns were neatly mowed. Rickey turned expertly into the narrow driveway of Number 24.

The garage was attached to the house. They got out of the car and went through a door which led into a small hall.

Wade called, "Evalina!"

A soft voice from the kitchen said, "Yassuh."

"Ham and eggs," said Wade. "And coffee. Hot coffee, Evalina."

A swinging door creaked and a black head stuck itself out into the hall. Wrathful brown eyes stared at Wade. Evalina's wool stood up in righteous indignation. She said, "Mist' John, you nevah have nothin' *but* hot coffee—and you knows it! Sometimes, Mist' John, you makes me so mad I could tell the cops on you."

Wade chuckled. "Go ahead, tell 'em. I just paid them off."

Evalina stepped into the hall. She was as tall as John Wade and was sturdier. She put her black hands on her hips and said, "I declare, Mist' John, it ain't no sense. We take these suckahs and we seperates 'em fum their cash and then we pays it for protection. It ain't sense, Mist' John."

Wade said, "Evalina, you got something there. Now cook me something, will you, like a good girl?"

"Seems t' me," said the colored woman, retreating in good form, "us might as well be honest as pay off all de time."

It was there again, nagging him, making him restless. He went into the small, comfortable living room. There was nothing unusual, nothing elaborate or luxurious about the house. It was an ordinary establishment, apparently that of a small business man, modern, well-equipped without sumptuousness.

The front door was barred and there was no entrance save through the garage, which held a storm door reinforced and wired for sound. But these facts could not be discerned. Also, there was a tunnel under the house which led to a heavily wooded vacant lot on the next corner. The house, to all appearances, was just a house and no one knew that John Wade owned its neighbor on either side as well as the aforesaid wooded lot.

Rickey flopped onto a divan and propped his head on a cushion. He said, "That new guy on our right. You know him?"

The neighbors were always a problem. It was necessary that they be harmless-seeming. Yet they must have a past, one known to John Wade or to Rickey. They must be legitimate now, so that no police raids attract attention to Avery Place. It would seem impossible to easily find people of that description.

IT WAS easy to find them. Wade knew that the town was full of them. The difficulty was to keep them in one place and not let their pasts catch up with them.

He had been successful with the house on the left. For two years a pair of ex-cons named Corrigan, man and wife, had lived there quietly and conducted a tavern in town which was ultra-respectable. There was never trouble with the aging Corrigans, who asked nothing but peace and an opportunity to live out their days together after a life of many vicissitudes.

The other house had been vacated suddenly by an English couple when a gentleman from Scotland Yard had appeared.

Wade answered Rickey's query. "He came with papers. Names Parsons. Got a cute wife."

"Cute?" said Rickey enthusiastically. "She ain't cute. She's beeootiful!"

Wade said, "Well, lay off her. We got trouble enough without you playing Cassanova in the neighborhood."

"Her name ain't Cassanova," explained Rickey. "It's Jean. Jean Parsons. Her husband's a little guy, ain't he?"

"He used to hold up banks in the West," said Wade drily. "I hear he's got chair-heat on him from twenty years back."

Rickey said, "That's dangerous stuff, John. Suppose they ketch up on him?"

Wade said wearily, "I don't show as owner of that joint, Rickey. But they won't catch up with Parsons. They don't even catch up with mobsters on the lam for homicide right here in this town. They don't catch anybody that's got a dime or an in where he can find a dime. They'll take two bucks from a dip and two grand from a murderer. The cops… the prosecutor's gang—anybody in office will take it."

Rickey said virtuously, "It ain't right, John. Us citizens pay them guys outa our taxes."

Wade read the evening paper. There had been a jail break. Red Gomper and Eddie Fultz had gone over the wall of City Prison. The guards had fired but missed. A mysterious black sedan (the inevitable black sedan, thought Wade) had picked them up and spirited them away. The police expected to recapture them any minute.

He laughed shortly. The police expected! The guards had fired machine guns at two men in a narrow street in broad daylight and missed!

Two hardened killers, this morning faced with certain conviction and the chair, were loose in Midburg. And in John Wade's mind there was no doubt that two or three prison screws and a couple of politicians were richer in pocket by several hundreds of dollars. Four thousand dollars, he had heard, was the price. Four grand to let you go over the wall while the turnkeys were looking the other way.

Dirt cheap, he thought.

Evalina had the ham and eggs ready. He went out into the spacious, electrically equipped kitchen and sat in the breakfast nook with Rickey and ate. No one spoke. Even Evalina seemed morose. He found he wasn't very hungry. He pushed his plate back.

"Nuts," he said. "I can't go out because the heat may still be on. If I stay in here I'll go rammy."

Rickey said. "You could go next door and look over your new neighbors. That Mrs. Parsons is worth lookin' over, John."

Wade said, "To hell with Mrs. Parsons and her bank-robbin' husband."

He went into the living room again. He smoked a cigarette and thought of Al Perryman, the fat slug, spending his end of the five thousand in bars and night clubs. He wondered fretfully if the stout crook would pass enough of it to clear him with the cops. He wouldn't know until tomorrow at Pete's Place. He was irked with a criss-cross of strange impulses. He got up impatiently and went out through the garage and across the driveway to the small house next door.

CHAPTER TWO
THE GIRL WITH
THE GUN

THE GIRL who opened the door was tiny and blonde and slim. She peered at him standing there in the dimness of late evening and said doubtfully, "Who is it, please?"

He said, "It's John Wade. Your next-door neighbor. Is your—husband home?"

She said, "Oh, Mr. Wade. Yes. Come in, please."

She was like a kitten, all fluffy and spotless in something white. Her eyes were round and violet and her lips were red and slightly parted. She was very serious and polite. She ushered him into the attractive room.

"Sam, Mr. Wade to see you," she said.

Sam Parsons got up out of a low club chair and came forward slowly. He was a little man with hair greying at the temples. He must be, John thought, twenty years older than his wife. He had sharp features and faded blue eyes and an air of competence. He said, "Glad to see you. Mr. Wade. I'll get a drink."

John sat down. The girl perched on a straight chair and solemnly surveyed him. She said, "The house is nice. I like it."

John said, "The owner will be pleased. I'm only the renting agent, you know."

She said, "I know. But I thought I ought to tell you. It's fun, keeping house with all those electric gadgets."

She rattled on. Her voice was pitched a trifle too loud, Wade thought. He came alive in every fibre of him on the instant. His ears strained. He heard nothing but the pleasant clinking of glasses and ice. He listened carefully, but there was no alarming sound.

Parsons came in with a small tray holding two glasses, a siphon and decanter. He said, "Jean doesn't drink. Soda?"

John said, "Yes. And not much liquor. You like it here too, Parsons?"

The little man said gravely, "It suits my purpose. And Jean likes the gadgets."

Wade sipped at his drink. He said significantly, "You came well recommended. I hope everything is quiet enough for you."

"It's been quiet for years," said Parsons. "Jean knows about it. You don't have to be cagey."

The girl sat straight, her big eyes upon Wade. She said, "Yes, Sam is all right now. They won't ever bother him. He's been straight for years."

Wade said, unconsciously, "They won't bother him unless they think he's got something."

"Yes," agreed Parsons quietly. "If they knew I had a dime they'd be after me quick. They're on the take in this town. But that's the only place a lamster is safe. This burg's full of us."

Wade said, "Don't I know."

They chatted of other things while the tall clock in the corner ticked off the minutes. The girl joined in freely. She was, John thought, surprisingly intelligent in spots. She seemed to know a little of everything and her remarks were pertinent. He began to wonder about her. She was very young, certainly not over twenty-two. Yet she knew many things which most young girls never learn.

The feeling of uneasiness returned. At eleven he stood up. He said, "It's been pleasant. You must come over and sample Evalina's cooking. Rickey and I get fat on it."

Mrs. Parsons said, "We'd love to. Rickey—is he out tonight? He's a droll one."

"Yes," said Wade ironically, "Rickey is amusing."

"He *has* gone out?" she persisted.

The danger signal rang clearly then. If Parsons had not been so vigorously recommended by unimpeachable underworld figures, if the girl were harder, older, it would be a nice set-up. Of course, nothing was impossible, he thought. His brain was racing madly. He kept his eyes on Parsons, still sitting in the low chair, and stepped towards the door.

The girl's voice said, "Hold it, Wade. You're not leaving just yet."

He had let her slip to the side, out of range of his vision. He did not look at her. He did not reach for the gun under his arm. He just stood motionless, immaculate in his well-cut clothing, his face wooden.

He said, "What is it, Parsons, a heist?"

The little man said, "You'll find out in five minutes."

Wade let his eyes travel to the clock. It was ten minutes past eleven. He said, "You cut it pretty fine."

"Mrs. Parsons is a good talker," grinned the little man.

HE DIDN'T look so mousey now. He looked more like a wire-haired fox terrier. He bounced out of the chair and went to the front door. He opened it on a crack and peered out.

He came back and said, "Relax, Wade. You're in no danger."

"I've been milked for five grand already today," said Wade bitterly. "You had the best of references. There will be some people pay for this."

Parsons said softly. "I think not. You'll feel differently later, Wade."

John managed to edge around so that he could see the girl. She held a large revolver in her ridiculously small hand. The big clock ticked away the seconds. Parsons was tremendously interested in the window and the door. He kept getting up and going to look out into the dark street.

The gun was too heavy for the girl. Her wrist was beginning to tire. Parsons had not shown a weapon. John Wade began to gather his muscles together. He could make the girl in one leap, though she might get hurt—might even throw a slug into him or into Parsons in the confusion.

If she did, there would be more cop heat. He cursed savagely. Someone had been smart. Someone had literally taken him where he lived. He hesitated, slow anger burning in him.

He had been inviolate so many years. He had been too clever for them. He had milked the suckers up and down the state and across all lines and been safe in Midburg, the city of crooked politicians, the capital of Midstate, the state of venal statesmen. And now he was being milked right and left by the crooks. First by crooks in office, next by astute denizens of the underworld itself.

Rickey must have gone out. They had been sure of that or they wouldn't have pulled it. Asking him about the big muscle guy was the signal for them to pull it, prearranged between them. They had let him walk, uninvited, right into the web. He was beginning to see red. In another second or two, he thought angrily, he would make a play and to hell with who got hurt and how many cops came down on his ears.

Parsons said suddenly, "Here he comes. Hold everything."

He turned out the porch light. A car rolled to a stop outside. A man's rapid footsteps sounded on the walk. Parsons had the door on a crack, ready to open and close it in a hurry, his hand on the knob.

Mrs. Parsons said tightly, "Don't make a move, Wade. I'll shoot you dead if you move a muscle."

Parsons opened the door. A topcoated figure, with upturned collar and pulled-down hat came hastily through. Parsons jammed the door shut behind the newcomer. There was a second of dynamic silence in the room.

Then a voice said from the door to the kitchen. "Baby, you better drop that gat. I got two of 'em on your husband and his pal."

John Wade said, "Attaboy, Rick!"

The girl said, "Oh—*oh!* Don't shoot. For God's sake, don't shoot. It's the governor!"

John Wade almost started out of his polished black shoes. The man in the topcoat slowly reached up and turned down the coat collar. He was a handsome, broad-chested man with an iron jaw and his grey eyes were fearless under shaggy brows.

He said in a heavy, unfrightened voice, "Tableau. Let's cut out the monkeyshines and get down to business."

Rickey Boles said flatly, "Governor or no governor, I'm workin' for John Wade. I'd as soon shoot a lousy politician as a rat."

He came into the room with the two guns still levelled. The girl had dropped her hand to her side. She was very pale and quite beautiful. She said, "Please—we only want to talk."

Rickey leered, "Talk damn fast then. Nobody's gonna make no sap outa John Wade, see? Not while I work for him they ain't."

The governor turned to John. He said incisively, "Call off your gorilla, Wade. This is the only way I could get to you without certain parties knowing it. I mean you no harm."

John Wade hesitated. He knew little of this new man who sat in the governor's chair. He was Castle Fortney; he was a lawyer who had been successful in corporation work; he was new to politics, a figurehead, it was said, for the Old Liners, the gang which had run the state for so many years.

He had been in office only a few months. He had been very quiet, had engaged in no wrangles, in nothing of great moment. He was thought to be another somnolent incumbent, content to let the grafters go their ways.

John Wade said, "What's the play, Governor?"

The big man calmly removed his coat and hat. His hair was iron-grey and plentiful. He had, Wade thought, the strongest face he had ever seen upon a man in public office.

He said, "You'll be amazed. Let's get comfortable and talk."

John said almost unwillingly, "Put up the rods, Rickey. But stick around."

The governor raised his eyebrows. "You want Boles in on this? No matter what it is?"

JOHN WADE relaxed. There was something about Fortney which gave him confidence. He said engagingly. "Governor, there ought to be one honest man in the room. Rickey is the only man I know who can be thoroughly trusted."

The governor said, "Touché! Sit down, all of you."

He dominated them without effort, without seeming to. He said easily, "Five thousand dollars is a lot of money, Wade."

"Yes," admitted John.

"Nice state of affairs in Midburg," said the governor conversationally. "You buy what you want: freedom, immunity. Nice things for you—er—adventurers."

John said bluntly, "Not adventurers. Crooks. Don't mince words, Governor. You're among pals."

"Meaning that a politician is a crook, too," assented Castle Fortney readily. "And how right you are. But, Wade, do you think all politicians want to be crooks? Do you think they like to be grafters?"

"It doesn't hurt them any," said John aggressively.

The governor sighed. Parsons moved restlessly, eyeing Rickey. The big man held his guns in his lap and watched stolidly.

The girl broke in heatedly, "You're unfair, Wade. The fault is not entirety with men in office. The whole system is wrong. The system which allows crooks to build political machines, to force aspirants to office into depending upon them for election."

Wade said calmly, "So what? Are you going to try to change the system? Don't let's be naive. What do you want from me?"

The governor said, "You're an intelligent man, Wade. You have been a clever crook. Parsons, who knows all about crooks, says so. You've made a lot of money fleecing men who thought they were turning a crooked penny. You have been smart enough to capitalize upon the avarice of humankind. How much of that money do you have now?"

"Not a lot," admitted Wade.

"The law got it," said the governor. He grinned like a small boy. He said, "John Wade takes the gullible and the crooks in public office take John Wade. Vicious circle, isn't it?"

John Wade said, "You express my thoughts exactly, sir."

The governor was silent for a moment. He looked for a moment at Rickey Boles. The big man shifted uneasily, but kept his two guns in plain sight. The governor said, "Wade, we've got you. Parsons here is a detective. He is not a story book detective. He is just a human ferret who can tie a crook into a knot and throw him in jail and keep him there. Parsons is employed by me."

Rickey Boles barked, "You ain't puttin' John in no can. He ain't never been in one and he ain't startin'."

The governor said soothingly, "I don't want John in the can. I want him on my side."

"He ain't no stoolie, neither," said Rickey belligerently.

The governor stood up and looked down at the silent Wade. He said forcefully, quietly, "You can't tell me that you like your life. You are an intelligent man. Surely you see the *cul de sac* into which you are walking—the inevitable end at the hands of a gunman when the pay-off isn't there, when Rickey relaxes vigilance. Surely you don't approve of paying off men in office. Certainly you can see the evil of political machines controlled by mobs of gangsters, dope peddlers, vice operators."

John Wade said stubbornly. "I have my racket. You have yours. Don't give me that stuff about the system. You can't change it."

The governor said, "I can't? I've got four years, Wade. Four long years. I've got Parsons and Jean over there. I've got the National Guard—armed citizens, Wade, the

National Guard. Maybe I can't change it. But, Wade, I'm going to make a hell of a dent in it!"

John scoffed, "And commit political suicide!"

The girl spoke again, heatedly, coming forward. Her eyes were bright and her lips moist. She looked straight at John as she spoke.

"The governor does not want politics if they are as dirty as this state's politics. Who wants to preside over a pig-sty?"

Fortney said drily, "And in case you doubt my altruism, Wade, bethink you of the young man in another state who is doing very well politically in spite of his vigorous prosecution of criminals in office."

He felt it, then, inside him. It was a flickering little thing which had been smouldering there, keeping him on edge, restless. It kindled and flamed a little. He said, "Now wait a minute. This is a fast one."

THE GOVERNOR ripped on, "Wade, you're no recidivist. You are dishonest deliberately, by choice, because you see no honesty anywhere. You are a product of this vicious city in this vicious state. You think all men are vile and that the price is the thing. Yet you have said that Rickey Boles is an honest man.

"You are right—about the men in office in Midburg. I know you are right. That is why I am here. I have two good operators, Wade. I have Parsons here, who was smart enough to turn you up—smart enough to know that you paid five thousand dollars to Aloysius Perryman this morning for protection. I have Jean Morrow, who is the cleverest woman in the state...."

Wade said, "Wait a minute, Governor. Jean Morrow? The girl who won the prizes at State College a few years back? This is Jean Morrow?"

"Miss Morrow is the perfect foil for Parsons," Fortney said. "Parsons can work with the F.B.I., with my own complete crime laboratory which is in my home. Now I need someone who is completely aware of the crooked men in office. I need someone who does not have to ferret, who can say, 'that is the man who takes graft.' I need a man who hates political corruption and can give us the slant of the underworld. I want you, John Wade."

Wade said, "No."

The governor sat down in the easy chair. He said, "But I say *yes.*"

Wade said, "I'm no stool pigeon. You can't make one of me. Why should I rat on a crook?"

"Why shouldn't you?" asked Fortney equably. "Do you owe anything to any of them?"

Wade said, "No. If anything they owe me. But there is something about an informer that stinks."

Fortney leaned forward. He said, "Now wait, I don't want you to play informer. I want you to help us break up this political set-up. I want you to actively take part in a crusade to dissociate crime from politics."

John Wade stood up and shook out the creases of his pleated trousers. He adjusted his lapels carefully and touched his cravat.

"Governor," he said, "I could tell you to scram. I could lam out of here and work somewhere else. I don't know why, but I can't do it. I think you are probably screwy. But lately, I've had screwy notions myself."

He looked at the girl, at Rickey, at the bristling little man called Parsons. He said, "Work this thing up. Figure it out so that I do not have to turn in anyone who has given me his confidence willingly. Then let's meet again."

Rickey Boles said in shocked accents, "John! You can't play ball with these citizens. These are legit people. We ain't got any right playin' with legit people."

John Wade said, "You'll play on my side, won't you, Rickey?"

"Well, but…" Rickey said unhappily.

"It may get us in trouble," grinned John Wade. "The cops won't like it. The mobs will be very upset. The governor can't protect us very much."

Rickey said. "Just us five? Just the five of us against the mobs and the cops?"

"And the politicians," nodded John.

Rickey made a quick motion and the guns disappeared from his big hands as if by magic. He said expansively, "Well—that's different. That's like a game. Hell, me, I don't care so long as it's tough enough. I'm with you, Governor. Shake!"

The governor gripped the big man's hand. He was grinning more broadly, now. He held out his left hand to John Wade. He said, "Parsons will work it out. You understand—I must appear to be a stuffed shirt. I can't show my backing. This is all undercover. It is dangerous—there is no pay except what I can scrape out for expenses and my own private means—which will be spent to the last penny, I assure you."

Wade said. "I don't want pay. I want my conscience soothed. I feel like a Benedict Arnold already."

Castle Fortney sobered. He put back his fine head and his voice was vibrant. He said. "Wade, I'm no purist. I'm a practical man who happens to despise underhandedness, who believes that this community, this country, deserves better men in the jobs which it dispenses at the polls. To attain something better than we have, I will do anything. I will adopt any measures.

"Wade, I believe that if you join us you will be making a step which will change your whole life. Remember, I am not making you a promise of immunity. I am not asking you to suddenly reform and suddenly become a limb of the law. I am leaving that to you. I want you to work with Parsons. The rest is your private affair. You take your own chances. But I want you with us."

John Wade said, "I haven't been very happy… it's been a pleasure to meet you."

The handsome governor showed his teeth. He put on his topcoat, adjusted his snap brim hat. A car purred outside. It was, John saw, exactly midnight. The governor made a gesture and was gone through the door like a shadow in the night. The automobile gears meshed quietly. The four were alone.

JOHN WADE looked at the girl. He said, "Well, Miss Morrow, it has been exciting."

The girl said, "I'm sorry about the gun and everything. We had to make sure of you. Rickey fooled us by pretending to go out."

Rickey said, "You ain't Mrs. Parsons, then?"

John said, "Miss Morrow is the girl who won three scholarships at Woman's State and don't ask me how I know that."

"It was in all the papers," smiled the girl. She seemed even younger when she smiled.

Rickey was indignant. He said, "Why, Miss Morrow. You ain't got no right livin' here with this gee if you ain't married to him. Why, Miss Morrow, I am ashamed of you.

What will people think? This is no way for a young girl to carry on, I—"

Parsons and the girl rocked with laughter. John said, "Rickey is a very moral guy. With other people's morals."

Parsons, silent until now, said, "Wade, are you really with us?"

John looked at him. He said, "I'm sick of being rooked by every ham in a political job. I'm with you, all right."

Parsons sighed. He said, "It was tough catching up with you. I had to dig pretty deep to get stuff on you. How about that Perryman dough? Will that buy you clear?"

John nodded. "Perryman has to come through. I'll get word in the morning. In Pete's Place."

Parsons hesitated. Then he said, "Look, Wade, about Pete. He's one of my men."

John whistled. He said, "Pete? Why Pete hides out every mobster in the state. Pete's one of the real cover-ups."

Parsons said, "Pete and I knew each other west. He framed my introduction to you after I told him why. Pete lost his eye in a fight we had one time. With a sheriff's posse."

John Wade said, "Oh."

Then he said. "You were on the take yourself once, huh Parsons?"

The little man nodded grimly. He said, "I got ten years to think it over, Wade. In a federal prison."

John Wade said musingly, "That makes it easier, Parsons. Pete, too, huh? I always liked Pete."

"He won't rap on a right guy, crooked or straight," said Parsons. "Pete just doesn't like politicians. He's had to grease too many. So have you. That's why you're with us."

John Wade said, "It's a shock. I dunno. Maybe I can't make it. Let's wait'll the cop heat is off me tomorrow and talk again. Let's call it a night."

They parted, quietly, as if they were old friends. Rickey and John went out the front door and across the lawn to their own house. It was like returning home after visiting with a neighbor—a real neighbor, a guy who went to business every day and came home to relax and enjoy his nightly leisure.

Rickey yawned and said, "You don't like Perryman and Roscoe Yarning and that bunch. So you turn Law."

Wade said, "You can quit me, Rickey."

Rickey said indignantly, "I wouldn't quit. What the hell do I care? I'm no crook and I never was. If the Law wants t' hire you and me that's okay. But why the hell don't you admit it?"

"Admit what?" asked Wade innocently.

"You don't like crooks!" sneered Rickey. "You mean you DO like that babe. As soon as you find out she ain't Mrs. Parsons you get very indignant, you do. You become very John Law, you do. You can't kid me, John Wade."

John sat and stared at his hands. The restlessness was worse, now. The change, the danger, the difficulties of maintaining his psychological balance in this new venture bore down upon him. He said, "She's nice, isn't she, Rickey?"

"Nice?" roared Rickey. "She's the nuts, that's what she is. But she's a smart babe. She wins prizes. John, you don't wanta mess with no smart babes. In this world there ain't nothin' so dangerous as a babe with brains. You know that, John. In fack, it was you tol' me that."

John said, "Different times, different people, different ideas, different thoughts. Go to bed, Rickey. And Rickey—"

"Yeah?" said the big man.

"Don't break it too abruptly to Evalina that we are going straight. She will faint and there will be no breakfast."

CHAPTER THREE
PERRYMAN TURNS UP

JOHN WADE arose early. Evalina had breakfast ready. Rickey was lounging in the breakfast nook, having finished even earlier.

Evalina said accusingly, "Mist' Rickey done tol' me about this new bizness, Mist' John. Where is we gonna git our cake money fum now?"

"You could take in washing," suggested John.

Evalina said, "I quit. I c'n go back to mah husband and do that."

John said, "You'd better stay awhile and see what happens, Evalina. I'll bet we find some money around and about."

"Honest money?" said Evalina unbelievingly.

"If there is any such," grinned John. "Or if not—anything that happens to stick to our fingers."

They went down in the cellar, which was fitted out as a small gymnasium. Rickey took to the chest weights and John worked out on the bars, horizontal and parallels. They boxed four fast rounds at the end of which Rickey grumbled, "I wish you would park that left on Al Perryman instead of me."

John said, "Perryman is taking off cop heat. I can't have cop heat in this new business. Cops are still our enemies."

He showered and dressed carefully in a grey, single-breasted suit and a white shirt with a dark red tie. He went into the garage but did not take the car. He went out onto Avery Place and looked casually at the house on the right. There was no sign of life. He wondered what Jean Morrow was doing, if she got meals for the little under-cover man.

He went down to the corner and picked up a cab and rode to Pete's Place. It was only eleven o'clock and there was no one in the bar but the one-eyed proprietor. John went to the end of the bar and leaned on the mahogany.

Pete drifted down and looked unhappy. John said, "No phone call for me, Pete?"

The single orb rolled and the walrus moustache quivered. Pete said, "And there won't be none, I'm afraid."

John said, "What's the angle, Pete?"

"I hear," said Pete painfully, "that Al Perryman took a trip somewheres."

"Oh," said John. "Like that, huh?"

"I wouldn't know," said Pete, "nothin'. Except that he ain't around no more, I heard."

"You wouldn't know if Perryman saw a certain party before he left, would you?" asked John.

"I don't think he did," said Pete miserably. "On account of there is two prosecutor's men in the back room right now. And they ain't lookin' for me."

John said, "Well don't cry about it, Pete. You can't help a thing like that. I'll talk to them."

He walked straight to the back room and opened the door. They were waiting for him, right enough. Big Hans Wolfgang had his gun out, but Tony Maretta looked sheepish and displayed no weapon.

John said, "Hiya, men? What's the beef?"

Wolfgang, who weighed two hundred and thirty pounds, said, "Frisk the mugg, Tony."

Maretta said disgustedly. "John don't pack heat like a mobster. Put your rod away, Hans."

The big prosecutor's detective held onto the gun and said stubbornly, "Wade's a smart guy."

Tony cut in, "The Boss wants you should come down, John."

Wade temporised, "Yarnell wants me? What in the world for, Tony?"

Tony squirmed. He said, "Aw—you know how the Boss is, John. He feels tough about that Simon—his cousin."

John sighed. Hans Wolfgang said, "Frisk him, Tony."

"You got a rod, John?" asked Tony diffidently.

"No," said John absently. "So Yarnell wants me, eh? And Al Perryman is gone with the breezes? Lemme make a call."

Before they could stop him he had the telephone and was dialing the number. Rickey's voice answered immediately. John said, "The prosecutor wants me. Got it?"

Rickey said, "Okay, pal," and hung up.

John said to the detectives, "Let's go down and get it over with. Hans, you better put that gun away. It makes me nervous. I am not a guy who is used to guns."

Wolfgang said, "You are a smart guy, Wade. I do not trust you too much, see?"

THEY WENT outside. The detectives had a small car. Wolfgang put the gun in his pocket but kept his hand on it. They drove downtown to the courthouse and went up to a second floor office marked, "Oscar Yarnell, County Prosecutor." The girl in the ante room nodded at them and they went right on into the back room.

Oscar Yarnell was an imposing figure behind the big desk. He was a man who looked like a bear and he wore the tweeds to go with his burly body and thick shoulders. He even smoked a pipe and roared when he spoke.

He was A Friend Of The Common People, this Oscar Yarnell. He was a vote-getter—a Plain Man, One of the Boys. He had a cold eye and a rugged jaw, and ever since he had been an overgrown lout in primary schools, he'd been a bully.

He snapped, "So you've got Wade. Fine work, men. Fine work. That's what we need around here. Fast pick-ups on these damn criminals."

The two detectives shuffled their feet. Tony Maretta said mildly, "We didn't have any trouble with Wade, Boss."

"Trouble? Of course you didn't have trouble," shouted Yarnell. "Crooks are all yella. I never saw one yet wasn't yella."

He glared at John. He said, "So—a wise guy, eh? A smart con-guy. Pickin' on out-of-towners with an old gag like the wire-tappin' steer. Thought you were smart, eh?"

John shrugged his shoulders and said, "All right, Yarnell. Let's stop the palaver and get down to business."

Yarnell said savagely, "This office don't do business. Understand, Wade? You're goin' to jail. What's more, you're stayin' in jail. I've had enough of you criminals in this town."

The creases in Wade's face fell into disgusted lines. He said, "You mean you took my five grand from Perryman and chased him out of town and now you're going to welsh on me? Why, Yarnell, even you couldn't do that?"

Yarnell blustered, "Don't give me that Perryman business, Wade. You can't ring that stuff in around here. That's another crook, that Perryman. If you gave him money, you threw it away."

John said, "You don't say! It was never thrown away before."

Yarnell said, "Ah! You admit you gave him money before—that shyster, that blackmailer."

"You oughta know," grinned John. "You got yours."

Yarnell leaped to his feet, sending his swivel chair against the wall. He roared, "Seize this man. Take him downstairs. I want to question him. Question him—understand?"

Tony Maretta was clumsy, getting in Wolfgang's way. John Wade's mind whirled kaleidoscopically. He had no illusions as to what awaited him in the small room downstairs. Wolfgang was noted for sadistic ruthlessness when a victim could not fight back—or pay off.

Once down there in the hands of a Wolfgang and Yarnell, Rickey, nor Sam Parsons, nor the girl, nor even the governor, could help him. He moved backwards a step, keeping the friendly little Tony between him and Wolfgang.

Yarnell was out from behind the desk. John could not resist the opportunity. He stepped forward, feinting with his right.

Yarnell tried to cover. John let the wicked left hook sing through the air. It caught the prosecutor on the button. He canted sideways and fell against Tony Maretta.

Tony threw his arms around Wolfgang. The big detective was tugging at the gun in his coat pocket, but Tony clung to him tightly. John threw the right fist with all he had. He hit Wolfgang behind the ear. That worthy lost all interest in the proceedings.

Tony said, "Hit me on the button and scram, John. Get outa town. I can't do a thing for you."

John said, "Perryman?"

"I dunno," said Tony. "The heat's terrific on you, John. I ain't never forgot that time you helped me outa that jam with my cousin, or I wouldn't dare do this. Gwan, tap me."

John swung his left as gently as possible. It would make a slight bruise on Tony's jaw. The little man dived to a soft spot on the carpet and said, "Beat it, John."

John said, "It's lucky you had a cousin, too, pal. Yarnell's cousin jams me and yours gets me loose. See you later."

He walked quietly through the ante room. The girl looked at him curiously, but said nothing. John went down the hall and found the stair-well. He leaped down the one flight to the street level and went out the side door onto the sidewalk.

The familiar red coupé was at the curb with the motor running. Rickey Boles gunned it up and John slid into the seat. The coupé went over a side street and doubled back, then circled the courthouse.

John said, "Let's take a ride, Rickey. Out to Attersbee's."

"The hide-out?" said Rickey. "You in a jam, John?"

John took a thick wallet from his pocket and opened it. He said, "Look, money. The prosecutor had five grand in his pocketbook. Now isn't that a coincidence?"

RICKEY BOLES said reprovingly, "Now John, don't tell me you went and lifted Yarnell's leather. It ain't honest to do things like that, John. Besides, it's beneath your dignity to be goin' around actin' like a common dip. I don't know where you ever learned that stuff. It's—it's degradin'."

"When I hit him on the chin he sorta fell sideways," said John. "So I grabbed this thing from his pocket. After all, Rickey, it's my own dough."

"You hit the D.A. on the chin?" gasped Rickey.

"I didn't miss," said John, gratified.

They drove out on the highway, into the country, beyond the limits of Midburg. Pleasant country sprang up around them and the road narrowed to a two-way macadam, winding lane which had once been a trail through a woods of pine and fir trees.

Rickey said, "Did you hit him with a right or a left?"

"A left hook," said John gravely.

Rickey said, "That is very good. If you had to hit him, I am glad it was a left hook. You hit very good left hooks. How do you figure that is your dough, John?"

"If Al Perryman was the pay-off man and Al is missing and Yarnell has exactly the sum in his wallet which I gave to Al—what would you make of it?"

Rickey said, "You think Yarnell would take your dough from Perryman and then welch on you? Why, even a prosecutor would not do a dishonest thing like that. Besides, Perryman would squawk very loudly. It would make Perryman look bad. That shyster cannot afford to look bad, John."

"Pete says that Al Perryman has gone on a journey, Rickey," explained John. "Maybe Al Perryman will not return from this trip."

Rickey swung the coupé off the macadam and slowed down as they hit the dirt road. He did not like to drive the red car over dirt roads as it was bad for the paint job. Rickey was very proud of the powerful car and its shiny paint job. He ruminated, "Things is happenin' too fast. I wonder if that bank heist had somethin' to do with it, too."

John said, "What bank heist, Rickey? What do you mean?"

"It come over the radio while I was waitin' for your call," said Rickey. "The First National got rapped off. Four muggs waited for the janitor and pushed it in. Regular mob

M.O. What with Red Gomper and Eddie Fultz lammin' outa the pen yesterday—"

John finished, "And Bones Magill and Itzy Schloff showin' around town. And Al Perryman bankin' in the First National. Rickey, I am very glad you told me about that bank robbery. You have the mind of a detective. You put things together."

Rickey said sulkily, "You do not have to insult me, John. I know I am dumb but not as dumb as plenty of detectives and you know it damn well."

John said soothingly, "You are a very smart guy. Park the car up in here—off the road behind those bushes."

Rickey made the car do a quick circle. They were in a small clearing with branches overhanging the coupé and effactually concealing it from casual passersby. The road was deserted and when Rickey cut the motor there were no sounds save the chirping of crickets and the cry of a small bird or two in the treetops.

John said, "Attersbee's is over the hill. I was there once when Perryman was hiding from the cops the time the Bar Association finally gave up protecting him. We'll walk. It'll be hard on my shoeshine, but it will be quieter."

Rickey said, "You expect to find people here ahead of us, huh, John?"

"I think," said Wade, "that you had better get out that old machine gun of yours. And you better give me a gun. I don't like guns. But this is one of those times when one might be handy."

The big man went around to the back of the coupé and manipulated a complicated lock. He came back with a large blue-barreled revolver which he handed to John, and a compact machine gun in a canvas bag. He took the machine gun from its covering and assembled it swiftly, saying, "Ain't used Thomas since I came to work for you, John. I'm all outa practice. Say—tell me somethin'. Are we in this for ourselves or for—you know. The Big Guy that was around last night?"

John considered a moment. Then he said, "Well, I'm no use to anybody down under the jail with cops hitting me on the nose. On the other hand, the Governor might not approve of what we may have to do now. Let's say a little of each, huh?"

"It don't really matter," said Rickey apologetically. I just like to know which side I'm on.

"Right now," said John, "I am most interested in Al Perryman."

THEY WALKED up the road a ways, then struck into a dim automobile trail which went wandering off among the trees. The ground sloped sharply upward after awhile, so that they were climbing. Attersbee had built his retreat upon a hilltop the better to command a view of all who approached. It would be no easy task to come up unseen to the log cabin hideout, Wade knew.

It hove within sight in a few moments. It was above the treetops, on a knoll of land. Rickey said, "Attersbee knew somethin' when he put that joint up there. He is related to the sheriff and I hear he owns this whole woods."

"Nepotism again," murmured John.

"I don't know about any disease," said Rickey, "but when the sheriff's cousin staches hot guys all over the country, it ain't fair. I know that much."

John was staring at the log cabin from behind a tree. There seemed to be no sentinel posted as lookout. Yet there was smoke coming from the chimney. After a moment he could pick out a car parked alongside the building. It was a black sedan.

He said, "Just like a movie. Rickey, Al Perryman isn't up there. Not unless he's got company."

The big man said, "Let's go. I will walk up there and turn Thomas loose and we will take over this joint until the heat cools off."

John said, "No. I think we will go around the back, Rickey. It seems like it would be better to go around the back. Where the woods are thicker."

They made a detour through the woods. They could keep the cabin in sight while they moved. They went slowly. The gun felt strange but comforting in John's hand. He had never carried a gun in his life. He had never shot at anybody and had never had any desire to do so.

They came finally to a spot on the hillside which was bare of vegetation. John paused and stared. There was a brick fireplace built in the middle of the clearing and there had been a fire so recently that the odor of burned embers was noticeable.

To one side someone had carelessly flung a spade. There was a pile of dirt, freshly turned. It seemed that labor had been interrupted or abandoned and that the laborers would of necessity be back to finish the job.

John said, "How about digging a little, Rickey?"

Rickey was poking the fire. His broad face was a trifle pale in the afternoon light. He had a sharp stick and was pulling something from the remains of the fire. John went close and saw that it was a piece of cloth, a tiny piece with a button attached.

Rickey said hoarsely, "I would not care to dig, John. This cloth looks like that checkered suit a certain guy was always wearing about town."

John looked at the button. It was a square button, the kind that is used on fancy checked suits which are usually to be found at race tracks. It was indubitably the kind of button that he had seen yesterday upon Al Perryman's coat sleeve.

Rickey said hoarsely, "I seen a guy once. It was years ago. This gee was took out for a ride. After they had done the job on him they took him and poured gasoline down his throat. And then they set fire to him. I would not like to dig in that spot, John, as I did not like looking at that other guy."

John said, faintly, "We will not dig. We'll go and see what is doing at that cabin."

THEY WENT hastily from the clearing. John was amazed at his steadiness. His pulse pounded unmercifully but his hands were cool and firm. He wondered vaguely whether being approximately on the side of law and order gave him confidence. This was all new to him, this stalking of men. He wondered if cops felt as he did now when they were closing in on criminals.

He stopped wondering about anything. They were getting close to the back of the cabin. It was growing late in the afternoon. Smoke still curled against the sky from the fieldstone chimney, but no one appeared at the windows or about the house.

He said, "Cover me. Rick. I'm going up there and look."

Rickey expostulated, "Now wait, John. Lemme take Thomas up there. You ain't used to this business. If Gomper—"

John said grimly, "I might as well start gettin' used to it. Cover me."

He went, bent over, running. He could run very fast and on this occasion he was sure that he outdid his best previous time. He covered the fifty yards across the cleared space to the cabin in something less than seven seconds.

When he was close to the rough logs of the large cabin he stopped. He could hear his heart pounding in his chest. He hoped no one else could hear it but it seemed impossible that they could not. He crouched under an open window and waited, straining his ears.

Then he heard the familiar sound. He could not believe it. He listened for a long moment. There was no question about it. Chips were rattling. Cards were slapping on a wooden table.

He took off his grey felt hat and raised his head slowly, peeking through the window with one eye. They were all there, seated around a deal table. There were Gomper and Fultz, the escaped cons. They were thugs, beetle-browed, coarse skinned. There were Magill and Schloff, the brains, the slick guys. They had piles of greenbacks on the table and they were playing poker. Even as John watched Itzy Schloff dealt a second to his partner Magill and the dark-haired bank robber raised the pot a hundred bucks.

John almost chuckled aloud. Schloff couldn't play straight even among his pals. He was a crook in his heart. John longed to point out the betraying flash of the middle knuckle to Gomper and Fultz, to show them how Itzy was laying them into Magill's hands for the cleanup. It would, John knew, save him a lot of trouble.

However, he made a signal to Rickey to go around and approach the front door. Then he waited while the big man disappeared into the trees. He thumbed back the hammer of the big revolver. If Rickey made a noise coming up they would all be out there shooting. He wondered if he could handle them. He hoped shooting at men was not different from shooting at targets in a gallery. He was all right in a gallery.

Rickey did not make a noise. He walked into the clearing at the front quite quietly, the machine gun cradled under one big arm, his finger ready to turn it loose. Before they caught sight of him John rose to his full height and leaned negligently on the window sill.

His shadow fell athwart the game. The players sprang back and Itzy Schloff yelled, "Get him. It's that con guy."

"Why should you want to get me, Itsy?" asked John curiously. He had the big gun pointed at them, holding it steady. "I never did you muggs for anything."

He might have held them if it hadn't been for Schloff's genuine panic. The bank robber tried to duck down and grab for his gun. John had no choice in the method of his procedure. He aimed the revolver and squeezed carefully on the trigger.

OUT OF the corner of his eye he saw Gomper tearing at a gun in the waistband of his trousers. Magill had dropped behind a chair and Eddie Fultz was reaching under his arm. John tried to get his own weapon around to fire but he could not take his eyes from Itzy Schloff.

The bank robber was spinning slowly around. There was an amazed expression on his face and a hole marred the line of his nose. Blood spurted, and John could no longer see what his face looked like. Schloff seemed to gather himself into a heap and flatten out upon the board floor.

Gomper was almost ready to turn loose. Bones Magill flipped a shot from behind the chair and hot lead slammed into the window frame at John's head, throwing splinters into his hair. He still stared at Itzy Schloff, bleeding upon the floor.

A coughing chatter broke loose from the front. Rickey had arrived. Rickey had the tommy-gun on burst firing and was spraying the room with lead. John got himself away from the window and went over and sat down on a stump. He wasn't interested in what happened further. He was quite sure that Rickey could handle it. He felt dazed and ill.

The firing stopped almost immediately. Rickey strolled around the corner of the house and said, "Got 'em, John. Like shootin' sittin' rabbits. What do we do next?"

John looked up at the big man. He said, "I killed Itzy Schloff. I shot him in the nose and killed him."

Rickey said blithely, "We don't give out no cigars. How could you miss 'im from that distance? C'mon, John, snap out of it. Whatta we do now?"

John said, "I never fired at a man before. I had to turn legit to kill a man. It doesn't seem right."

Rickey said querulously, "Look, John, this is not exackly a desert island. Maybe there are people hereabouts. What do we do, sit here and get pinched?"

John made himself get up. His legs were a little wobbly. He got inside the cabin and looked around. Rickey had done a very good job indeed. There seemed to be dead men all over the place.

He rummaged in a closet and found a leather bag. He broke open the lock and found it to be full of clean, crisp currency. He scooped the money off the table and put it in his pocket. The bank loot was probably intact and he would need money later, when the pinch of not working the rackets began to manifest itself.

He searched for documents. He searched the cabin from top to bottom and from stem to stern. He came finally to the fireplace. The fire was out now. John bent close to look at it. There was a packet of black, charred paper.

He grunted in dismay. Yarnell had seen to it that Perryman's incriminating legacy was looted from the bank, then immediately burned.

He said dolefully,

"We shouldn't have killed all these guys, Rickey. They might have talked. I am afraid that we make lousy cops."

Rickey said, "These muggs would not have sung, John. I know these muggs. They are very clammy guys."

John said, "Well, there are the papers we came after. And such as they are, they go with us."

He worked very painstakingly, with a couple of shingles that he found. He managed to get the charred papers between the shingles. Then he tied them together and carried them carefully out and down the trail to the red coupé. Rickey followed with the bag of money and the guns. The big man said, "I don't see what good it done us. It ain't honest to keep the dough. They killed Perryman all right but we can't do nothin' about that. There ain't a thing to tie 'em to Yarnell."

John said grimly, "I guess you're right, Rickey. But let's see what Parsons says."

"That guy," said Rickey. "He's a cold fish."

"He's supposed to be smart," said John. "We are not smart. We are too new at this business to be cop-smart."

"Cops," said Rickey, "are not smart. They are just plentiful. And they got a book. If we had a book to go by we would be all right too."

"If you could read," said John gravely.

CHAPTER FOUR
THE PROSECUTOR'S SONG

PARSONS WAS very quiet. He nodded while John related all that happened. The girl perched on the edge of a chair and her eyes were very bright. But when John was finished Parsons said, "It's bad, Wade. You still got heat on you. Yarnell is in the clear. Even that bag of dough is bad for you to be totin'."

John said, "I know. I was dumb to rush in that way."

Parsons said, "We're supposed to be workin' together. You went off half-cocked."

Jean Morrow said, "Just a minute. Those papers. It was smart to bring them back."

"They're charred black," said John.

"The governor has an infra-red camera in his private lab," said Jean. "I'll take these over right now and make some pictures. They're not poked up enough to have been entirely burned. There's a bare chance we might be able to use them."

John said, "Perryman had the dope on Yarnell. Parsons, I tell you Perryman is buried out there, what's left of him, and Yarnell is guilty of his death."

The little man said satirically, "So you knock off the only possible witnesses, you and that ape of yours."

John said, "So all right, we knocked them off. They needed it, didn't they?"

"It was undiplomatic," complained Parsons. "I can't hand you much for that job. Now you'll have to go in hiding and we'll have to cover you somehow until the police bungle around and try to piece this thing together. And if they don't, you'll be hot right on."

John was beginning to feel indignant. He said coldly, "You don't have to cover me, Parsons. I'll take care of myself."

"With the prosecutor raving for your blood," said Parsons, "and every cop in town looking for you."

John snapped, "Yes, right in their teeth. And I'll do it right now."

He was gone before they could stop him. Parsons said, "Now where has that damn fool gone?"

Rickey looked blank. He said, "I wouldn't know. But probably down to the prosecutor's office."

Jean Morrow said, "He can't do that. They may shoot him on sight. Yarnell would stop at nothing now."

Rickey said, "That wouldn't stop John. Parsons made him mad. He's tough when he's mad...."

John was at the wheel of the coupé, slamming it through traffic. He passed a red light out of sheer defiance. He was thoroughly angry.

He had turned legitimate and tried to scrape up a case against an obviously venal prosecutor. He had been forced to shoot a man, which was not a pleasant experience. He had retrieved thousands of dollars of stolen money. And still he was a hunted thing and Parsons had bawled him out in front of Jean Morrow.

He skidded the car to a stop at the curb in front of the courthouse, smack against a No Parking sign. He put the keys in his pocket and strode into the building.

No one noticed him. They were all out looking for him in strange places. He went unhindered through the corridors and up the stairway and into the office of Oscar Yarnell.

The girl was gone home, but the prosecutor was in his back office. John Wade went right on in without knocking.

Yarnell leaped up from his chair and shouted, "Here he is, boys. Come and get him."

Wolfgang and Maretta were in the next room. They came in with drawn guns. Wolfgang licked his thick lips in anticipation. Tony Maretta looked sorrowful.

John said, "Did you miss your wallet, Yarnell? The wallet with my five grand in it?"

"You stole my wallet," said Yarnell loudly. "Grab him, men. Take him downstairs and start working him over. This is going to be a real pleasure, ain't it. Wolfgang?"

The big man started forward but John put out his hand. Wolfgang leveled the gun. John said, "Don't shoot it at me, stupid. There'll be an awful kick-back. Your Boss is in a jam."

"Grab him," shouted Yarnell.

John said, "That five thousand dollars is in good hands, Yarnell. I had it marked and registered, you know."

Yarnell put both hands on the desk. He said, "You what?"

John went on easily, "We knocked off Gomper and Magill and the others and got back the bank money and the papers. And my money was marked when I gave it to Perryman. That ties you in with Perryman's murder. You had the dough in your wallet."

Yarnell said, "Wolfgang! Grab him!"

There was something strange in the prosecutor's voice. Even the thick-witted Hans hesitated. Tony Maretta said quickly, "Is that the goods, John?"

"Look at him," said John. "He's scared to death. When they turn up that stuff of Perryman's on him, Yarnell's motive will be obvious. He'll burn in the chair, Tony. You're gonna get a new boss, believe me."

Yarnell's hand had fallen out of sight. The drawer was half open. It suddenly occurred to John that he could do nothing about it. If there was a gun at his hand, the prosecutor could shoot him.

EVEN IF Tony and Wolfgang dared to talk, Yarnell would out-shout them. John knew that all the burly attorney had to do was pull the trigger and eliminate him and leave the rest to fate. The marked money was the main detail. Yarnell *must* be aware of that.

John said sharply. "Don't start shooting, Yarnell. I'll make a deal. I want the heat off."

Yarnell relaxed a trifle. He said, "Wolfgang. Maretta. You want to wait outside a moment? I'll see you boys later."

John said, "I don't want them outside. I want them to know the heat is off."

Yarnell said softly, "All right, Wade. The heat is off. Give me back the five thousand and call it even."

John said, "Give you back nothing. I—"

Yarnell made his play. His hand had been creeping closer and closer to the gun while he temporized. He made a fast grab and the gun came up above the desk.

Then a voice from the door behind them said, "Drop it, Yarnell. Drop it quick."

Yarnell dropped the gun. It clattered on the glass desk top. Rickey walked into the room with the tommy-gun under his arm.

Rickey said, "There's a guy to see you, Yarnell."

Sam Parsons came in. He was more like a wire-haired terrier than ever.

He said in crisp accents, "The governor has the papers in the Perryman case. You're through, Yarnell."

The prosecutor stammered, "They're—they're burned."

"The boys didn't succeed in destroying them," said Parsons. "The black light camera brought them up again, Yarnell. Perryman had affidavits, you know. Why, even the police of this town are cooperating."

The big man sat down as if his knees had suddenly given out. Parsons said, "We're going to leave you, Yarnell. This means the chair at least. You can't escape. There isn't a place you can hide—not even Attersbee's."

"It can't be," said Yarnell dully. "I'm a big man in this town. You can't touch me. I carry weight in this community."

Parsons said, "You did carry weight. Like a lot of other rotten politicians. You thought you couldn't be touched. Your power went to your head. You had a man murdered. You can't get away with murder Yarnell. Not even in Midburg you can't."

Parsons deliberately turned his back and walked out. The others followed, silently. Even Wolfgang came lumbering into the ante room. They waited there. It seemed a long time to John Wade but it was only a moment before the gun roared in the room they had just left.

Parsons said tightly, "Let's go, John. We don't want to be here when they find him. Tony can cover for us."

John said, "This Wolfgang. He's yellow."

Rickey said, "Hans won't peep. Hans knows me."

He tapped the machine gun significantly.

Wolfgang, white and trembling, said eagerly, "I never seen you guys. I don't know nothin'."

"Right for once," nodded Rickey.

They went out and got into the coupé, the three of them. They had little to say en route to the Avery Street house.

The governor was there, waiting. It was quite dark outside. When the tale was told, the chief executive said, "It was haphazard, but it's a beginning. Yarnell was a key man and one of the worst. We will be better organized next time. I'm satisfied for now."

When the big car had rolled up and he was gone, John said, "It feels good to know he's satisfied. He's a man."

Parsons said, "The best."

John went on, "What I want to know, how did you get that infra-red ray camera stuff done so quick?"

Parsons looked sheepish. Rickey grinned. Jean Morrow said cheerfully, "Well, it was pretty certain what was in the papers. It was worth a gamble. I—" she paused, confused.

Rickey said gleefully, "She was worried about you. So she made us go down and make out like the job was done. Those pitchers ain't even developed yet."

John said, "Well I'll be damned. And I thought I was pullin' a fast one when I told him that five grand was marked dough!"

JOHN WADE AND THE CORPSE CRUSADE

THE CROOKED COPS OF
MIDBURG DIDN'T KNOW
THAT JOHN WADE, SMART
EX-CONMAN, WAS ON THE
GOVERNOR'S STAFF. SO THEY
HUNG A DOUBLE MURDER RAP
ON HIM THAT ONLY TOOTHY
ABE SCHECHTEL, MIDBURG'S
KING-PIN CRIMINAL, COULD
BREAK—FOR A PRICE
IMPOSSIBLE TO PAY!

CHAPTER ONE
A COP IS KILLED

THE FOUR sat waiting in the living room of the modest house on Avery Place and the waiting did not suit John Wade. He looked at the little man and at the pretty girl. Then he looked at Rickey Bole and snapped, "Pull down your vest, you big lug."

Rickey thumbed his dilapidated nose and sighed, his feelings injured. He said, "You got gnats in your bloomers, John."

The girl said softly, "We'll hear something tonight, John."

Sam Parsons, who made John Wade think of a wire-haired terrier, said, "It takes time and patience."

John shrugged shoulders perfectly draped in an English jacket. He fixed deep-set eyes on the girl. It was better if he just looked at her and didn't think.

She was very beautiful, this Jean Morrow. She had round blue eyes and the fair skin of the very young, and fluffy yellow hair which curled in the new baby hairdo. She was all soft curves and; but most amazing, she possessed a brilliant mind.

John said in brittle accent, "It's all right for you guys: Sam ferrets; Jean potters in the lab; Rickey just follows me around and looks important. That suits you all. I had more

action when I used to work the suckers. I can't stand this inaction. It drives me nuts."

John Wade said, "No, Ricky. That
thing he's got is loaded."

Sam Parsons said bluntly, "We are under direct orders
from the governor of this state, John. We are engaged in a
fight against the toughest of forces—"

"Talk," interrupted John. His seamed face was bitter. "Sneak and talk, while Toothy Abe Schechtel runs the town. You got yourself an honest D.A. and think everything's gonna be right. What can he do while Schechtel owns the cops? Look—I turned square to help chuck the mobsters out of politics. All I'm doing is moping around marking time."

The clock struck eleven. Outside a car purred to a stop. Sam Parsons leaped to the door, careful that the light should not shine through upon the man who came unhurriedly down the path. John took a deep breath and held it.

The man who entered was large and handsome and his white hair was a vigorous shock like the mane of a lion. He sat in a large chair and said, "This is the only place I can relax. It's so hard to play stupid and keep my mouth shut sometimes."

Sam said soothingly, "Sure, Governor. We know. John was just sayin'...."

Governor Fortney Castle said kindly, "I know John likes action. But we must proceed slowly. I've learned a new expression: 'wired in.' Men like Abe Schechtel are wired in so well we can't move directly upon them. My own office—"

Rickey Bole said, "You didn't know what 'wired in' meant, Gov? You really didn't know?"

The governor grinned at the big bodyguard. He said, "There's a lot I don't know, Rickey. But I'm willing to learn. This is a tough job we've got. Schechtel will not come into the open. He owns the police in this town. I have no one in the state government I can trust. The state is owned lock, stock and barrel by crooks who are clever enough to garner votes for their stooges. And Midburg is the principal haven of corruption."

John said flatly, "We know all that, Governor. But let Rickey and me have this Schechtel. We'll put him in wrong and knock him off somehow or other. This is too slow, this diggin' for facts and figures."

"Nevertheless," said the governor equably, "we must have facts and figures. I want a real case when I proceed. I cannot come into the open without every facet clear-cut. I am surrounded by crooks and spies. We must be sure."

John said drily, "I am sure: My friends, you must excuse me. I can't stand another one of these conferences. Walking in circles makes me dizzy."

He swung on his heel and went out of the room. Sam Parsons started after him, his fierce eyes enraged. Governor Castle said quietly, "Leave him alone, Sam. He may be right. We are getting nowhere on this Schechtel business. Let him take a rest while we look around some more."

Rickey Bole shifted uneasily. He said, "I don't like it for John to go off like that. He gets in trouble."

Sam Parsons said grimly, "Take your hand away from that gun and sit quiet, Rickey.... I don't know, Governor. I'm having plenty of trouble with this army. Nobody wants to take orders."

Jean Morrow said softly, "John's impatient. But he is very clever. Let's discuss what evidence we have gathered so far and leave John to work out his own salvation. He misses his former life."

"Of fleecing suckers," snorted Sam Parsons.

Rickey Bole did not move in the chair. But his voice was like a whiplash, "The suckers asked for it, Parsons."

The governor frowned. He said, "I don't like this. We are at each other's throats every moment. There will be no conference tonight. I am leaving now. Pull yourselves together. We cannot have this cross-fire among ourselves.

Only by working closely together can we hope to make a gain against the men who are corrupting our institutions."

He rose, a fine figure of a man. He turned his worried eyes on each of them in turn. He said softly, "I'll see you all as soon as something develops. Take it easy—forget the need of haste. We must pull together every minute."

He was gone in another minute. Rickey Bole said soberly, "A good guy. Whyn't you lay off wise crackin', Sam? You made the gov unhappy."

Parsons said hopelessly, "I give up. Let's go to bed—all of us. We've got to work something out of this. I'll see John...."

IT WAS the next afternoon in Pete's Place. Behind the mahogany, Pete's walrus moustache drooped as he parked his paunch against the service sink and allowed his single eye to solemnly survey John Wade across the bar. There were no other occupants of the sidestreet gin mill this fall afternoon in Midburg. Outside there was no wind and the October air was warm and tranquil.

Pete ventured, "Things is quiet lately."

John nodded, the lines in his face deepening in discontent. Inaction seemed to him to widen the chasm between himself and Jean Morrow. He told himself for the thousandth time that he was not enamored of the former State College student phenomenon; that he had neither the right nor the urge to love or be loved by any one woman.

He told himself that it was a matter of loyalty to the governor which held him in line, that his ever-burning hatred of chiselers and double-timers made him long to act against the Schechtels of Midstate.

The rear door of the tavern opened and Pete said drily, "C'mon in, Patsy. You know you don't have to sneak no beers in this burg. Come in open. Nobody gives a damn."

A thick-bodied patrolman entered. He sucked at the amber beer which Pete proffered and fell into complaining at once. "It's that new rookie. Makes me thirsty. Wants to try every door on the beat. Pokes his nose in every alley. Got the book by heart. Kid Regulation, I calls him."

Pete said sententiously, "Billy Mulloy is a nice boy. He has got a nice wife and a nice baby. The Force needs plenty more like Billy. He will get some place on the cops. When you are still carryin' a log among the goats, Billy will be wearin' stripes."

Patsy Kelley sniffed into his beer. He said, "Pete, sometimes you talk like a citizen. I bet you believe in the Easter Bunny and Sandy Claus, too."

John Wade said, "Toothy Abe Schechtel doesn't promote a cop for ability, does he, Patsy?"

Kelley hooded his blue eyes and made his face wooden. He said, "I wouldn't know nothin' about Abe Schechtel."

John nodded. "Of course not, Kelley. I heard about that note you had with the money lenders. Abe fixed it for you okay, didn't he?"

Kelley said stonily, "You know too much, Wade. Some day...."

There were sudden sounds out in the street in front of Pete's Place. An automobile slammed into second gear and the motor raced. The sounds came again, rattling coughs as though the car had backfired many times, once off-key.

Kelley turned pale and said, "Migawd, one of them shots was a service gun."

John Wade was already running through the door. He paused on the sidewalk. The car, a heavy sedan, was just turning the corner on two wheels, shooting fire from the exhaust. It was, he noted resignedly, another black sedan. It was always a black sedan. Life insisted upon holding the mirror up to fiction.

Across the street was a small tailor shop. Inside, a light was burning. John moved swiftly on his long legs. He checked himself at the curb. He bent and picked up a bright, brass cartridge, still hot. He put it in his coat pocket and went on.

He hesitated at the door to the tailor shop, wrapping the blue silk handkerchief around his fist before touching the knob, protecting possible latent finger prints against obliteration. Then he opened the door and went inside.

On the floor lay two men. One, a small figure with a mop of bushy hair, was trying to arise. Blood ran through his hair and down the side of the man's face. John recognized Herman Kavinsky, mild little owner of the shop.

He moved to go to the tailor's aid but a glance at the second form held him in his tracks. The face turned to the ceiling was vacant, staring. The eyes were wide but they saw not. There were three small, neat holes in the forehead.

This man wore a blue uniform. His brass buttons gleamed brightly, his black shoes were polished until they shone. He had been a young man with an eager, intelligent face. He had been Billy Mulloy, whose wife and child were at home awaiting his return from the night patrol. He was as dead as Adam.

JOHN SUPPRESSED the choking in his throat and knelt beside Herman Kavinsky, raising the tailor's head. Kavinsky tried to speak, fighting for every breath.

"Billy Mulloy... he shouldn't of did it. I couldn't pay off.... They was pushing me around... but they would not of killed me.... Poor Billy... trying to save me, yet.... A good keed, Billy...."

He dropped back against John's arm, his blood marring the impeccability of the English jacket. He closed his eyes, opened them and stared up at John. He said, "Ach, Mr. Vade... that fine goots... Don't get it doity, yet....'T's a fine piece from goots..." And Herman Kavinsky died there on the floor of his shop and Patsy Kelley, his pot belly quivering under the Sam Browne belt of officialdom, came closer and said, wanly, "There'll be hell to pay about this. Billy was crazy."

John snapped, "Sure he was crazy, buttin' in on Abe Schechtel's collectors. He got killed for it. If you'd been on the job instead of guzzlin' beer in Pete's—"

Kelley said, "You think I wanted any part of this, Wade? Don't be a Boy Scout."

John let Herman Kavinsky's head gently to the floor. The two dead faces seemed to stare appealingly to him. He said indignantly:

"A citizen and a copper dead and nothin' will be done about it. There will be headlines and indignation for a couple days and then there will be quiet and Herman Kavinsky and Billy Mulloy will be forgotten."

Kelley picked the telephone from its place and called Headquarters without further display of emotion. John looked carefully around the shop. He wished Jean Morrow were here with her complete detective's field kit: that the sharp, experienced Parsons could prowl the scene. He knew enough to search for more cartridges, but the killers had evidently taken the time to retrieve all but the one he had found in the gutter. Since the F.B.I. in Washington had been known to possess records of almost every machine gun in circulation, mobsters had grown careful of their cartridges.

He thought that he could visualize the killing. There must have been at least three men. Two would have been roughing Herman Kavinsky, who could not pay off. One would be at the wheel of the car. Billy Mulloy had appeared and the man in the car had unlimbered the machine gun. Somehow Billy had turned to face that danger.

The men in the shop, forewarned, had of course hit the deck on their bellies. The gunner had aimed high, contrary to practice, to avoid enfilading them with his fire. Billy had caught the first lead, then Herman had been unable to duck.

Billy Mulloy's gun, clutched in his right hand even in death, would show one bullet exploded. John wondered where that bullet had found a home. He wished he could get the bullets from the bodies of Herman and the dead cop. He had no faith in the willingness of Police Headquarters to trace them to their source.

There was a siren in the street and brakes squealed. John suddenly realized that he should not be on the scene when the detectives arrived. True, Kelley would tell his story, but the brass cartridge should be delivered to Parsons at once. He was too late to make a getaway. The door slammed open and John noted cynically that no one bothered to preserve the prints he had so carefully salvaged.

CAPTAIN MOSE Belfry of the Homicide Division led the invasion. He was a bulky man with a hooked nose incongruously riding a fat face. He was reputedly a smart detective. He was, to John's knowledge, a ruffian with a sadistic streak a yard wide. He stared down at Billy Mulloy for a moment without comment.

Then he turned to the men who crowded behind him and said roughly, "Take your pictures, dust the joint for prints an' get the corpses down to the morgue. Snap into it before a mob collects. Patsy, go outside and don't let nobody near. Wade—what's your story?"

John said, "I heard the shots from Pete's and came over. Billy was dead when I got here. Herman died right after."

Belfry's expression did not change as he stared down at Billy Mulloy. After a moment he said, "Damn funny you should be on the ground. You got your nose in too much stuff lately."

John retorted, "There's a dead cop on the floor, Belfry. Aren't you interested?"

Belfry took a step forward, his jaw jutting. "You're damn right I'm interested. I'm interested in knowin' what the hell you know about this business."

"Lookin' for a fall guy already?" sneered John. "You know more about it than I do. Herman talked before he died but he didn't tell me anything you don't know right this minute."

Belfry took a deep breath. His voice got cold and hard. He said, "Consider yourself under arrest as a material witness, Wade."

"I wish I was a witness," snapped John. "I wish I'd seen Schechtel's hoods in here pushin' poor Herman around. There'd be dead Schechtel men to keep Billy and Herman company."

At the mention of that omnipotent name, Belfry's expression froze. He said slowly, "Tryin' to pull a bum beef, huh, Wade? Maybe I can figger this thing right here an' now. Maybe these stick-up men had this job fingered. Maybe you were the guy. You were in the gin mill. Was Kelley in there as usual, knockin' off a beer?"

John said boredly, "Ask Kelley."

Belfry's voice rose, "Maybe you held Kelley in the grog shop, not knowin' about Billy bein' along today. Your pals stick up Herman. Billy comes in and gets lead. That makes you an accessory, Wade."

John said, "Yeah. Only there was a car and Pete heard it and every day for two years when I am in town I take a drink about this time in Pete's and Kelley told us about Mulloy while I stood there. That is a very bad beef indeed, wise guy."

"It'll do me," said Belfry with satisfaction. "You're it, Wade."

Before he could move, two detectives had him by the arms, jerking his wrists together behind him. Belfry snapped handcuffs with a resounding click. John stood helpless, knowing suddenly that he was in a precarious fix.

They would need a Patsy for Abe Schechtel. The police, owned lock, stock and barrel by Toothy Abe, would have to make gestures with one of their own lying in the morgue. Poor little Herman could be laid at the door of casual stick-up men and easily forgotten. But a cop-killer is another thing.

Belfry was openly exultant. The husky captain was one of Schechtel's promotions, since the racketeer had taken over the Department. There were, of course, many men on the Force who could not be classed as Schechtel's cohorts, but Belfry was not one of them.

There was no escape now. John wished desperately for Rickey Boles. Even in a roomful of cops the big body-guard and his handy guns would have had an even chance of effecting a rescue. Rickey was out with John's red coupé and was not due at Pete's for an hour.

The photographers shot off their flashbulbs, the finger-print men desultorily dusted places where no prints of value would be found, men with notebooks made crude diagrams with X marking the position of each body. They searched the premises perfunctorily and John wondered sadly when they would search him and find the precious brass cartridge.

He fastened his thoughts upon that object. Somehow he must get it to Parsons. The under-cover man would examine it with Jean in Governor Castle's private laboratory, take pictures and send them to Washington. If the machine gun could be identified, if it had been used before or was used again, this check-up could be invaluable. It could, he realized with rising excitement, even lead to the undoing of Toothy Abe Schechtel. If the gun could be traced to one of Schechtel's mob and thence to the Big Boss....

THE MORGUE attendants came in, bearing their long, wicker basket with careless efficiency. John pointed his chin at Billy Mulloy, being unceremoniously tumbled into limbo and said, "You're lettin' a cop go unavenged by pinning this ridiculous charge on me, Belfry. I never knew a dick to be so rotten yellow he'd condone a cop-killer."

Belfry's red face went liverish. His big hand came up and slapped resoundingly against John's jaw, jarring him to his heels. The detective snarled, "You fingered him yourself, you rat. You're the guy'll pay for Mulloy's death."

John shook his head, trying to throw off the effects of the blow. He said, "Toothy Abe Schechtel's hoods collect this district this afternoon and you know it. Why don't you look them up, Belfry? You're scared, you big baboon."

Belfry grabbed him by the back of the neck and the slack of his trousers. John, helpless, had to stand for the shag which landed him on the sidewalk. He saw Pete's one eye watching expressionlessly across the street and carefully made no sign. Belfry slammed him into the squad car.

"That's just a piece of it, wise guy," he roared. "Before I get through with you, you'll sing and we'll have the other guys. And you'll wish you were never born, Wade, I promise you that personally."

The ride to Headquarters was a nightmare of shrieking siren and narrow escape from collision as a taciturn detective known as "Boffo" Cassidy trod on the accelerator. They hustled John in through the side entrance and down a flight of steps.

They did not book him and he knew at once where he was headed.

There was a corridor which was lighted only from the hall above, which would be dark when the door was closed. A cell door clanked open and Belfry shoved him once more, so that he flew inside and collided with the back wall.

Belfry said, "Cool off, punk. I'll heat you up later."

John gathered himself together. He could find no piece of furniture in the blackness. He was in a basement cell six feet by three with a damp floor and no place to lie or sit. He was in the detention pen next to the infamous room called "Coney Island."

He had no illusions as to what would happen to him now. In his years as a confidence man, always on the thin edge of the law, he had managed to walk safely without incarceration, because he had been clever and because he had been willing to pay the fixers. But he had heard plenty about Coney Island. He knew the tortures that could be inflicted upon suspects by a man like Mose Belfry.

There was no out. They had not booked him, therefore Rickey, Parsons, Jean—even the Governor could not find him. He would be worked over by the Headquarters force with impunity. If wind got about that he was here, they could whisk him from precinct to precinct, always a step ahead of a *habeas corpus*.

He had always sworn that if they caught him he would confess all and repudiate his statement later when he could get in touch with his lawyer. Even this avenue was closed now. A confessed copkiller would never survive the round of the police stations. They would beat him insane and swear he had fallen down a flight of steps.

He wondered how much he could take, if he could hold out against them without cracking. Perspiration ran down his back, between his shoulder blades. He had not known fear before. It was a very real thing now, very real and very unwholesome. He hated being afraid, but he could hold no hope, and without hope there is always leering fear.

Time slipped by. He paced the narrow length of the cell, trying to keep his circulation normal. They had not removed the handcuffs. Neither had they searched him, he realized suddenly. They had patted him for a weapon but they had not taken his effects, knowing him to be helpless in the shackles. He twisted in the English jacket, aided by its loose cut.

He got the brass cartridge in his fingers, clutching it. He felt along the floor of the cell, ran his fingers over the wall. At the back he found a depression where the floor met the imperfect wall. Erosion had worn a small crevice. He poked the cartridge carefully into the hole.

IT WOULD be safe enough in the darkness, he thought. These cells below stairs were seldom used, especially since Abe Schechtel's time when gangsters were given the run of Headquarters. When he wanted it he would get it, somehow. There was a good chance, he thought ruefully, that he might never again have sense enough to know what to do with it. Repeated beatings bring a dullness to the brain....

An indirect beam of light sprang down the corridor. John tightened his lean face. They were coming for him. He shut his mobile lips tightly. He had to hold out now, at the beginning. He must never confess to evade punishment. His only chance was to make his treatment a martyrdom, to come back if possible for his revenge.

Boffo Cassidy, the dour detective, opened the door. He jerked his head and said, "Out, killer."

John tried to shrug his jacket into something resembling jauntiness. He got his chin up and stepped out briskly. Cassidy grabbed him and slammed him against the wall as though he were a sack of potatoes. A door next to the cell was open. Cassidy caught him on the first bounce and pitched him through it.

Mose Belfry was in the room, grinning with anticipation. There were several chairs and alongside a bare table was one which was under a strong, white light. Cassidy used his bulk once more and John lit jarringly into that seat with the light burning fiercely upon him. Outside its rays were shadowy, bulky figures of men in shirt sleeves. John tried to pull himself erect.

Belfry said, "Relax, Wade. You'll last longer. I want cha t'last. It'll be more fun."

He moved into the circle of light and a limber, black thing dangled from his hand. It was the leaded hose of which John had heard, which would stun without leaving a mark. Belfry lashed out with it without warning, slashing at John's head.

John ducked instinctively. The blow fell upon his neck muscles, numbing them, sending pain through his lean body. Belfry's voice was thick with pleasure.

"Duck, you so and so. Keep duckin'. It makes fun."

John braced himself and said steadily, "Have your fun now, Belfry. This is your only chance."

"I'll murder you right here," roared Belfry, hauling back with the vicious length of hose. "I'll take it out for Billy Mulloy right now."

The door to Coney Island swung open behind the enraged detective captain. A whining voice said, "What's goin' on here?"

Without looking around Belfry snarled, "H'lo, Chief. Got the finger guy for the Mulloy job here. Just givin' him a lil' workout, thassall."

Another voice said harshly, "Speak up, Belfry. I can't hear you. Snap out of it!"

Belfry swung around as if a bee had stung him. Smiling Joey Watson, the fat, figurehead Chief of Police stood to one side of the open door, grinning vacuously. In the doorway stood a beefy man of great height. He had a mouthful of teeth which partly protruded from thick lips. He wore a hundred dollar suit of clothes and a twelve dollar shirt and yet he looked like a man clothed by the Salvation Army.

Belfry stammered, "Yes, Mr. Schechtel. I didn't know it was you, sir."

John Wade sat and stared at Toothy Abe Schechtel. This was the man who had started in life as a truck driver. He had organized his fellow-drivers long ago and that had been his beginning. Gaily they had sabotaged the owners into recognizing their independent union and its boss, Toothy Abe.

His rise had been swift.... The chicken men, the fish-mongers. Gangsters to aid in rounding up the taxi-men, who had been tough, but not tough enough. Organization of the imported mobsters into protective associations which preyed upon the Herman Kavinskys.

Then came the inevitable move into politics so that the rackets could persist untrammelled by the law. The First Ward, where Abe had always lived, had been easy. Abe knew the needs of the poverty-stricken denizens of the First Ward.

TONS OF coal and baskets of food had been dispensed with his ill-gotten gains. Then law services, loans to the needy without exorbitant interest. Outings for all, athletics for the young, drink for the drunken. And Abe Schechtel's INDEPENDENT VOTERS LEAGUE, avowedly "wearing no man's collar" but voting for the best man—the best man for Toothy Abe.

The First Ward had been easy. Boris Melinsky had seen the possibilities and had thrown in with the Second Ward. The Ghetto, without representation until now, had come over whole-heartedly.

Then Abe had hired Manning Endicott for his legal counsel. And Endicott had amazingly succeeded in welding the white collars of the Fourth Ward, that other forgotten group of humble but proud people, into an auxiliary known as the VOTERS INDEPENDENT CLUB, as wholly Abe's as the Ghetto or the reliable First.

That solid bloc of voters bought with puny gifts paid for by money stolen from them had been enough. Abe had shrewdly not attempted to control the town. He had made deals in high places, John knew. To get his votes, respectable stuffed shirts had been forced to do business.

Then Abe had taken over the Police Department. Abe's rackets were safe, Abe's income secure. He was a Hitler, a Mussolini in Midburg.

Yet, John knew, Abe Schechtel did not own every cop. No man can own an entire Police Department because always there are officers who are more than men working at a job. Always there are men who are cops in their hearts, because they believe in law enforcement. Abe Schechtel had these men walking the goat districts with aching feet, but they were at hand when and if Abe's power should slip.

Chief Smiling Joe Watson was not one of these. His perpetual, inane grin did not change as he said to Belfry, "A cop-killer, huh?"

"Fingered the job," nodded Belfry. "Just as bad. I'll have the answer outa him in a jiffy."

The words were addressed to Watson but Belfry's eye was upon Abe Schechtel, fawning, beaming. The toothy man came forward, shambling on flat feet in custom-made shoes. He peered down at John Wade and his black eyes were surprisingly sharp and interested as John stared back at him.

Schechtel said, "John Wade, ain't it? I know Wade."

John shrugged. He was mildly surprised, knowing that he had never exchanged words with the Big Boss. He said briefly, "I had nothing to do with the job and Belfry knows it. I'm playin' patsy."

Belfry said triumphantly, "He says! You know what, Mr. Schechtel? He even tried to say Kavinsky made a statement layin' it on a couple your boys. Said they was pushin' the kike around when Billy went for 'em."

Schechtel said thoughtfully, "That right, Wade?"

John took a deep breath. He said steadily, hopelessly, "That's what Kavinsky said before he died."

Abe Schechtel nodded. He said, "I heard you had plenty moxie, Wade. You didn't finger that job?"

John said shortly, "I'm no geezer, Schechtel."

Toothy Abe raised a long, bony finger and placed it alongside his prominent nose. He ran the tip slowly up towards his eyebrow, then back down to the corner of his loose lips. No one moved or spoke while he stood there, considering John Wade.

At last he said easily, "Why no, Wade. I don't believe you are. I heard you had a couple bum beefs on con rackets. But nobody ever made one of them stand up. You want a mouthpiece?"

Mose Belfry opened his mouth and closed it and opened it again like a big fish. Smiling Joe Watson's grimace never altered a jot. John tried to keep the eagerness from his voice. He said, "I don't want a chocolate soda, Schechtel."

Toothy Abe nodded. "I'll have Endicott down here in half an hour. You know me, Wade. Always with the under-dog. It's my weakness."

He smiled and posed before the detectives, preening his ego in their silent acquiescence. He said to the Chief, "Or maybe you'd like t'turn him loose in my custody, huh, Joe?"

The Chief said, "Why now, that's an idea, Abe. You'll be responsible for him?"

"Cert'ny, cert'ny," said Schechtel, waving his truck-driv-er's hand. "Take care of it, Joe. Take care of it."

That was all. Schechtel stalked out, Smiling Joe toddling behind like a Pomeranian after a police dog. Mose Belfry's mouth had stopped on "open," his eyes goggling. John got up from the chair.

He turned his back and thrust out his arms. He said, "Come, come, my good man. Take 'em off and make it snappy. You would not want to be walking the goat district with a log of wood, would you? You heard the Master speak, did you not?"

Belfry choked and came forward with a key. The detectives beyond the white circle of light were still nebulous, disembodied spirits.

John Wade suddenly felt very good about the whole thing.

CHAPTER TWO
ANOTHER STRANGE
ROLE

THE AIR, the blessed, free air of the street where people went unhindered about their business, was balm to frazzled nerve ends. John Wade went down the steps and walked aimlessly for moments, enjoying newly precious freedom. It was scarcely midnight, yet it seemed days since he had been tucked into the cell next to Coney Island.

A car swung into the curb just ahead. He recognized the vehicle as a sedan, as a black sedan. His gorge rose, then died into cold rage. He walked directly towards it.

There was the snout of a big revolver. It was trained on John's middle. There were three men in the car. John recognized them as Ikey Bittel, Schlonk Krag and Bootsy Bannigan, who was at the wheel. They were slick-haired, pasty-faced and wore sports clothes. They looked like three grown-up pool room idlers upon whom affluence had miraculously descended. They were three of Toothy Abe Schechtel's "collectors."

John said flatly, "Put up that rod, Schlonk. I'm not taking anything from you punks right now."

Krag had intelligent eyes and a quick tongue. He put the gun away under his Norfolk jacket and said propitiatingly, "Sorry, Wade. Force o' habit. Abe wants to see you."

John tried to scan the sedan without seeming to display interest too acute. He stood upon the curbing, debating with himself. His eye caught a round hole in the smooth surface at the rear of the car.

He said, "Abe's got a right to see me. He pulled me out of a jam. But don't get careless with guns, Schlonk. I'm a nervous man around guns."

He got into the car. Bootsy Bannigan, a strong, silent hoodlum with a reputation for snapping arms like twigs when the pay-off was not ready for Schechtel, drove off.

Ikey Bittel was jumpy as usual. He was a little cokey, very quick on the trigger, John had heard. He sat beside Bannigan and jittered as the big man coolly ignored Midburg's traffic laws.

Schlonk said, "Abe speaks good about you, Wade. He thinks you're plenty smart."

The car turned up Prince Street and turned into narrow Elm, which led to the First Ward. Abe Schechtel had never deserted his humble beginnings.

"Yeah," John said, "Abe's plenty smart himself. Too smart for a guy like me."

"Abe's never too smart for a guy he likes," said Krag pointedly. "Abe never went back on a pal in his life."

John nodded slowly. "It's a good thing to remember. I always heard that about Abe. I won't forget it."

Krag grinned thinly. The car drew up before a frame building on a block filled with teeming tenements, a three story house startlingly white in squalid surroundings. There was a wooden sign, the letters of which spelled, "INDE-PENDENT VOTER'S LEAGUE." John went up the steps and into the building.

The ceilings of the old house were high and there was a broad hall down the middle. Downstairs were two large rooms furnished with comfortable, sturdy chairs, magazine racks, card tables and the inevitable pool table. There were stairs going above. John mounted them slowly and came to a hall from which led a veritable maze of doors.

Krag moved to one of the identical portals and knocked. Abe Schechtel's voice rumbled, "C'mon in, Schlonky."

It was a moderate-sized chamber with plain, mahogany office fixtures and one deep leather chair. It also held twin doors at its rear, which in turn must have led to other chambers cunningly cut to intermix like a Chinese box puzzle. It was apparent that a curious person would be hard put to make sense of the architectural set-up of Schechtel's retreat.

THE BIG Boss sat behind the desk, his necktie slightly askew, a cigar tilted at an angle from his loose mouth. He said, "Hiya, pal? Howja like your trip to Coney?"

"Very un-good," admitted John. "Those boys play too rough."

Abe nodded comfortably. "Smart guys like you ain't got no business down under the jail like that."

"I do not claim to be a real smart guy," said John.

"They never made a rap stand up on you," chuckled Abe. "I know your record, pal. I know plenty things. You are smart enough."

John said pleasantly, "You wouldn't be making me a proposition, would you Abe?"

"Well," said Schechtel, allowing the cigar to roll about between his rubbery lips in a gymnastic pattern of parabolas, "I gotta be careful, if ya know what I mean. My boys are all nice boys with clean noses. But I think I could use you, Wade. A guy smart enough to wear clothes like you can't, be dumb. Sometimes I think I could use a front now and again. Know what I mean?"

He nodded pontifically, beaming as though he were bestowing the highest of accolades. John made himself sound impressed. He said, "If I was wired in right there are angles, Abe. Smart angles."

Abe said, "Where you stayin' at?"

"The Montrose Hotel," said John. "Rickey Bole and I got a couple of rooms there."

"I heard of Bole. He is a guy who is handy with a—a lot of things, huh, John? I could use Bole, too."

"That's good," said John. "You hirin' me to dress you, Abe?"

Schechtel dusted the ash of the cigar, narrowly missing his vest. He said, "Get me straight, pal. I sprung you outa the can because you got brains and I can afford to hire brains. I got brains of my own, y'unnastand. But a real smart guy never sells brains short. Don't sell me short, Wade."

"Okay, Abe," said John passively. "What do I do next?"

"Schlonk Krag will get in touch with you," said Abe. "You wait at the Montrose 'til you hear from me. Say, tell me somethin' Wade. Who makes them swell suits for you? I'd like to get me a suit made by your tailor."

John said lightly, not taking his eyes from the Big Boss's face, "You're too late, Abe. Herman Kavinsky made my clothes for years."

Abe never flickered an eyelid. He said, "Kavinsky? That's the poor Hebe got knocked off, ain't it? Too bad. Well— when ya get another one like 'im, lemme know, you hear?"

"Yeah," said John. "Sure, Abe."

He leaned across the desk and reached out his hands. Abe's face turned pale and he jerked backwards. John said gently, "Your necktie. Abe. It's crooked."

He pulled the knot up slowly. Schechtel's eyes were hooded, inscrutable, but he did not stir. John gave the cravat a final flick and said, "Got to go and change this suit, now. See? Kavinksy's blood all over the sleeve."

He smiled upon Schechtel and went out, leaving the racketeer staring hard at his back. He went downstairs and got into a taxi which he knew was owned by one of Schechtel's corporations. He went directly to the Montrose Hotel.

The lobby seemed filled with Rickey Boles. The crooked-nosed, giant bodyguard was stalking up and down taking up more room than a battleship, staring suspiciously at everyone in sight. The room clerk looked nervous; the assistant manager saw John Wade and threw up his hands in relief.

John said, "Hey, Rickey. What makes?"

The big man whirled and his eyes were filled with great joy upon the instant. He said, plaintively, "You could of let a guy know. Pete tells me this Belfry lugged you off to the can and what happens? They give me the stalleroo. So after I hit the copper—"

John said, "Not Belfry? You didn't hit Belfry?"

"I could not find the Captain," said Rickey regretfully. "I found a guy named Boffo Cassidy, though, and he gets tough. So I clips him and then they did not like me around Headquarters any more. So I hear Abe Schechtel has got you and then I give you an hour before I shall take Mr. Thomas and go after Schechtel."

John said, "It was a good idea to sock Cassidy, at that. I owe him a couple. I owe Belfry more."

He moved his shoulder uneasily. It hurt still where the loaded hose had landed. He went on, "But don't unlimber that tommy-gun of yours until I give you the word. Tommy-guns spell trouble these days. Besides, we are working for Abe Schechtel now and he can furnish his own materials...."

Rickey's slice of a mouth hung wide open. He gasped, "Schechtel? You an' me an' Schechtel? No, John."

John said, "Ixnay on the ackscray, uckersay. Get upstairs."

THEY TOOK the elevator to the sixth floor and their comfortable two-room suite. John said, "Parsons was right when he made us take this place and leave an out for the Avery Place house. I wouldn't like Schechtel comin' down on Avery Place."

Rickey said, "Now look here, John. I do not like this business of workin' for Schechtel. No good will come of it. Abe is not honest!"

"No," said John, amused as ever at Rickey Boles's peculiar private standards of morality. "I understand he takes money under false pretenses."

"That ain't it," said Rickey stubbornly, furrowing his low brow. "Abe Schechtel is a wrongo. He is strickly dishonest in all his dealings."

John said, "I hear he never crosses a pal."

"He would cross his favorite grandmother, only he has not got a grandmother," said Rickey flatly. "He has not even got a legit father."

"You are probably quite correct," said John. "As a matter of fact, Rickey, we are not actually becoming members of Schechter's organization. If he accepts us we are pretending to do so. But actually we are looking for a certain tommy-gun."

Rickey looked hugely pleased. "Undercover guys? Like G-Men?" he said eagerly.

"Right," said John. "I knew you'd enjoy it."

He started for the telephone to call Sam Parsons in the second house on Avery Place, then stopped. He said, "Rickey, I have an idea our phone is tapped. I imagine Mr. Schechtel will be checking hard on us today. I tell you, I'll write a message. You leave it at Pete's Place—and keep your eyes open. You'll be tailed undoubtedly."

Rickey said, "If I had one dime for every time I shook a tail...."

John wrote his message to Parsons and Jean Morrow on a piece of hotel stationery, folded it and handed it to the big bodyguard. He said, "If one of Abe's men gets too close to you, hang onto the note until you shake him."

Rickey said, "I can't sock him?"

"You're supposed to be joinin' them, you mug," said John.

"Oh yeah," nodded Rickey soberly. "I almost forgot. Look, can I sock Captain Belfry?"

"I sincerely hope so," said John, "But not until I say so."

"Just so's I can look forward to it," said Rickey cheerfully. He departed with the message.

John shook his head, but immediately put the matter of the delivery of the note from his mind. Rickey would deliver it. Rickey's apparent simplicity induced underestimation of his canny if transparent nature. He was utterly and thoroughly reliable.

John turned his attention to bathing and re-dressing, carefully, tender of each detail. He was immaculate by nature; but his brain actively dwelt upon the problem at hand.

Until his advent into the ranks of law and order under-cover men, John Wade had been a stranger to scenes of violence and carnage. His own smooth work in selling oil stocks, phony race track tips and other genteel swindling plots had never led him into the darker alleys of crime. The scene in Herman Kavinsky's shop had etched deeply upon his mind.

The useless slaughter of Billy Mulloy filled him with increasing nausea. The thought of Abe Schechtel, sitting like a huge toad, dispensing his orders through a half-witted chief of police was revolting.

The trail of the brass cartridge cached in the cell next to Coney Island seemed hot to him. He had a feeling that Sam Parsons would not approve of his joining Schechtel's outfit on such slim evidence; that Governor Castle might not be too pleased at such a drastic maneuver. He himself did not relish the role of stool pigeon.

He did not, indeed, appreciate any of the circumstances of the set-up. But he could not shake off the picture of the dying little tailor, or the bravely polished shoes and shining brass buttons of Billy Mulloy.

CHAPTER THREE
A GUN AND A HOLE

IT WAS the morning after the twin killing in Kavinsky's shop. John Wade and Rickey Boles had breakfasted at eleven in their rooms. Rickey complained, "This joint has not got hot-cakes which are like Evalina's hot cakes. They are more like flannel blankets."

John sighed and wondered when he would again see black, devoted Evalina and the comfortable small retreat on Avery Place where for so long he had cloaked himself in an atmosphere of quiet respectability.

"Inferior flannel at that," he said. "We are here until this case breaks, Rickey, Did you deliver the note?"

Rickey said, "A hood they call Bootsy Bannigan folleyed me into Pete's place. I give Pete a ten-spot with the note folded inside. Of course I wait until this Bootsy is in the men's room before I do this. He does not see me at all."

"If Parsons calls here it will be bad," mused John. "We can't involve Pete any further. He's too useful to us. Rickey, we've got to find that tommy-gun."

Rickey said, "I hope there is not a gee hanging onto the trigger of this heater when we find it."

"Schechtel's men will be all around us until he makes up his mind we are okay," said John. "We've got to be very careful, Rickey."

The telephone rang. John motioned at Rickey for attentive silence and picked up the instrument. Abe Schechtel's voice, was hearty, confidential.

"Wade? Hiya, pal?… Look, come down here t'night about ten. I'll have somethin' for you."

John said. "Thank you, Mr. Jones. Tonight at ten? I'll be there, Mr. Jones."

Schechtel chuckled, "I said you was smart. You'll do, Wade. I'm pretty sure it'll be all right."

John hung up. He said rapidly to Rickey, "That's the blow-off. You know how these mobs work. Tonight Abe'll send me out on a job with a couple of his hoods. It's bound to be something that will definitely tie me to his gang, like beating up or terrorizing a citizen.

"I can't afford that. The cops don't like me now and the honest ones would never learn to like me even if we succeeded in busting up Schechtel's wagon. I can't come out in the open as one of Castle's operators or my usefulness will be ended.

"So before ten o'clock tonight we've got to find that machine gun, get a cartridge out of a cell at Headquarters, turn everything over to Parsons and lam out of town. While we're gone Parsons and Jean can clean up the case and nail the murderers of Billy Mulloy—and through them, Schechtel."

"It sounds to me," said Rickey judiciously, "like we do all the work and Parsons has all the fun."

"We've got to get going," insisted John. "You'll—"

There was a rap on the door of the room. John pushed back the wheeled table bearing the breakfast dishes. Rickey bounded to the shoulder holster strung carelessly over a chair.

There was another imperative knock. John took the handle of the door in his hand, turned it silently. Then he jerked it towards him, leaving Rickey to cover the portal with his big gun.

A blonde, pretty girl with violet eyes walked into the room. She was below middle height and of a slimness which would have adorned the stage of any Broadway show. Her expression, habitually serene, was perplexed as she spied Rickey crouched behind the .45 Colt revolver. She was Jean Morrow, the cleverest young woman in the state.

Sam Parsons followed on her heels. The little, fox-terrier man's pointed features and faded grey eyes had the instinctive alertness of the dog he so closely resembled. He said distastefully, "What's all this hullabaloo?"

"You didn't get my message?" said John tensely.

"We heard you were in trouble with the police," said Jean Morrow. "We came down to check up."

"What message?" demanded Parsons.

John said, "Rickey, Bannigan saw you. They've got Pete. Did you call Pete, Sam?"

Parsons said, "I called him a half hour ago but no one answered. He doesn't open that joint until noon, does he?"

"He won't open it today," said John. "I sent you a message telling you the whole story. Schechtel's hoods must have seen Rickey pass it. The fat, folks, is now in the fire."

Parsons said tersely, "Let's have it, Wade."

The little man's eyes grew hard as John told him. He said when the tale was done, "Half-cocked again. We've been carefully gathering evidence from the other end—Schechtel's in goes all the way to the Governor's staff, Wade. How are you going to break it with one lousy brass cartridge?"

JEAN MORROW interrupted smoothly, "That's beside the point, Sam. John is into it, now. Schechtel knows something about us all. We are in danger right now. The Avery Place houses, our work for the Governor—everything is all endangered. We must figure a way out."

John said feverishly, "Schechtel gave me until ten o'clock tonight. Maybe he figures to take us for a ride. Maybe he's framin' a job where we can be conveniently killed by some of his cops. But he won't act until ten o'clock."

"We figgered on cleanin' it up by ten o'clock," explained Rickey brightly. "So what's the difference?"

"We also figured on Sam and Jean winding up the case," pointed out John. "Now they are in as much danger as we."

Rickey got up and sauntered about the room. Parsons repeated, "Half-cocked. Wade, we're in a hell of a jam. The Governor can't be dragged into this, you know. He has too many enemies."

Rickey was at the door of the bedroom of the suite, which was closed. He made a sudden move and the door came wide. A small figure tumbled into the room. Rickey made one brief motion with his right fist. The figure straightened out and lay quietly upon the carpeted floor.

John said, "Ikey Bittel. He must have come up the fire escape. Nice work, Rickey."

"I got ears like a gnat," said Rickey, not explaining what kind of ears a gnat possesses. "Do we bump this mug off or take him for a ride?"

"We do neither," said John promptly. "Look—Schechtel is on to us all. There are two more of these mugs around town. Schechtel is going to hold off until ten tonight. Evidently only he and these three hoods know about us."

Parsons nodded, "We tie this one up and hold him."

"You and Jean stay right here," went on John. "Rickey and I will see what we can do."

Rickey said, "I still think we should bump this hero. He is a cokey and cokey's are not nice people."

Nevertheless the big man utilized light cord, sheeting and some adhesive tape. Soon the hapless Ikey was a bundle of wrappings. Rickey stood him carefully in a closet and shut the door.

Jean Morrow said to John, "Are you sure you know what you are doing?"

"Nope," said John readily. "I am the world's lousiest detective. But I know underworld minds like Schechtel's. His ego will tempt him to clean up on us with his own clique so that he can brag about it later. That gives us some time."

The girl said, "It will take time to check up on that cartridge. We can prove it with our equipment to our own satisfaction, but it must be wired to Washington for official confirmation, even if you are correct."

"We've got to chance that," said John.

Parsons said, "Too big. The chance is too long."

Jean Morrow said softly, "John's awfully lucky. And he's right about the Schechtel psychology. Good-luck, boys."

JOHN ADJUSTED the single breasted grey jacket over the unaccustomed bulge of the shoulder holster which contained the .32 revolver he scarcely knew how to use. He said grimly, "Thanks, Jean, we'll need it. If you don't hear from us pretty soon you better make a move."

"We'll be here—one of us," she promised him, and her big eyes were tender for a moment so that his pulse fluttered and quick blood surged in his lined face. He nodded curtly to cover his agitation and followed Rickey into the hall.

All the way through the lobby they half-expected trouble. Not until they were on the sidewalk were they sure that Ikey had been sent alone on his errand of spying.

Safely outdoors, John said, "Rickey, if you were a machine gun belongin' to Abe Schechtel's mob, where would you be?"

Rickey scratched his crinkly black hair. Then he said seriously, "If I would have just burned a copper I would be sloughed into a lake or somethin'."

John shook his head. "Machine guns are too scarce, and Schechtel's too big. They don't have to slough a hot gun."

"Then," said Rickey triumphantly, "I'd be stached in a heap. That's where my Mr. Thomas stays at."

John snapped his fingers. "The inevitable black sedan. Rickey, this is a pushover."

"I ain't bright," said Rickey, "but sometimes I am quick. So I ask you, where is this black see-dan?"

John stood for a moment, fingering his lapel. He said slowly, "Ikey Bittel upstairs… how would he get away? I have a hunch that if we stood here long enough this sedan would drive right up in front of us."

Rickey said, "So what do we do then? We cannot stop a see-dan belonging to Abe Schechtel and case it in broad daylight. Not in this town we can't."

John said, "Get our car from the parkin' lot. Bring it around and keep your eye on me."

"I do not like this," frowned Rickey. "Those Schechtel mobsters are tough people, John."

"I've met them," said John. "Get goin', will you?"

Rickey went. A few moments later John could see his red coupé nosed in at the curb, the big man peering tensely from behind the wheel. The moments went by until the corner clock said one, and the crowds of office workers in the downtown district began sifting back into the large buildings.

He had almost given up when the big black car at last appeared, pushing contemptuously through lesser traffic. He stepped to the curb, adorning his lean features with a welcoming smile. Bootsy Bannigan was driving. Schlonk Krag was on the back seat.

John moved with the suddenness which was sometimes paralyzing to the beholder. He had the car door open and closed and was on the rear seat with Krag before either hoodlum could blink.

He said pleasantly, "Let's take a lil' ride, huh, boys? See the town. It's a nice town in spite of some people we both know."

Bannigan sat with open mouth but Schlonk's hand darted rapidly to the holster under his left arm. It did not occur to John to match draws with the gangster. True to his training, he lashed out with his left fist. His wrist flicked in a practiced gesture and his bony, solid fist went home on the point of Krag's jaw. The mobster sagged.

John plucked the gun from Krag's hand. He said softly, "Don't try it, Bootsy. Just drive. Nice and slow and where I tell you to drive."

Bannigan's hands returned unwillingly to the wheel. He growled, "Say, you punk—you can't do this."

"Straight ahead 'til I tell you to turn, Bootsy," said John stonily. "There's that little matter of Pete. I could square up whatever you did with Pete—right here."

BANNIGAN STARTED the car, his red face wooden. Krag jerked convulsively, returning to consciousness. John hit him again, without regret, behind the ear. Krag went back to sleep.

Behind, the red coupé picked up the trail. John said, "Out Morgan Road, Bannigan. Straight out, into the sub-development. And no funny business."

The streets were deserted except for some half-completed houses in the subdevelopment. Bannigan said, "You better take it easy, Wade. You can't buck Abe Schechtel."

"I take smarter uckersays than Schechtel every day in the week," said John. "Pull over here, behind these trees."

An empty house frowned down and no human stirred in sight. Rickey tooled the red coupé around the corner and came abreast.

John said, "Take Bannigan, Rickey. I've got Krag."

Rickey boiled out of the car and came fast. Bannigan was reaching under the dash of the sedan. Rickey hit him with a fist like a ham and Bannigan rolled over. John dropped Krag out into the street. Rickey reached in and got Bannigan by the foot. In a second the two lay dusty in the road, bleeding slightly from the hard-knuckled blows.

John was inside the big sedan, searching feverishly. He found rolls of adhesive tape; soft, pliable wire; bandages for the eyes; he even found a pre-constructed gag for each hood. He said, "What the well-equipped mob car will wear. Tie 'em up. Rickey."

Rickey straightened, bearing an automatic pistol and a long knife which he had found upon Bannigan. He complained, "Tie 'em up, tie 'em up! What are we gonna do with all these apes when we get them tied up?"

John was tearing the cushions of the sedan apart. He called, "Maybe they would like to talk. Maybe they would like to tell you where they keep that tommy-gun with which they killed Mulloy and Herman Kavinsky."

Rickey looked at the two gangsters. They were completely and thoroughly unable to talk even had they been willing. Rickey's hands were deft and strong and practised in tying people securely. He said doubtfully, "I would untie them and urge them but I do not think these mugs are talkative people."

The back cushion came loose in John's hands. The machine gun was not carefully hidden. It lay secure in its case behind the seat. John could have kissed it. He lifted it out carefully, watching the eyes of the two mobsters. Neither showed any emotion other than blank indifference. John pondered briefly on the courage of cornered rats.

He went outside and again examined the small hole in the metal of the car, which was not armored. He plunged again into the interior, taking Bootsy Bannigan's knife. The abused back cushion gave under his slashing. He probed around in the springs and excelsior with his fingers until he found what he sought. He put the pellet of lead in his pocket and wondered ruefully if enough markings would be left on its crushed surfaces to identify it with Billy Mulloy's gun.

It was another link, he thought. The chain was being slowly forged. If only he had time.... The F.B.I. would co-operate, but they had no jurisdiction. He must proceed undercover, relying upon Jean Morrow's speed and skill in the Governor's private laboratory and the breaks of the game.

Rickey said, "I ask you, John, what are we going to do with these people? Can't we just bump them and leave 'em in one of these empty joints?"

John said. "I want them handy, where we can produce them when we need them."

"I can't lug them around," protested Rickey.

John said thoughtfully, "If we only had a couple of boxes or crates or somethin'...."

"Oh," said Rickey, relieved, "is that all? A pushover. I got a pal who owns a lumber yard."

"No questions asked?" queried John.

"Pals of mine don't ask no questions," said Rickey. "I will see to it that he drives the truck himself."

"That," said John, his dark eyes gleaming, "will be just too ducky."

CHAPTER FOUR
CRATE OF KILLERS

IT WAS three-thirty-five. Rickey said, "We drive around and we don't do nothing. How are we gonna snatch that cartridge outa that cell?"

John said, "I think we'll have a drink on that."

"Scotch?" asked Rickey hopefully.

"Scotch," assented John.

They went into a side street bar which they believed was not one of Schechtel's places. They had been driving around town keeping out of sight of any stray Schechtel men. They ordered a couple of Scotches. They drank them slowly. When the hands of the clock pointed to four. Rickey frowned and said, "Six hours is not enough time for what we got to do. We should right now be getting ready to lam town."

John said, "Young fellow, you're drunk."

Rickey guffawed. "On a bottle of this you could not get me drunk. Not good and drunk."

"You are drunk," reiterated John. "You will now go down to Headquarters. You will claim that Cassidy has wronged you. You will sock Cassidy again, unless you can sock Belfry."

Rickey perked up. He said, "And you will be in there with Mr. Thomas to cover me. You an' me and my Mr. Thomas can stick up the station and grab that cartridge."

"Your precious Mr. Thomas will stay in its case," said John inexorably. "We are not hi-jacking Police Headquarters with a machine gun to find a machine gun bullet. It wouldn't make sense and anyway someone would pop us off. You will just sock Cassidy, or preferably Belfry, and let events take their course."

Rickey complained, "And have them dumb cops rake me over in Coney Island? I do not like this, John."

"But you'll do it," said John firmly.

"I oughta have another drink to make me seem drunker," stalled Rickey. "I can't even play drunk on one drink."

He took the bottle standing on the bar and tilted it. John watched, fascinated, as the amber liquid vanished. Almost a pint had disappeared when he finally seized Rickey's arm and made him stop guzzling. The big man grinned and said,

"Well—I always wanted to sock a cop right in Headquarters. Let us go and do this thing."

John drove. A block from the station he said, "Okay, pal. Let's see you stagger."

Rickey said, "Drunk as a mice. Whoop-pee!"

He clambered out of the car. He went weaving down the sidewalk, swaying convincingly. For a disturbing moment John wondered if he had not sold his idea too well—if Rickey were really too drunk to carry out instructions. He shrugged and waited fifteen minutes. He would have to make sure. The police, he felt, would not have anything on him. He still had time to bluff. Ten o'clock would be the deadline.

When the quarter hour was up he started the car, parked it in front of Headquarters against a No Parking sign and sauntered inside. In the corridor he came upon Boffo Cassidy. The tough detective was groping his way along toward the Infirmary. One eye was closed as a result of the morning's encounter. The other was obscured by a hand-kerchief which Cassidy held against it.

John beamed with satisfaction. It was probably, he thought, all for the best that Rickey had encountered Cassidy instead of Belfry. The Captain was a tough customer and handy with a blackjack. He might have nailed Rickey with that weapon. He went on inside.

Belfry was leaning against the rail, gesticulating at the lieutenant in charge.

John said loudly, "You seen my boy Rickey Boles around here?"

Belfry whirled around as if a large bee had stung him. He glared at John. John's eyes popped wide in mock dismay as he said, "Why, Belfry! Don't tell me you tried to mess with Rickey without usin' your mace?"

BELFRY'S LEFT eye was growing very black. His nose was swollen to alarming proportions. He said thickly, "You dirty lousy so and so. You sent that crazy gunman in here. I'll—"

He made a jump for John, who gave ground, stepping sideways. Belfry tried to check himself and John hit him with a left, a right and a left. The lieutenant, a man named Ogilva, long in the service, said chidingly, "You shouldn't do that, Wade. It's against regulations."

Belfry hit the floor in a heap. John explained, "He gave it to me yesterday when I was handcuffed."

"I heard," nodded the lieutenant. "I'll have to arrest you, though, Wade."

John nodded, "Sure. But I can telephone?"

The lieutenant temporized, "Who would you be callin', Wade? Anybody I know?"

"Well," hesitated John, "either Endicott or—Abe."

Ogilva sighed. He said, "I heard. Well—ain't no use in you callin' and wastin' that time. You better take Boles. He's about tearin' down the cell by now."

"He's impulsive," explained John ingenuously. "He learned about Cassidy and Belfry workin' me over yesterday."

"Yeah," said Ogilva. "I gathered that. He yells a lot when he's drunk."

"I suppose he's downstairs? Where I was?" said John, off-handedly, holding his breath for the answer meanwhile.

Ogilva said, "Where else?"

John nodded sympathetically. "You guys have your problems these days. Say—isn't Tony your nephew or somethin'?"

Ogilva nodded. "You mean Tony Maretta from the prosecutor's office? Yeah, I heard him say you was all right. Let's get your pal before Mose wakes up."

There was a tremendous sound below stairs as they approached the cell. John listened for a moment. Then he said, "Rickey's singing."

"He's singin' 'Old Man Mose Is Dead,'" nodded Ogilva. "It made Belfry awful mad."

John said, "Impulsive, that's Rickey."

Ogilva opened the door. Rickey plunged from the dimness of the cell like an enraged bull. Ogilva ducked and said hastily, "Hey! Tell him I'm a pal, Wade."

John soothed, "Lay off, Rickey. These cops are on the same payroll as we are these days. Lay off, I say."

"I won't be on same payroll with coppers," roared Rickey. "Coppers is crooks."

John said, "He will have his fun. Come on now, Rick. Quit playin'. Abe has work for us to do."

They got him up the stairs and into the main corridor. There were several people about, citizens upon business, police officials and officers going about their duties. Ogilva said, "Maybe you better ease him out the side door, Wade."

"Yeah," said John. "Thanks, pal. Do somethin' for you some day."

"Just remember me to Abe," murmured Ogilva. "Abe ain't never noticed me yet."

John nodded gravely, "I'll remember that, pal."

He raced around front, hauling Rickey by the arm. They piled into the coupé and John drove rapidly through the downtown streets towards the Montrose Hotel. Rickey kept saying, "Boy, oh, boy, oh boy. Ain't had so much fun since Kirby died…. Ain't had so much fun since m' kid brother ate a copperhead… Boy, oh boy, oh boy!"

John said, "The cartridge?"

"In me kick," chortled Rickey. "I hits Cassidy in the hall. Just as he lights on his neck, Belfry comes at me with that black thing. I take the black thing and I bend it around his ear. Then I up-end 'im with a right and level him out with the left. Mister, I ain't had so much fun since my aunt had that accident with the wringer."

John said beatifically, "I had doings with Mr. Belfry myself."

"I sang 'Old Man Mose' and he come in the cell at me," chortled Rickey. "I socked him in there, an' Ogilva had t' lug 'im out. I wouldn't stop singin'—"

"I clipped him with two lefts and a right."

Rickey said with huge enthusiasm, "A good left, John?"

"Two good lefts," corrected John.

Rickey said, "Oh boy, oh boy, oh boy!" Then he sobered. He said, "Look, John."

"I'm lookin'," said John good-humoredly.

"THIS CARTRIDGE," said Rickey. "Suppose we tie it to that tommy-gun those characters had. They have not got that tommy-gun now. We have got it right in this car."

"They'll have it," said John grimly. "If this cartridge came out of their gun, they will be found some place with the gun in their laps. That is why I kept them handy. I'll frame them so tight the 'cutor's office'll walk home with the case, and the hell with the police."

Rickey frowned, "This framin' guys. It is not strickly honest, John. Since we are law and order guys we do lots of things which go against me, John."

"If the gun and cartridge matches up, they murdered Billy Mulloy and Kavinsky, didn't they?" John pointed out patiently. "You don't object to tyin' murders to killers, do you?"

"I would rather bump them off and let it go at that," said Rickey simply. "For two pins I would take Mr. Thomas and line up them three and kiss them goodbye with lead. I would throw in Mr. Abe Schechtel for one pin more."

"Neat idea," nodded John, "but impractical. The Governor and Sam and Jean would not like it."

"They are amachoors," said Rickey sadly. "That is the worst of workin' with amachoors."

In the hotel room Jean Morrow and Sam Parsons were not conducting themselves like amateurs of intrigue. They were calmly playing 500 rummy on a small table and Jean was winning Sam Parsons' money hand over fist.

John said, "We got it. Clean as a whistle."

He handed the cartridge to Jean and the cased gun to Sam Parsons. He said eagerly, "Match 'em up fast and rush it to Washington. Rickey and I will scram as soon as we get the news and attend to a couple of small details. Did a man come with a crate?"

"Yeah," nodded Parsons. "Are you screwy, Wade?"

"You'll find out," chortled John.

He dragged the long crate out of the bedroom where they had stored it. He opened the closet door and found Ike Bittel still propped in the corner. He lifted him out, mercifully ungagged him and gave him some water. Ikey eyed the crate and said, "Gimme a shot, cancha, pal? I could take it if you gimme one shot."

"If I had it," said John honestly, "you could take one, Ike."

The little hop-head muttered, "So what the hell? Abe'll give you worse'n this."

John cheerfully re-gagged him and picked him easily off his feet. He laid him in the crate and packed him carefully in loose bindings, allowing room for air. To Rickey he said, "Have your pal take him to his friends. I want them handy when this cartridge proves out."

Jean Morrow said, "You've done wonders, John. But how you're going to tie it to Abe Schechtel I still don't quite see."

Parsons added dourly. "And if the cartridge didn't come from that gun...."

John produced the piece of lead he had dug from the black sedan. He said, "This clinches that part of it, Sam. Billy Mulloy fired once and got a shot into their car. This is it. It was Schechtel's car, driven by Bootsy Bannigan and containing Krag and Bittel. They killed Mulloy and Kavinsky with that gun. All you have to do is go to the Governor's lab and prove it. We'll do the rest after the F.B.I. confirms it. We'll put these three mugs and that gun on Schechtel's doorstep and have Tony Maretta pick 'em up. With this evidence, the D.A. will go to glory."

Parsons complained, "We can't show. We have to stay under cover."

"The new prosecutor can show," said John. "Let the Governor fix that. Stop worryin', Sam. It's in the bag."

Jean Morrow said, "I hope so. You make it sound convincing, John. Bring the gun, Sam, and let's hurry. We must break it as quickly as possible. At ten Schechtel will be looking for his three men and John. At ten-thirty Schechtel will be looking for all of us—with a mob of killers."

"We'll wait for you at Avery Place," grinned John. "Chicken from Evalina's skillet."

Sam Parsons said gloomily, "Pete turned up. They held him awhile and he lied out of it. Pete's cute that way."

John said, "I'll buy a bottle from him, and we'll celebrate."

CHAPTER FIVE
DEAD MAN'S LEAD

THE LIVING room at 22 Avery Place was HOME. John Wade sank gratefully into his favorite club chair and stretched long legs. His creases, he saw with satisfaction, had not been spoiled by the day's activity. In the kitchen Evalina gave out on "The Oldtime Religion" while the chicken sizzled. Rickey sprawled on a divan, and the radio softly hummed.

The little hideaway house was the only home John had ever known. He had built it and those on each side of it with the money from a Texas oil well proposition which had made no one any money but John Wade and Rickey Boles. Nevertheless, they were comfortable, respectable little samples of suburbia.

One of them held a couple named Corrigan, an elderly couple known by John alone to have a criminal past, but who were now conducting a respectable small tavern in Midburg. The one to the right, number 34, housed Sam Parsons and the girl who posed as Sam's wife, Jean Morrow.

John dreamed of certain revisions in the scheme of things as he lolled there, enjoying the home sounds and smells. If Rickey and Parsons could live together and Jean could move into number 22 Avery Place, everything would be just as convenient. They could go right on working together. It would be much nicer to have Jean pose as

John's wife. Parsons was obviously too old for her, too dull and dour for the youth and beauty and brains which was Jean Morrow.

The clock chimed six in unison with the suave radio voice naming that hour. John roused himself and said, "They oughta make it in time for the chicken."

Rickey said comfortably, "You and that broad. You get more jittery over that gal every day. Whyn'cha marry the dame an' get it over with?"

John said with dignity, "Miss Morrow is not a broad nor a dame."

Rickey sighed. "Love! Nothin' in this world but love."

"You know better than that," said John wistfully. "You know what chance a guy with my past would have with a girl like Miss Morrow."

"Eve'ry time you forget yourself an' call her 'babe' or 'honey', she purrs like a pussy cat," said Rickey disgustedly. "Love. That's what it is. Pah! It makes me very sick."

A taxi pulled up at the house next door. John leaped across the room and peered out from behind the curtains. Jean and Parsons got out of the cab and waited, stalling while it pulled away. Then they came directly across the lawn, Parsons carrying the machine-gun case. There was something in their lagging steps, in the droop to Jean's shoulders which sent an icy shiver to the pit of John's stomach.

He worked the trick triple bolts of the door with trembling fingers. The pair came slowly up the steps and into the house. Parsons was grim, Jean's face was pale and worn.

John said, "What is it? What went wrong?"

Jean lifted her hands, let them drop helplessly. She said, "The cartridge. It—it doesn't match, John."

John's head went around in a circle, very swiftly, then stopped. He stared at them, his expression vacantly silly. He said, "Now—now wait. The hole in the sedan—it must have been their car. They *must* have done it, I tell you."

Parsons said in his dry voice, "I'm afraid you've under-estimated Schechtel and his mob, Wade. I believe, as you do, that Bittel and Krag and Bannigan in that black sedan, pulled the job on Kavinsky and Mulloy. But they were also smart enough not to carry around a hot gun. They have undoubtedly dumped that gun in a river somewhere—we'll never know where."

John muttered, "Such a quick switch—they didn't even carry that gun twenty-four hours. I can't believe they bothered to hide it."

"It is true, John," said Jean softly. "The bullet you dug out of the car is a .38 and could be out of a service gun. But it is so badly mashed we couldn't prove it came from Mulloy's revolver even if we had that weapon. Actually, we have no worthwhile evidence against Schechtel or his men."

JOHN FOUND he could walk. He paced the floor, back and forth in the pleasant little living room. He said finally, "You took the lead leeds? You fired the gun?"

Parsons said, "Certainly. We sent pictures of the lead and the cartridge to Washington as a matter of formality. If Schechtel was not so damn smart there would be a possibility that the gun was used in a previous crime. Then the F.B.I. could place it. The numbers had been filed, of course, but we brought them up with acid. We sent all the dope in. But you'll find that it belonged to some fool deputy sheriff. When those birds retire they sell their weapons to anyone who has cash. It may have gone through four or five hands before a gun-legger procured it for Schechtel. Toothy Abe is cautious—that's why he lasts."

John felt the stubbornness rising in him. He fought to control it, knowing it would lead him to say things which could not stand up before the logic of the Governor's laboratory and the sharp mind of Sam Parsons.

Evalina stuck her frizzled head in the door and announced serenely, "Come git suppah, folks. Now! Chicken won't wait on yoall."

John said, "We may as well eat the last meal together."

He got his smile working and his thin face broke into the myriad of wrinkles which the sun and life had etched into it. He said pleadingly, "Please eat. I feel a stubborn streak coming on. Maybe food will soothe it."

Parsons said ominously, "It had better. You're ridin' for a fall right now, Wade. You should let us handle these things from the top. The Governor knows how to dig down and underinine this rotten mess in Midburg. You're too damn hasty."

Jean Morrow said gaily, "Sam Parsons, stop being a stuffed shirt and come in and eat before Evalina kills us. Besides, food spurs the imagination—or something."

It was a silent meal. Evalina regarded them suspiciously, knowing that the chicken was perfect. John said, "It's all right, Evalina. We're all just thinkin' about something."

Evalina sniffed. "Bettah be thinkin' about some money-makin'. I ain't convinced about dis yeah legitimacey we is into. Plenty grits an' gravy an' watermelyons when we was jes' good, plain crooks."

Jean Morrow was eyeing him, her lips soft in an understanding smile as the red flowed into his face. John laughed un-mirthfully as Rickey roared and even Sam Parsons grinned.

Always there was that reminder. He choked on his food, watching her loveliness. She was preoccupied, silent. He chewed slowly, unable to concentrate on the problem of Abe Schechtel and the bullets which didn't match. Bullets? Not bullets! Cartridges. He stared at Jean Morrow.

She, at that moment, raised her eyes and stared at him. He lifted his eyebrows and purposely refrained from speaking, holding his breath, waiting for her. She nodded firmly at him. She said in a matter-of-fact voice, "I know what you're thinking. It's plain, isn't it?"

He said, "The lead. The bullets."

Parsons was staring from one to the other in bewilderment. Jean went on, "It struck me at the same instant. I could see it in your eyes, John."

He whispered, "Go on. Go on, baby."

She smiled slightly and went on, "The bullets out of Billy Mulloy or Herman Kavinsky. If we could get them. I think—I'm sure it would solve the case. It's more than a hunch. I remember reading something...."

"Cooper's book," said John hoarsely. "You loaned it to me. You marked that page."

John was already getting up from the table. She nodded again, childish almost in the smooth simplicity of line which was her beauty and her grace. She said, "You'll get it—somehow. You always bring it to us—the thing we need."

Parsons said harshly, "You're crazy. That gang at Headquarters'll hold you for Schechtel. We can't get you out if the cops nail you."

John's eyes were on the girl. He spoke directly to her. "We'll get it. We'll be back...."

He was going out on his long legs. The red coupé was parked at the curb. Rickey followed as a matter of course, gnawing on a chicken leg.

Parsons looked at Jean Morrow and said, "He never parks that car on the street here. I wonder what he's got up his sleeve."

"He is a daring man," she said in a small voice. "He always has something—some last desperate scheme when all seems lost."

"He made his living by his wits for years," nodded Parsons. "He's a smart cookie, Jean. I have to keep giving him the 'No!' because like all con men he is a great optimist. But he's a damn valuable man and when he gets killed—which he will because he is rash and reckless—I'll miss him."

"Yes," she said. "I'll miss him, too. Very much."

She did not eat any more of Evalina's chicken. She went into the living room and sat in John's favorite chair. It seemed a good place to her. She stayed there as the moments slipped by.

CHAPTER SIX
DEATH UNDER THE MOON

RICKEY SAID, "Where to, pal? Right at them guys?"

John said thoughtfully, "I think this is where the D.A.'s office comes in. Let's try Tony Maretta's house."

Rickey said helpfully, "Tony's got an uncle. Ogilva."

"I met him," grinned John. "Get goin', pal."

Tony Maretta lived on the other side of town. It was eight o'clock before they got there. Tony was a dark, small-ish man with a hard face. He was a prosecutor's detective and once John Wade had been able to help his uncle in a way which is another story.

Tony listened to them and said doubtfully, "They won't let evidence go to the prosecutor's men. We don't stand good with the cops."

John said, "I can blackmail Schechtel into anything with that lead, Tony. You know that would be a good idea."

Tony said, "Yeah. Anything you get outa Toothy Abe would be velvet. I could see my uncle."

John folded a hundred dollar bill and said, "Is one C-note enough?"

"Too much," said Tony.

"I'll cut you in later," said John tentatively. He was not ready to have the prosecutor's man know his own connection with law and order.

Tony said, "I'm not on the clip, John. But I'd like to see Abe get it."

In a street near Headquarters Rickey dug out his faithful "Mr. Thomas" and assembled it. He kept the machine gun oiled and polished until it shone. He had used it only once since coming to work with John Wade but he could write his name with it any time the going got tough.

He said, "John, if Tony does not get this lead I have got an idea. I have got an idea I will take Mr. Thomas right into Headquarters and make them spit out this lead. I am getting very tired of this lamming around and about and getting nowheres."

John said bitterly, "I am getting more than tired of it. Take it easy, Rickey, you make me nervous with that thing, I can't get used to guns."

"Working for the Governor it seems to me a guy needs a gun," said Rickey defensively. "If we do not get this lead and Mr. Abe Schechtel starts his hoods after us I *know* we will need guns."

"Schechtel has a big head," said John thoughtfully. "He thinks right now that Bittel and Krag and Bannigan have got us holed up somewhere. He thinks that at ten o'clock we will be a pushover for him. I am making plans on Schechtel's overweening ego, Rickey. I am playing like he is a Dictator, only not so smart."

"You played like he was not so smart and got fooled, too," pointed out Rickey morosely.

"I can't always be wrong," grinned John.

After awhile time began to skip along too swiftly. At nine o'clock John was sweating a little. Tony Maretta's appearance at the side of the car startled him half out of his shoes. He said sharply, "Did you get it, Tony?"

Tony shook his head slowly. Rickey said, "Lemme in there. I'll blast it outa them coppers in there."

Tony said, "No use, Rickey. It ain't there."

John said, "What?"

"If that lead was in Headquarters my uncle could put his mitts on it," said Tony positively. "My uncle is a very smart gent, John. Somebody got to that lead and snaked it outa the evidence room. It's gone."

John said, "Gone? Tony—keep that dough. Split it with your uncle. Use part of it for taxi-fare. I gotta go."

Tony waved his hand. "Sorry, pal. I'd sure like to see you hang it on Abe Schechtel."

John said, "Go straight home, Tony. Sit on the phone. If a guy named Parsons calls you, get another hack and follow his instructions."

"Parsons?" said Tony. "The little guy that bristles?"

"You know him. And keep your mouth shut," said John.

Tony nodded and said, "I always make that way."

John was slamming the car into gear. Rickey protested as they lurched away, "You don't know how to handle a crate, John. You'll ruin this heap."

"We'll all be ruined if we don't hustle," said John. "It's after nine."

Rickey clung to the machine gun. He said, "I'm sure glad we got Mr. Thomas. There's gonna be hell to pay tonight."

"Hell," said John grimly, "is a comparative state. Somethin' worse than hell is on right now."

HE STOPPED in front of 22 Avery Place. He had to see Parsons and Jean before he went into action. He couldn't spare much time. He wanted to be at Schechtel's before ten if possible, to look over the architectural discrepancies of that second floor. But Parsons always accused him of going off half-cocked. He would see Parsons. And Jean. He might never see Jean again, he thought, heading for the door.

Rickey came slowly after, saying, "I can at least get a hunk of that pie Evalina had in the oven. Mr. Thomas, you wait here and be good. I will be right back and feed you some lead."

John said absently, his thoughts still upon Jean Morrow's violet eyes, "You shouldn't leave that tommy-gun around like it was a toy, Rickey."

"Safest place for it," said Rickey blithely.

John rapped on the door, using the brass knocker, spelling out the code upon which they had agreed. He heard the triple bolts slide back and stepped into the room, his eyes searching for the girl.

Something in her attitude, her stiffness, warned him, but Rickey, coming fast behind him for his pie, spoiled any play he might have made. The door slammed behind them and Abe Schechtel's toothy face was triumphant behind a sub-machine gun which rested gently in his hairy hands.

Parsons was on the floor, his scalp bleeding on John's rug. Schechtel was, to all appearances, alone. Evalina sat grim-mouthed on a straight chair. Jean still was in John's chair, the comfortable one by the radio. The radio still played softly.

Schechtel said, "A couple of smart operators. Thought you were runnin' a frame on Abie, eh?"

John said, "You copped the lead from Headquarters, didn't you, Abe?"

"I own Headquarters," sneered the Big Boss. "You should have known better, Wade. You should have known you can't buck a real smart man."

John said, "I got three of your men, Schechtel. I'd have had you if I hadn't counted on that ten o'clock deadline."

Rickey was breathing heavily behind him. Without moving a finger John said, "No, Rickey. That thing he's got is loaded."

"Sure it's loaded," said Schechtel pleasantly. "And in a little while it'll go off. When that noisy program comes on the air. An old gag, but a good one, Wade. The cops'll find the four of you—and a couple of hot machine guns. Four crooks fightin' it out, the colored gal killed in the battle."

Wade said, "Not bad. Not good, either. You haven't got Bittel and Krag and Bannigan."

"I'll get 'em," nodded Schechtel, his eyes bright. "I'll make you a deal for 'em."

"I don't deal," shrugged John. "When those punks are picked up, the D.A. will nose in. They're your men, Schechtel. You can't get away from that."

Schechtel nodded. The big, slouching man was almost jovial. He said, "I'm smart enough to know that, Wade. That's one thing I couldn't dope out—what you done with them mugs. Not that I need 'em, unnastand. I get my results by doin' things myself when they need doin' right."

He paused and cocked an eye at John amusedly. He said, "Like figurin' the boys should have called in. An' tailin' you here from the Montrose this afternoon. I been pretty busy, Wade." His voice changed, grew harder, colder. "But I got to have those boys to take the heat off me. I know you got somethin'. You couldn't hold it back yesterday, in my office. That stuff about the clothes—and Kavinsky. I'm smart, Wade."

"I was afraid of that," sighed John. "Too smart."

Abe said generously: "I'll deal with you, Wade. Gimme my men and I'll let the gal go."

John kept his voice indifferent. "Why should I deal for Parsons' girl? I'm no apsay, Abe."

ABE GRINNED so that he seemed to have more teeth than a horse. He said, "Don't con me. Wade. I seen you look at her a coupla times. You heard me. Abe Schechtel always keeps his word. The girl goes loose if you gimme my men back. And I mean dead or alive. I just want 'em safe from the D.A."

John heard the quick intake of breath from his favorite chair but did not make a move.

Schechtel would kill them with as little compunction as he would kill so many cockroaches. But just as certainly, Abe would spare the girl. Jean Morrow would go free— to the Governor. Abe certainly did not suspect them of other than some complicated plot to blackmail him out of a large sum of money. He had not had time to check on their tie-up with the law. He would have no reason to think Jean was other than a moll.

Rickey was beginning to get restless again. John said quickly, "Okay, Abe—it's a deal."

Abe said, "I thought you'd do it, Wade. It's kinda nice of you, at that. Ain't it, babe?"

Jean Morrow said faintly, "No. Don't do it, John."

John ignored her. He said, "I've got your sedan and I've got your men."

"Just tell me where," said Abe negligently. "I can check 'em over the phone. I got men here and there. I ain't got 'em right here because I don't let nobody know when I got a job like this to do."

He nodded brightly, pleased with his own acumen. John shook his head. He said, "You're a cold-blooded murderer, Abe. I gotta hand it to you. Your men are right here. You don't have to check on 'em."

Abe said, "You don't say? Here, huh?"

John said, "They're in the garage. The entrance to my garage is behind you. Don't try to work it because you can't. Now—or after you kill us. That is my getaway door. It can only be worked by me and by Rickey."

Abe said, "Oh yeah?"

He reached behind him and wrenched with his strong, truck-driver's hands. The door, leading from the small foyer in which Rickey and John and Schechtel were standing, resisted without quivering. Abe said, "Steel, huh? Pretty smart, Wade. Okay, open it."

John reached for the button which controlled the door. He pressed it once, twice.

There was a moment's pause, then the door swung slowly open, into the spacious garage. John went down the steps and a light glowed automatically, illuminating the interior sharply.

Jean came down, then Rickey, mumbling rebelliously under his breath; then Evalina, stoical, unafraid. The black sedan was in the garage. In front of it, piled against the wall, were three long crates. John stopped stock still and said loudly, dramatically:

"There are your men, Abe. Crated and ready to ship to hell!"

ABE HAD paused in the doorway. John's words held him there, peering cautiously, the machine gun balanced in his hands. Rickey balanced, his small eyes sharp upon Schechtel. Jean was pale but calm.

Schechtel said, "You'll have to turn them loose, Wade. I can't mess with them crates."

"You could give me a hand," complained John, not moving.

"I could but I ain't," grinned Schechtel. "I'm stayin' right here where you can't close that door with a trick switch."

John said resignedly, "Okay; Abe. I guess you're too clever, at that. Outside of that cop-killin' you never made a mistake—and you didn't trigger that job I guess."

Abe chuckled, "You'll never know. I fixed that, too. Open them crates. That program's on in ten minutes. Move!"

John moved forward. His toe pressed a switch in the floor which was just under the front right tire of the sedan. He made himself refrain from turning to look.

Then there was a shout and confused action behind him and he sprang about, running as quickly as he could around the front of the sedan.

Jean cried, "Rickey! The gun!"

Rickey had caught the play, John thought gratefully.

On the threshold lay Abe Schechtel. Pressing down against his body was an iron sheet of metal, like a guillotine. It pinned him there, like a huge, sprawling bug.

Jean stammered, "It was like something out of heaven—a judgment descending upon him."

John said gravely, "The poor chap who designed the door made allowances for one to go wrong. He put in a second door, which dropped from above. It travelled four feet before it struck our smart friend. I just pressed the switch and it finished our case."

Jean was standing very straight, looking at him. She said, "At the last moment—always you have something."

"I didn't plan it that way," John said honestly. She was very close to him, looking upward into his eyes. "I—had some hope of course. But I was just feeling every step, tryin' to put myself in his place, thinkin' what I'd do if I were he. I thought I might get us all in here and strand him in the house with that metal door between us. Rickey had his gun in the car...."

She said, "John, you are wonderful. Sam and I scheme and plot and take pictures and peer into mikes. But you just go ahead and do things. And Rickey, bless him. The way he leaped—just at the right second—to snatch that gun."

John had to pull himself away from her earnest eyes. He said, "Abe—is he dead, Rickey?"

The big man said happily, "Yep. Broke his damn neck."

"In the car," said John grimly.

THEY GATHERED him up, Rickey and John between them. He was very heavy. They put him in the back of the sedan. Evalina put aside the basin of water with which she was ministering to Sam Parsons and the little man staggered to his feet, calling weakly, "What the hell's goin' on here?"

"Schechtel's dead," John said matter-of-factly. "Now all you got to do is take some more pictures. You see this tommy-gun Abe obligingly brought here? If you fire it and check up you will find that someone switched bolts between this and the murder gun."

Parsons rubbed his head and said, "My skull hurts. So that's what you and Jean meant. Cooper's book. They disassembled the two machine guns after each job. They switched bolts. The cartridges then are scratched differently. The cartridge from the Mulloy killing will match this gun of Abe's. The lead from poor Mulloy's carcass will match our first gun."

"Right," said John.

"The lead," said Parsons. "You get the bullets out of Kavinsky and Mulloy from the cops?"

"Nope," said John blithely. "Abe beat me to it. But he brought them along like a good little smart guy. Abe's ego was so overwhelming that he discounted failure in advance. Rickey found the lead in his pocket. He didn't even snip off the official tags—it's still evidence."

Parsons said, "It'll hang Bittel and Krag and Bannigan if we can get them."

"Get them?" said John. "Oh—I forgot. You didn't know. They're out there. But they didn't kill Mulloy. Abe killed him. They're just accessories."

"How do you know that?" demanded Parsons sharply, peering frowningly into the garage where Rickey was unpacking the long crates.

"Abe said, 'When I want a job done I do it myself,'" said John. "He said, 'You'll never know who killed Mulloy. I fixed that.' But what convinced me that Abe had triggered that job happened yesterday when I was in his office."

He paused. Jean's admiring eyes were distracting. He went on slowly, "We'd been talking. I leaned over quickly to fix his necktie. His tie was always cockeyed. I saw it in his eyes, then. Down deep he was afraid."

"You can't prove that rubbish," said Parsons disgustedly.

Parsons insisted, "That wouldn't stand up in court. It's not evidence."

Jean Morrow said, "But it's true. I know it is true. You can't judge the intangibles on the basis of legal evidence."

"You don't need to," grinned John. "Rickey will take care of everything. He'll drive Schechtel and his hoods and the two guns out to the sub-development off Morgan Road. He will leave 'em among the other unfinished business out there. The D.A.'s men will find them and hold the evidence until you get word from Washington. Schechtel is dead—as dead as Billy Mulloy and Herman Kavinsky. Those three killers will get theirs. That's what counts with me."

Rickey came into the living room sweating, grinning. He said, "What a loada junk. Look, pal, whadda I do after I drop these tomatoes?"

"Walk back two blocks. I'll pick you up," said John.

Rickey was gone. Sam Parsons was gone. The living room was very quiet while Evalina cleaned up in the kitchen to her own rendition of "Swing Low Sweet Chariot" and all was as if nothing had happened.

John relaxed in his favorite chair. Jean sat across the room, her hands and feet folded primly.

The radio broke forth into ominous sound, crackling in mock battle as hoodlums and police fought their battle in the current installment of the Crime Wave series. John tried his muscles, stiff from the tension of the past hours. He arose, switched off the set.

"Gotta pick Rickey up," he said.

She said, "Yes, John."

He said, "Well, baby—how about ridin' with me?"

She said, looking up at him, "Yes, John."

They went out under the moon and got into the red coupé. John Wade's past rose up and rode his left shoulder, prodding him with remorse.

But against his right shoulder the blonde head of the girl sank nearer... and nearer....

JOHN WADE— CORPSE ATTORNEY

EX CON-MAN JOHN WADE,
RECENTLY TURNED
CRIME CRUSADER ON THE
GOVERNOR'S SUICIDE SQUAD,
BECAME A MIDDLEMAN FOR
MURDER WHEN HE SOUGHT TO
CRUSH A COMBINE HEADED
BY A MAN ACCUSTOMED
TO BLINDING THE EYES OF
JUSTICE WITH BLOOD-SOAKED
BANDAGES!

CHAPTER ONE
THE CORPSE
GOES TO BED

JOHN WADE said, "I don't like it. Even the Governor has no right to bring in outsiders. It's dangerous."

Blond, beauteous Jean Morrow surveyed him anxiously. They were all in the living room of the little house on Avery Place where John Wade posed as a business man, with Rickey Boles as his assistant. Next door, Sam Parsons, undercover man for the Governor, dwelt with Miss Morrow who pretended to be his young wife. It was a Council of War against Crime and they awaited the Governor of the State, their minds alert.

Rickey Boles said bluntly, "This is a sweet lay. If there's a leak, John'll lose his hideaway and plenty dough. Dough ain't easy since John went straight. We gotta be careful."

The big, tough bodyguard was completely serious. It never occurred to him that Rickey Boles himself was not an honest man. Rickey had never stolen a penny in his life—not even from the corpses which Rickey had from time to time, in the interests of his job as bodyguard, been forced to create. John Wade had been a con-man before he enlisted with Governor Fortney Castle to clean up crooks from the underworld and the political scene. But Rickey had always been an honest killer.

Sam Parsons said doggedly, "If the Governor wants Mike Stormley in, Mike is in. Stormley, Levine and Stormley have more knowledge of the underworld than anybody—that firm has represented half the crooks in the state."

"I can't say anything about that," John retorted. "The Governor played football or somethin' with Stormley and believes in him. But the Governor don't know Mink Levine, and Mink is Stormley's man. I don't like it, I tell you."

The guns spoke. They rattled and spat and the lead whistled....

The clock struck eleven. A car hummed outside, paused briefly, then went on. Sam Parsons scurried to the door like a swift gnome. It opened, closed, and was barred in a second. Two men had slipped into the room.

John's frown was thunderous. He was a sartorial symphony in browns tonight; brown suit, beautifully draped to his tall, spare form, brown tie, shoes and expensive silken hose. The other men seemed shabby beside him.

Jean Morrow touched his arm as Governor Castle smiled, pulling the stranger into the light.

The girl whispered. "It's done, now. Take it, John."

Governor Castle was saying, "Gentlemen, this is Red Mike Stormley. He may be a big shot to the legal profession, but to me, he's just a broken down end."

Stormley was tall and lanky. He had red hair and a jutting chin and there was an aura of success and strength about the man. He shook hands with John Wade and his grasp was firm and frank. He had especially long fingers and his nails were sharp and well kept. John said:

"I nearly hired Stormley, Levine and Stormley when I was in Dutch one time."

Mike Stormley grinned engagingly. He said, "I've kept dumber crooks than you out of jail."

Governor Castle said hastily, "But Mike has seen that keeping crooks out of jails when they are known criminals is merely postponing the inevitable and inviting trouble for citizens. Mike is going to drop most of his criminal practice and devote his efforts to cleaning up politics with us. Mike, my friends, will some day be District Attorney of this county. Then we will indeed achieve our ends."

John said bluntly, "Meantime we have crooked judges, crooked lawyers, a stupid prosecutor—and plenty muggs like Perch Puddle and Riley Gorgon and the rest to take over as we eliminate their predecessors. We're gettin' no place fast."

Governor Castle's strong face went intent, serious. He said, "That is Mike's job. We take our cases to Mike before we act hereafter. Instead of you and Rickey being forced to act as executioners, you gather the evidence and take it to Mike. He'll tell us how to get convictions. I tell you, friends, it is a wonderful thing to have Mike with us."

Rickey Boles said suddenly, "How about Mink Levine?"

THERE WAS a flat silence. Then Mike Stormley said decisively, "This is an undercover campaign, as Fort tells me. We can't come out in the open. They would crucify Governor Castle if it were known he plotted against the crooked politicoes of Midstate. So we let Mink go ahead. He can handle the criminal cases for Stormley, Levine and Stormley, while I work on your side behind the scenes."

The lanky lawyer paused and said ruefully, "It seems unfair—like doublecrossing. But the power of gangdom is a terrible thing. The end will justify them. If we can eliminate men like Perch Puddle and Riley Gorgon we can cut the feet from under the men at the top—the politicians who buy the judges and prosecutors."

"Right!" exclaimed Governor Castle. "Now my idea of procedure is this...."

John Wade listened somberly. He was thinking of Mink Levine, who was Mike Stormley's partner. The astute, beaverlike little lawyer was known the length and breadth of Midstate as "the Big Little Mouthpiece." He was the man to see when a buy was made. He was the springer of criminals from the Big House.

He wondered how much Mink Levine knew of Mike Stormley's plans. He wondered if the red-haired big man was smart enough and strong enough to control Mink. He wondered lots of things before the half hour chimed and the car came to bear the Governor away as quickly and silently as he had come.

When the four of them, Sam, Rickey, John and the very pretty and clever Jean Morrow were alone, John Wade said, "I don't like it. I don't like it one bit."

Sam Parsons said, "You don't have to like it. But it's right. The Governor...."

John got up. He said to Jean Morrow, "Ride?"

Jean said regretfully, "I have some work—reports on that crime-poverty survey."

John said, "C'mon, Rickey."

The telephone rang. John answered it. A voice said, "John? Pete. A certain biggie is in Milton on a conflab. Another one of the mob is on his way out."

John said, "Okay, pal."

He hung up. That was Pete of Pete's Place. The information was valuable. John knew he should share it with Sam Parsons. He glared around the room, annoyed with the trend of events, angered and hurt that Jean could not take a moonlight ride in his big coupé. He said, "Dammit, Rickey, get out the car. I'm ridin'."

He swung out of the room. The clock said eleven-forty-five.

IN THE hotel room a man looked at his wrist watch and saw that it was eleven-forty-four. The other two occupants of the room were arguing steadily. The man with the strap watch took no part in the colloquy.

One said, "You can't pull this on me, you dirty rat. I knew you when you were a scared mouse. Now you have growed to be a scurvy big rat. You can't—"

The second man produced the gun as if by magic. Without warning, without a single word he thrust it against the body of the one before him and pulled the trigger. The sound of the shot was partly muffled by the proximity of the muzzle against the cloth but the report was nevertheless loud in the ears of the third man in the room.

The wounded man opened his mouth in a round O. His eyes bulged, his hands gripped his middle. He said thickly, "You gunned me, you filthy rat… you gunned me…."

After a moment he lay down on the floor, groaning, but not loud, just moaning in pain. The man who had shot him pocketed the gun and moved deliberately into the bathroom. He returned with towels, a large armful of them.

He placed the towels where they would catch the blood of the now helpless man. He straightened and stared down at his victim. The bloodlust was slowly dying from his half-maddened eyes.

The third man was equally nonchalant. He was at the door now, listening. He said quietly, "You damn fool."

The killer said, "He had it comin'."

The man at the door listened hard. His words were slow, weighted with thought. "This floor is largely unoccupied at this time of year. If no one comes in five minutes you may get away with it temporarily. But you know what it means to me."

The murderer repeated stubbornly, "He got me hot. And he had it comin' anyway."

The third man shook his head impatiently. He said, "Stupidity—always stupidity. There's no one coming. I'll be leaving you, my friend."

The killer said, "Yeah. You better scram. Nobody knows you're even here. Get an alibi. It'll be all right."

The other man said, "My God! All right!"

Then he slipped into the deserted corridor and was gone like a wraith in the night.

Inside the room the killer was pre-occupied. One of the towels had slipped a little. He could not leave a trace of blood on the floor. He did not have to give the boys the office because the boys were coming anyway. But he had to be careful not to leave any trace of the killing in the room.

The Law could place him in the room easy enough, if it got suspicious. The pansy desk clerk and the bell hop would be dangerous witnesses. But the crime could not be proven to have taken place in the room—if the boys came through and all traces were removed.

There was a furtive knock on the door. The man sighed in relief. He opened the door. Three men came in. One cocked an eye at the corpse and said, "Saved us a job, huh?"

The killer said, "Make it good. Down on Route Seven, where the river's deep. Tie rocks to him."

They picked up the dead man, being careful with the towels. They perched his hat on his head, disarranged his hair and draped an arm over the shoulder of two of them.

"Our drunken pal," one said satirically.

"Got to put him to beddy-bye."

They were gone with the corpse. The killer remained to take one more look, to wipe all surfaces clean of finger prints with the one remaining towel. He peered at the spot where the slain man had fallen. He cursed.

There was a spot of blood on the wood. No amount of wiping could remove the tenacious stain. Some had dripped into the cracks between the boards. There was no way to remove it.

The man stood up, sat down. He sat a moment, thinking. Then he shrugged and went into the bathroom again. He came out with a drinking glass. Deliberately he stood above the stained floor and broke the glass in his hand. The cut bled immediately. He was careful to let it drop directly on the spot made by the gore of his victim.

CHAPTER TWO
THE THIRD KILLER

RICKY BOLES nursed the accelerator under his big foot. The coupé rolled at sixty-five without a murmur. Rickey loved the powerful sixteen cylinder car.

"Pete always knows," he said. "But I don't see much sense snoopin' around like this. I crave action."

"Milton's only a few miles away," said John absently. "If Perch Puddle and Riley Gorgon are out there it might mean a break."

He was thinking about Jean Morrow and how he would like it if she were along. He was not, he told himself for the thousandth time, in love with Jean. But she was such a swell kid—and smart, too—that he liked having her around. They were pals, he ruminated. That was it. It was swell to have a pal like Jean. Blonde, beautiful, with eyes like twinkling stars when she was amused....

Fifty feet ahead of the fast-traveling coupé a car jerked into action. It spun away from a standing start evidently in second gear and the tires scraped on the road. It seemed entirely oblivious of the coupé. Rickey jammed the brakes as John braced himself to meet the collision.

The coupé almost ran up the back of the car. It was an open job, a grey Panhard with a bent left fender. The hydraulic brakes took hold under Rickey's pressure. The coupé stopped. The open Panhard sped on without hesitation.

Rickey growled, "I'll get those birds. I'll run 'em in a ditch and hammer their ears down. I'll—"

John said, "No! Don't start again. Hold everything."

Rickey said, "They mighta dented us up. If any son dents up our heap—"

John said, "That car. There's a mobster crate in town that could be just like it. Let's take a look here, pally."

He got out the big flashlight and climbed down to the side of the road. Rickey grumbled, but followed.

John said, "Look—a road down to the river. Footprints, too. Don't be clumsy now, pally. Walk on the edge of the path."

The road led to the edge of the Monanga River. The footprints were scuffed and overlapping and went directly to the brink of the water. John said:

"There must have been three of them. And the prints are plenty deep. They could have been carrying something,"

He gingerly crept close and peered into the dark water. He brought the flash close to the surface of the sluggish stream. He said breathlessly, "Rick! Look! We fell right into it!"

"Don't fall into that drink," cautioned Rickey uneasily. "What you got there?"

He stared into the water. The flashlight threw a hard beam which penetrated the darkness of the river to a point a foot or two below the top. An object could be plainly discerned, swaying eerily, giving way with the motion of the water, swinging back reluctantly. It was undoubtedly the head of a man.

John said, "Grab that branch and reach, pally. Use that strong arm of yours."

Rickey got hold of the overhanging tree. He thrust one arm gingerly into the water. He grunted once and heaved with all his prodigious strength. The body came up and fell half onto the shore. John grabbed a flopping arm and dragged it in.

"Nobody but Mr. Riley Gorgon," he said, "shot in the guts. They over-estimated the depth of the stream and the swiftness of the tide. They tied rocks to him and just dropped him and ran. They are not smart, pally."

Rickey said, "Now what do you know about that? Riley Gorgon. He was the numbers racket in Midstate, John. I guess maybe somebody wanted them numbers, huh?"

"Yeah," said John. "Don't touch him—or anything, Rick. Let's go on to Milton. This is one case we are going to try to wind up right. I'll call Sam and Jean and let them take moulages of the footprints and pictures of the scene with their pretty cameras and stuff."

THEY HIT the outskirts of Milton in nothing flat, with Rickey driving the sixteen cylinders to their limit. John said, "There are two hotels—the Chico, in town, and the Empire House on that little lake near here. The Empire wouldn't be filled until later, in the summer. I think that would be the place, pally."

Rickey said approvingly, "I bet you it will, John."

John warned, "No monkey business, Rickey. This is all legit stuff."

Rickey said injuredly, "I would not ever shoot anybody unless they tried to shoot you or me first, John, and you know it."

"Not much you wouldn't," said John. "Here's the joint. Cover me while I phone."

Rickey dived into the convenient space behind the coupé seat and came out with two big, heavy revolvers. He slipped one into a holster under his arm and thrust the other into his left hand pocket.

"I am now ready for detecting, John. I always feel very much like detecting when I have my things on me."

John got out of the car and went across the small lawn beside the little resort hotel. The lobby was deserted except for a sleek-haired, dozing clerk. The phone booth was convenient to the entrance. He slid into it and closed the door. Rickey slumped into a large easy chair and pretended to be oblivious to all but a newspaper he found.

John got his number. Sam Parsons was sleepy and irritable. But when he heard John's news he said with glee, "We'll go right out there. After we get through we'll notify the cops. Then we'll come on and meet you at the Empire. Now don't do anything rash, Wade."

John said curtly, "This is legit—like you want. Step on it."

He hung up and came out of the phone booth. He went over to the desk and roused the sleeping clerk and said, "I'm looking for a man who should be registered here. He might have used any name—he's careless that way."

The clerk opened his eyes wide, then narrowed them. He said, "Fer gossakes, how do you expect me to answer a ridiculous inquiry like that?"

His accents were effeminate, his left hand strayed over his pompadour, his right hand poised on his hip.

John said, "You know exactly what I mean!"

Rickey, lounging up behind John, said in a high-pitched, exaggerated voice, "You tell us now, or papa slap."

"You can't kid me," the clerk shrilled. "I'll have you know it's against regulations to—"

Rickey leaned forward, his big paws outstretched on the desk. He said, "Sister, gimme the cards for tonight. Make it snappy."

The clerk looked at the hairy, great hands, at Rickey's twisted nose and craggy jaw. He bridled, simpered and said, "Oh, if you *really* want them...."

John leafed them over. There were only three. Two were on the second floor. One was on the third. He took the latter and examined it. It was signed, "P. Gerard and S. Smith, Midburg."

John said, "What did these two look like?"

"Go on up and see for yourself," said the clerk airily. "They haven't checked out." He giggled and went on, "That is, Mr. Gerard hasn't. Mr. Smith was taken a little drunk and had to be helped out by Mr. Gerard's friends."

Rickey said in awed accents, "Outa the mouths of babes an' pansies."

"Room Three-forty-five," nodded John.

"Shall I announce you?" asked the clerk merrily. "Mr. Gerard seems to be having more fun! One man sneaked in and out. I never even saw him. Then three more came and took Mr. Smith away and then they came back and now they're all up there. It's a party!"

"How cute," said John. "We'll surprise them. Don't give us away now!"

"Oh, I wouldn't," said the clerk. "I like fun!"

"He likes fun," muttered Rickey as they went up the stairs. "I bet he plays left stitch on the local knittin' club."

John said, "Now remember—no gunplay. I mean, don't kill anybody. We'll take these guys and if we can tie them to Riley Gorgon—if the clerk can identify him—we got 'em."

Rickey said joyfully, "We'll take 'em okay, pal."

THEY TIPTOED to Room 345. Standing there they could hear the rumble of voices. John tapped on the door and a voice said, "So what now?"

"I brought you some ice water," said John, trying to imitate the high voice of the clerk. "I thought you might need it, what with one thing and another."

Someone laughed coarsely and the door opened. John stepped aside and Rickey took over.

Rickey had the two guns levelled. John followed him into the room. The four assembled men raised their arms promptly. One said, "Migawd, that murderin' Boles."

Rickey said delightedly, "See, John? I don't have to shoot these muggs. They die of fright."

John was examining the occupants of the room with interest. He said, "Looky here! Ikey Bittel, Bootsy Bannigan and Schlonk Krag! All under indictment for murdering Billy Mulloy and Herman Kavinsky!"

The three gunmen, out now on *habeas corpi* while awaiting trial as accessories to the murder of Patrolman Mulloy and a tailor named Kavinsky, while working for the late Toothy Abe Schechtel, stood immobile. Toothy was a killer John and Rickey had removed from society. The fourth man thrust forward a fat, greasy countenance and growled, "You can't blackmail me, Wade. You got Schechtel in some kind of a jam but you can't do it to me."

He was a short man, with the barrel body of a freak, hard, evil in every lineament. His face was like that of an angry baby except that no baby could be so greasy. There was nothing smooth, nothing prepossessing about Perch Puddle. He was all rat.

John said, "We stopped Schechtel, but you took over his rackets. You got the heavy sugar. Why can't I cut in?"

Ikey Bittel said sharply, "Look out for him, Boss, that's how he got Abe. He'll bleed you, or Boles'll kill you. Don't let him in."

One of Puddle's hands was bandaged newly and a red spot showed through the white gauze. He half lowered his arms and said, "You can't pull this on me, Wade. You might as well put up them gats, Boles. I'm walkin' outa here."

His voice was hard. He sneered, "If you got the nerve to bump me off—go ahead. But I ain't payin' no hush dough to you or nobody else. And hereafter look where you're walkin', too, Wade, because you're liable to wind up in the can, you crook. I got the connections to put you there."

John's eyes narrowed. He said casually, "You sure you wouldn't rather bump me? Like you did Riley tonight?"

Perch Puddle's face did not change. He sneered, "Pipe dreamin', huh, Wade? You can't bleed me on no such a story."

"I suppose Riley Gorgon wasn't here tonight?" asked John easily.

"Sure he was here," snorted Puddle. "If it's any of your business. He never could drink. The boys hadda take him home. Or somewhere. I even broke a glass an' cut my hand tryin' to keep him from spillin' a drink. I was just gonna call a doctor when you come in."

John said, "I'll call him for you."

An oily grin spread over Perch Puddle's bulbous face. He said, "I won't bother now. It won't be necessary. And I'm still walkin' outa here—guns or no guns. C'mon, boys."

He did not entirely lower his arms. He held them shoulder high, careful not to make a motion to draw a weapon. But he lumbered courageously to the door. Rickey's finger tightened on the trigger, but John Wade said sharply. "Let him go, Rick. We'll see him again."

The others followed behind the fat boss like a herd of goats behind the bellwether. They piled out and John could hear Puddle's mocking laughter as they went down the hall.

Rickey swore violently, but John said, "Take it easy. Get down there and spot their crate."

Rickey thrust one gun under his armpit, put the other in his pocket, keeping his hand on it, and followed the four men. John Wade closed the door of the room and went over to the door of the bathroom and stood there, leaning against the jamb.

HIS EYES roved around the room. There would be little here for Mike Stormley, he feared. Perch Puddle would have every surface wiped clean.

Yet the scene was as clear as though he had been in the room. He knew as well as he knew anything what had happened.

Knowing and proving what one knows, John thought ruefully, was the trick he had never mastered. His was not the logically deductive mind. He was a hunch-player.

The ash trays were all suspiciously emptied. The place reeked of the fact that it had been cleaned with purpose by its late occupant.

It had undoubtedly been the scene of the murder of Riley Gorgon. Perch Puddle had lured Gorgon here for a conference and had killed him. There had been no witnesses, because if Krag and Bittel and Bannigan had been present the job would not have been done in the hotel; they would have taken the victim for the proverbial ride.

"One man sneaked in and out. I never even saw him...."

The words of the effeminate hotel clerk popped suddenly into the forefront of John's busy mind. At the same instant his eyes fell upon something tucked in between the carpet and the intersection of wall and floor.

The object was a paper match, one from a folder of the sort which is given away with cigarettes. Someone had been playing with this match. It had been burned, briefly, as though to light a cigarette. Then someone had been tearing at it. It was frayed into slivers.

John counted the tendrils. There were nine. Someone had been very painstaking. It was not easy to split a paper match into nine slivers, John thought. He found a piece of paper and folded it tenderly about the match, placing it in his vest pocket.

He locked the door behind him and hastened down the stairs. The clerk was sitting blandly in his cubby-hole, unaware of anything untoward. John said, "If there was a third man in Room Three-forty-five and you didn't see him, how did you know he was there?"

The clerk blinked and looked puzzled. Then he smiled seraphically and said, "Oh! I see what you mean. Well, after ten there are no bellboys here. We haven't enough business for them now. So I have to look after everything. It's terrible, really it is!"

John said impatiently, "How you suffer. Go on, how about this third man?"

The clerk said smugly, "I always try my best. I thought the party might want something. So I went up and paused outside the room. I heard voices. Three of them."

"You're sure?" John demanded.

"Oh, but aren't I?" said the clerk archly. "The other voice was so different! Educated, refined. Not like those other brutes!"

"Refined, eh?" said John thoughtfully. "Now how do you like that? Refined!"

He saw Rickey lumbering back into the hotel. He asked a question with raised eyebrows. Rickey nodded happily, indicating that the grey Panhard was the car in which the mobsters had departed.

John said, "Sit and rest, pally. We will wait for Jean and Sam and all their fine instruments of detection. We have now got a refined gent in the party."

Rickey listened to the tale. When John had finished the big man said only, "Mink Levine."

"We got to prove it," said John.

"The Governor made a blarney," said Rickey. "Stormley'll be in very bad standin' if this breaks."

"The Governor," nodded John, "will pay for this blarney if something is not done."

"Something like bumpin' off people," observed Rickey sagely.

CHAPTER THREE
SLAUGHTER IN THE LOBBY

IT WAS noon next day in the house on Avery Place. John Wade said, "We got Perch Puddle in the hotel. We got the grey Panhard at the spot where the body was found. Sam and Jean took those moulage businesses of everything. We got Gorgon in the hotel with Puddle—we got him dead in the river. Those things we have established. Yet we have no case!"

His lined face was bitter, dark. He was wearing sports clothes, a camel's hair tan jacket and grey slacks, a brilliant scarf knotted loosely about his neck in lieu of collar and tie. The others sat and looked at Mike Stormley.

All were there, Jean Morrow, rosy in spite of a night of hard work in the laboratory which was her special pride and joy; Sam Parsons, grey and weary; Rickey with his guns still bulging about his person, ready for Public reprisals; Michael Stormley in a dark business suit.

Stormley said patiently, "Remember, Puddle will have the shrewdest counsel money can buy. He will have alibi witnesses by the score to controvert your hotel clerk. The blood clue on the floor is no good because even if Gorgon's blood were spilled beneath the stain which Puddle made, no lab test can detect that fact. You have a fine case if your own testimony were allowed—but you cannot come out in the open."

John said bitterly, "What good am I, then? How can I help?"

Jean Morrow said instantly, "At least you brought us in what you found. Through Pete's tip we got onto the thing. Maybe something else will develop."

Mike Stormley said hopelessly, "The worst of it is—the longer these things go, the more chances the criminal has to escape. I wish I could do something, I really do. But your evidence, while it convinces me, would not stand up in a court of law. That is my legal opinion."

John Wade said slowly, "A court of law. I have had experience with the courts of law. For years I swindled people who willingly entered into crooked deals thinking to swindle others. And I never stood up in a court of law. I bought my way out of trouble. I know about these courts of law."

Rickey Boles rumbled, "We got a way. We just skip all that stuff. We just—"

"Stop!" Mike Stormley held up his hand, his pink face shocked. He said sternly, "Never confide in me when you plan anything like that, Boles. I am a sworn attorney at law. If I should listen to such a tale and you should actually commit a crime, it would be my duty to turn you in."

John Wade's hand stole to his vest pocket; then he realized that he was not wearing his vest. The match was still in tissue paper, still in the brown waistcoat. He had long since decided not to speak of that torn lucifer.

He had decided that neither Perch Puddle nor Riley Gorgon were the match-tearing type. He had concluded that the third man in the hotel room last night was, if any, the only one who could be logically believed to sit quietly and tear matches into thin slivers. He said now, "That would be bad, Counselor. I suppose if you were actually present at such a crime, you could be disbarred."

"Disbarred?" snapped Stormley. "I could be held as an accessory!"

"No!" said John silkily. "You see, Rickey? You embarrass the firm of Stormley, Levine and Stormley."

Rickey's face went bland. He said, "I'm just a dope, Counselor. 'Scuse me, please."

THE LAWYER took his departure, cautiously, slipping around the corner of Avery Place to his waiting runabout.

Jean Morrow said, "John! I know you're horribly disappointed."

Sam Parsons said, "I give you credit, John. You might have started something out there and killed the whole gang of them. The Governor doesn't want that. He wants to nail them in court and stir up the bigger rats behind them. He wants the connecting links between the Puddles and the political ins."

John Wade said nothing. He kept his face expressionless and one eye upon Rickey Boles. The big bodyguard tried hard to look downcast. Jean Morrow said, "Next time, John."

Sam opened the door for her and added, "We'll go back to the lab and work over that blood thing. Puddle was damn clever to cut himself and pull that one."

John said sadly, "Too clever for us, Sam. So-long, kids. Rickey and I will take a ride or somethin' and try to forget."

Jean smiled sweetly and commiseratingly upon him. He lowered his gaze and shuffled convincingly. The two left.

When the door had closed firmly, Rickey said, "Boy-o-boy! Levine!"

"We got to place him there," said John incisively. "Let's go out and try that clerk again. Then we'll come back and question every stoolie in town. We'll put the Ferret on his trail from now on. If we can establish the fact of Levine's presence down there while that murder was committed—"

"We c'n get Puddle easy," finished Rickey. "Because I c'n make that Levine talk as easy as pullin' teeth. His teeth!"

At two o'clock that afternoon they pulled up to the Empire House. John said, "Around back and park where no one will spot the car. I think this ape will talk plenty. He's the snooping kind,"

"I will park the heap and stick in the background," suggested Rickey. "If you need me to scare him, whistle."

John assented. They put the car up and went into the hotel. The clerk was newly pomaded, smirking behind the desk. Rickey went to the back of the lobby and prowled. John went to the desk.

The clerk was coy. He said primly, "I do not listen to the conversation of guests, really I don't!"

John said in a hard voice, "Now look, sister. There was a murder committed in that room last night. Anything you might have heard while you stood outside the door and listened to the man with the 'refined voice,' is evidence. I want you to talk and talk fast before I have you thrown in the can."

The clerk paled.

John said, "Sing, sister. I'm in a hurry."

The clerk swallowed hard. Then he said, "Well—I couldn't help but hear—and when they mentioned the Governor's name! After all, the Governor is a public figure—"

John said tensely, "Governor Castle? His name was mentioned?"

"Well—the man with the refined voice," said the clerk. "He said something about running Castle out of the state. He said that Castle was campaigning against something or other in an underhanded way. I don't believe it! Governor Castle is a fine, handsome man!"

"How true!" said John caustically. "Snap into it, sister. Give!"

"The other men sort of snarled—you know how they are," shuddered the clerk. "They said there were *ways*. The refined man said no; he said he had a scheme. He said the quietest way was the best. He said he had a scheme—"

There was the sound of a car outside. The clerk straightened and said importantly, "Customers. You'll have to wait, sir. Customers always come first."

He ran his hand over the slicked down cone of hair and preened himself importantly, looking expectantly at the entrance. John cursed under his breath and stepped aside. Three men came in the door abreast. John leaped six feet to a pillar of the lobby. He put his fingers in his mouth, boy-fashion. He blew a terrific whistling blast.

He yelled, "Duck, Thomas! Down, you fool."

The guns spoke. They rattled and spat and the lead whistled. John saw the effeminate clerk stiffen, seem to rise to the tip of his toes. A crimson stream formed on his immaculate shirt front. His face was blotted, suddenly, by a crimson mask.

John felt futilely for a gun. He hated guns because they spoiled the fit of his clothes. He was unaccustomed to their use and would not carry one. And now he was poorly sheltered behind a column, and in the doorway Krag and Bittel and Bannigan were peering through the smoke, trying to locate him. The clerk came down off his toes. He fell out of sight behind the desk.

Bootsy Bannigan shouted hoarsely. "There he is! Get the dirty stoolie!"

John shrank, feeling very unheroic and helpless. A voice behind him roared "Here's your target, you yella punks. Come and get it!"

John twisted his neck around and stared. Rickey had heard the whistle signal. Rickey was coming front and center.

The big man had his two revolvers in his hands. He was striding from the rear of the hotel, a large, plain target for the three gunmen. He was deliberately drawing their fire to save his boss. John gritted his teeth helplessly. They couldn't miss the loyal bodyguard.

Rickey's guns were already banging. Rickey was a careful workman. Unlike the gunman who sprays indiscriminate lead, Rickey was an artist. He called his shots.

BULLETS WHISTLED past John's ears, then ceased as the three gunmen turned on the menacing Rickey. Krag, who was first in Rickey's line of fire did a sudden nip-up and landed on his ear. Rickey had nailed him dead center. But Bannigan and Bittel dropped to their knees and levelled their automatics.

John took off laterally, shooting his long body out of range. He skidded over a lobby chair. He got completely out of the picture, to one side. Then he started back.

He picked up an ash stand as he came. He moved his long legs with incredible speed. Rickey, still unhurt, popped a shot which struck Ikey Bittel in the left eye. John saw it plainly, saw the eye disappear, saw Bittel die on his knees. But Bootsy Bannigan, teeth pulled back, was taking dead aim at the still oncoming Rickey.

John was afraid to let go of the ash stand. He held tight to it, flailing it, throwing his body behind it. He brought it down like a huge, two-handed sword, Straight for the skull of Bannigan. He felt it go home with a sickening thud.

Bannigan crashed to earth, flat as a pancake. His brains ran out of his broken head and stained the tiled floor.

Rickey said, "Gosh, John! I was snappin' an empty gat. One of 'em jammed on me and I missed a couple before I got the range. Gosh!"

John said, "You took the three of 'em off me. What the hell more do you want to do?"

Rickey said dolefully, "A hell of a bodyguard I am! A jammed gat! Gosh! They would of got me, John."

John said forcibly, "You damn fool, they would have made mince meat of me if you hadn't hollered."

John was already over beside the crumpled form behind the hotel desk. He took one look at the hotel clerk and straightened. He said, "Pally, our case is really shot, now. Puddle has eliminated our star witness."

Rickey said, "Gosh, John. The cops. The Milton cops'll grab us. We ain't got any standin', John. The Governor can't break us out of any jams."

John said, "And all our good work done for. All our legit clues shot. Dead people all over the joint. Ain't it hell?"

Rickey took a deep breath and came back to normal. He carefully put his two big guns on the floor beside the hotel clerk. He tenderly took the dead hand of the clerk and made prints on their butts.

He said philosophically, "It wouldn't fool a real smart detective. Or anybody that knew poor Thomas. But it'll stall 'em for awhile. Let's scram, huh, John?"

John said, "Yeah. Let's lam. There's only one thing left for us to do now."

Rickey said, "Mink Levine."

John said, "Mink Levine."

CHAPTER FOUR
MINK LEVINE

SAM PARSONS said severely, "Wade, you and Boles have done it again. There's a hue and cry all over the state for the men who engaged in a gun battle in the Empire House. You've messed it up again!"

John said, "Is the Governor coming?"

"He's coming," said Sam. "I hate to think what he will say to you."

It was eleven o'clock by the timepiece on the mantel of the Avery Place house. Jean Morrow was biting her red lips. Parsons was furious. Rickey was imperturbable, slouched in a big chair. John had changed to a dark blue, double-breasted worsted with a plain tie and black shoes. He said somberly, "Let him say it, then, Sam. Here he comes."

Sam admitted the Chief Executive. Fortney Castle's fine face was lined as if with fatigue. He said, without preamble, "I know you meant well, John. But you can't continue to take the law into your own hands like this."

John Wade said quietly, "Governor, we're going to take a ride. I'm going to tell you some things Rickey and I found out this afternoon among the city's stool pigeons and underworld characters. Then we are all getting into your car and going for that ride."

The Governor said, "I can't see—"

The ebullient Rickey said carefully, "You will, Gov., you will."

John Wade talked earnestly for fifteen minutes. The big car hummed softly outside. The Governor stood up. His face was even more weary; his eyes were sunken.

He said, "You'll have to prove it, John."

John Wade said, "Let's go."

The burly, personal chauffeur of the Governor drove swiftly through the streets of Midburg. He drove into the driveway of a fine house in an exclusive section of town. The Governor alighted and helped Jean Morrow to earth. Parsons and Rickey and John Wade followed him into the house.

There was a large, pleasant study. There was a man servant, a husky fellow with a broken nose, who peered askance at Rickey. There were two men in the study.

Michael E. Stormley said fretfully, "I can't understand this, Fort. I thought Mink was to be left out of it."

John Wade kept his eyes on the second man. He was a little man, slender, with sharp eyes. He had long, thin fingers and sharp nails. He was dapper, overdressed. He had the most intelligent face John had ever seen, with the tightest steel trap of a mouth. He was the famed Mink Levine.

Fortney Castle said heavily, "John has something to say to all of us."

Stormley said, "Mink, this is John Wade."

The little man's voice was smooth and vibrant. "I know of Wade. It is my business to know men like Wade. He is a very clever fellow."

John said mildly, "Thanks, Mink. The boys all speak well of you, too."

Levine gave him a sharp glance but did not respond. John grinned and went on, "We both have an extensive acquaintance in the underworld. I think we can go ahead with the knowledge that everyone I speak about is known to us all."

Mink Levine kept his bright eyes steady. He said, "I don't get this."

John said, "Let me explain. A guy got killed last night in a hotel in Milton. Then he got dunked in the Monanga River. Rickey and I found him. We traced him back to the hotel. We found Perch Puddle and three mobsters hanging around. We found… other things.

"When Riley Gorgon was killed in that hotel room there were two men present. One killed him. The other saw it done and got away. The man who got away is, of course, a material witness at best. At worst, he is an accessory."

Mink Levine said, "Right. Go ahead."

JOHN SAID easily, "We had a witness who could have identified the voice of that third man. He got killed by three men who didn't live to brag about it."

He broke off and said pleasantly, "How about a cigarette? Jean?" He passed the opened pack around, and watched Mink Levine take a thin white cylinder and light it with a paper match.

John went on. "The witness, Thomas Pilkington, overheard some of the conversation in the room. He heard enough to make clear that there is a plot afoot against Governor Castle."

Jean Morrow exhaled smoke, watching. Rickey had his hands near the fresh guns he had procured. No one spoke.

John said, "It seems there has been a recent leak. I take it that the leak inaugurated sometime since Mr. Michael E. Stormley became a member of our combination against crime."

Stormley said, "Is that fair?"

"Maybe not," grinned John. "But I choose to believe it. After all, Mr. Stormley, you have a partner—clerks in your office."

He was watching Mink. The little lawyer never blinked. He sat there as cool as ice, playing with the paper match. John kept his eyes on the nimble hands.

Levine had separated the match into four strands. John kept talking.

"The firm of Stormley, Levine and Stormley had managed the release of the three dead gunmen, Bittel, Krag and Bannigan. They are known to have represented certain crime interests in this city. They may even now be representing Perch Puddle, who certainly caused the deaths of Riley Gorgon and Thomas Pilkington—if we could only prove it. Governor Castle vouches for Michael E. Stormley. Who vouches for Mink Levine?"

He shot it at the man suddenly, and let it lay there.

Stormley protested vigorously, "Mink didn't know about us. It was impossible for Mink to find out anything."

John watched the little lawyer and the match. Mink Levine was bending the four strands. He bent them to make elbows and knees, so that the head of the match became the head of a stick man. He was meticulously putting feet on the awkward, stringy legs. Stormley, too, fingered a match.

John said, "So!"

No one moved. John took a deep breath and said, "So you vouch for Levine. It's a funny thing. Rickey and I combed the town this afternoon. Crooks have ways of knowing where people are—especially people important to them. Rickey and I couldn't place Levine at the scene of the crime to save us."

The little lawyer put down the match. His eyes were brighter than ever. He turned his complete attention upon John Wade as though waiting patiently.

John addressed himself to the intelligent face. He said, "Evidently you didn't go out to Empire House. You are Perch Puddle's counsel and he wanted you there. But you had your ear to the ground and you knew Riley Gorgon's number was up. You're too smart to have any part of a killing. You stayed away."

John turned around and faced the others. Behind the desk Michael Stormley looked puzzled. He said, "Then why this conflab, Wade? I don't get it."

John said, "Well, someone was there. Someone who left a tiny clue. Not a very good clue. Not one which would stand up in your courts of law. But still, someone who plotted against the Governor."

Stormley said, "So what?"

JOHN TOOK a long step and leaned forward. He plucked a frayed paper match off the desk in front of Stormley.

He said, "Funny stunt. Tearing paper matches into strands. I see Mink Levine makes strange looking men of his."

He reached into his vest pocket and produced a piece of paper. He unwrapped it slowly. He dropped the contents on the top of the desk.

"I found this one in the room at the Empire House. Funny how they compare, isn't it?"

The lights in the room went out. They were in complete blackness. John remembered the heavy hangings at the windows. He remembered the husky man servant. He dropped on his stomach on the floor. Rickey would be in action any moment now. Trust Rickey to know where to start.

He crawled as best he could to where the wall should be. If the lights had not been cut off outside there should be a switch. He thought of Jean Morrow somewhere in the dark chamber, her soft flesh susceptible to hot metal.

He got to a window. He could tear the hangings down, but that might make things worse. He had a gun tonight. He arose, inspired, and slipped behind the concealing curtain.

Stormley's voice said coldly, "The lights are coming on. This room is covered by plenty of guns. Don't any of you make a mistake."

The lights came on. John put away the knife with which he had slit an eyehole in the curtain and peered out. Only Rickey had moved. Rickey was against the far wall, a gun in each paw, as natural as life. The others still sat.

In the doorway stood Perch Puddle, a machine gun levelled in his fat paws. The husky man servant had a sho-sho gun and was at the far end, enfilading the group.

Stormley said, "We'll have to tie them up and get the plane out, Perch. We're through. There's a million in cash in my car. We'll do all right."

Puddle chuckled greasily, "Lemme bump 'em off, Chief. Lemme take 'em. It'd be a pleasure."

There was insanity in Stormley's protruding eyes. He said hesitantly, "Well, our neighbors are away.... Let me get out, Perch."

The lawyer unfolded his long frame from behind the desk. He passed in front of Mink Levine. He paused, suddenly staring. He said, "Where's Wade?"

Puddle cursed. They had just missed him, John thought grimly. He got the gun poked through the eye slit. He tore the fabric gently so that he could aim. He was not the best shot in the world. He thought that if he could get Puddle, Rickey would take his chances with the man servant. He squeezed on the trigger.

Before he quite completed the squeeze a shot rang out. It wasn't a loud shot, just a feeble crack. At the same moment Rickey's .45s went into action. John hauled down on Puddle hastily, firing twice.

Puddle fell sideways. The machine gun chattered and splinters flew as the bullets went harmlessly into the fine hard wood floor of Mike Stormley's home.

Rickey was firing steadily. The man servant never got the riot gun up. He went down on his face, riddled with Rickey's bullets.

John leaped into the room. Michael E. Stormley was draped over the desk. His face was blank and upon it was a very amazed expression. In the middle of his forehead was a small hole.

John said, "Now who in hell is carrying a popgun?"

Mink Levine's smooth voice was unruffled. He said. "He's dead, isn't he?"

John took a closer look and said judiciously. "He's as dead as if a shell hit him."

MINK LEVINE stood up and shook the wrinkles out of his suit. He said, "That was the idea."

He put a tiny, vest pocket revolver on the table. He said apologetically, "I always carry it. I'm a nervous man."

Rickey Boles picked the ridiculous weapon up in his big paws and stared at it. It lay in the palm of his hand without overlapping. He looked from it to the tall figure of the dead Stormley. He said, "Gosh! And my .45 jammed this afternoon and John could have got killed. And you pop a guy off with this! Gosh!"

Mink Levine said silkily, "Well, gentlemen. This is a mess. I assure you that Mike Stormley was indeed plotting against the Governor."

He remembered Jean and bowed to her in apology. He murmured, "My dear, you are beautiful."

Jean moved closer to John Wade, twisted her hand in his. Governor Castle said heavily, "I trusted that man."

Mink Levine said, "A mistake. The money he was taking is partly mine, you know. Mike was really crooked. I've known it for some time. This other business—he intended to be Governor in your place, sir."

Sam Parsons said eagerly, "He was the link between crime and politics. If he hoped to be Governor, he must have had connections. If we can find these connections…."

Mink Levine said deprecatingly, "I may be of some assistance. After all, I am on the inside now. Wade, who knew I was innocent and suspected Stormley, persuaded me to come here tonight; I assure you I would never have attended any meeting that Stormley called. I would have been afraid of Puddle and his gun-men. I think Wade had something in mind…."

Everyone looked at John. Jean squeezed his hand. John said, "Well. You all seemed to feel the need of legal advice. I asked around. The crooks all trust Mink. He allowed as how he wouldn't turn up one of his clients—it isn't fair. But if he were made District Attorney—and we worked with him…. And if at the next election Mink has built a

machine in his own peculiar way—among the right guys—
it'll be that much more strength for you, Governor."

Governor Castle slowly nodded. He said, "I was wrong.
Maybe you're right, John. But... this is all so horrible. I'd—
better get away. This shooting...."

John said easily, "Go ahead, Governor. Take your car and
lam. We'll clean this up. Mink Levine can handle the cops."

Levine gave John a rueful glance, but nodded assent.
John said, "Jean, let's you and me get out of here."

Jean said, "John, you're wonderful."

"Ahhh, if I could only believe that!"

"Bahh," said Rickey Boles, "Now I'll tell one."

JOHN WADE, MOB EXTERMINATOR

JOHN WADE, EX-CONMAN, AND HIS INIMITABLE PAL, RICKEY BOLES, WERE FAVORITES ON THE GOVERNOR'S SECRET RACKET SQUAD. BUT HIS EXCELLENCY ASKED JOHN AND RICKEY TO SOFT-PEDAL ON THE HOMICIDE.... UNTIL THE GIGANTIC FIVE MOBS CROWD SET UP SLAUGHTER-HOUSEKEEPING IN MIDBURG, AND NAILED JEAN MORROW FOR MURDER!

CHAPTER ONE
KILLER'S HATE

JOHN WADE sat in the spacious bar-lounge of the Carlton House and watched huge Rickey Boles with amused eyes. In a little while they would secretly visit the Governor of Midstate, for they had been summoned urgently. In an hour they would be launched on a mission which might bring anything from sudden death to horrible torture. But Rickey Boles was hungry for his beloved peanuts.

The big, scar-face bodyguard was amiably serious, plodding around the end of the bar with the glass dish in his great paw. He could eat a pound of nuts without blinking and drown them in a gallon of beer without showing the slightest effect. He bore the dish tenderly.

He turned the end of the bar and started towards the leather seat upon which John Wade lounged in sports clothes immaculate and correct. Rickey was a lumbering bear, compared to John's cleancut figure, the perfect foil for the elegant ex-confidence man.

Wade and the inimitable Rickey had been secretly working for the wise and fearless Governor Fortney Castle since he had convinced John Wade that he was squandering his talents and losing his self-respect as the state's smoothest and most successful con man. At that time John Wade was sick of splitting his profits with cops, crooks and lawyers—

The sour-faced matron was bringing
Jean from the filthy cell....

sick of living the existence of a fugitive, and he had been willing to listen to Governor Castle's plan. Working undercover for the Governor had restored John's self respect, given him back his belief in man, removed much of the cynicism which he had worn as a barrier against the world. It had thrown John with Jean Morrow, which—he occasionally reflected with a wry smile—was a mixed blessing.

He watched Rickey Boles affectionately, smiling. As the big man came forward, he saw a hand reach out. It reached across in front of Rickey. It snatched a big handful of the coveted peanuts from the dish. John sighed. There would, he knew, be trouble. Rickey loved peanuts too well.

Rickey stopped dead, staring down. John hitched forward, listening, watching. The man who had snatched, stared contemptuously up at the big bodyguard.

He was a little man. He wore fine clothes. A diamond sparkled on the fingers which clutched Rickey's peanuts. The man's face was swarthy and the skin seemed oily and unhealthy. The eyes were piercing and full of a peculiar venom. He was clean to the eye, yet John felt instinctively that upon the frame underneath the fine raiment there was dirty underwear.

Rickey said, "Why don't you get your own peanuts, pal?"

The little man said, "Scram, bum."

There were two others with the little man. They were bulky-shouldered men with cartilage lumps over their eyes. John recognized them. One was Chipmunk Daley. The other was Borsch Kazan. They were a couple of known hoodlums. At the rear of the bar, leaning against the wall was another of their ilk. He was Log Kazan, a shiv artist addicted to heroin and worse. John shook his head in despair. There was no rest for the weary, he concluded.

Rickey always tried to do right. They were, after all, on a secret mission. Rickey said, "I'll see you some other time, Buggy—"

His big face was solemn. He turned and walked towards John again. The little man reached out. He held a peanut between thumb and forefinger. He flipped it so that it struck Rickey on the back of the neck. The two hoods guffawed.

JOHN GOT up reluctantly. He took the flat gun from under his arm. He showed it significantly to Log Kazan, then shoved it into his pocket. Kazan did not move; his hot eyes were upon John, ignoring the scene at the bar.

Rickey wheeled slowly. He put the dish on the bar. He walked back to where his tormentor sat. He reached out and deliberately slapped with open hand. It was like being hit with a board.

The little man's head canted around. He slumped in the seat and his vest rumpled up under his chin. His mouth dropped open in amazement and pain.

The two hard-faced hoods started up. Rickey bent his elbow and slapped again, twice. The hoods sat down. Rickey said, "You wanta play and I will play with you. I will slap you dizzy. I will bat your cabbages around to the back of your necks."

The little man recovered his voice. He screamed hoarsely, "Log! Where are you, Log? Take this bum, Log!"

Rickey lazily slapped again, using the other hand. The little man began to assume a definitely lop-sided appearance. His face was bright scarlet. His hair fell over his eyes. John went forward, keeping Log Kazan within his line of vision. He said softly, "Now, Buggy. Mustn't holler cop when you started somethin' you can't finish!"

The little man stared up with baleful, half-crazed eyes. He spat, "You keep out of this, you slicker."

John said, "You look pretty silly, Buggy. You want Rickey to slap you again?"

The two hoods sat silent, their hands upon the table. Log Kazan did not move. Buggy Rutkin, gambling czar of Midburg, screamed, "What do I hire you guys for? Why doncha take these punks?"

Chipmunk Daley said expressionlessly, "This guy Wade packs heat in his kick. Boles can outdraw any gun in town. We'll see these punks later."

Borsch Kazan added, "Me brudder'd took 'em if Wade didn't have a gat on us. Be smart, Bug. We'll see these boids again. Sit easy, Bug." He spoke reassuringly, as to a child.

Rickey said, "I hope I am around when you see me again, pal. Even if my back is turned, I will gladly give it to you muggs. You been here too long now, small potatoes. Maybe we oughta move you out."

Buggy Rutkin sputtered like a wet live wire. He gasped, "You'll be dead before I make another move, you dirty little jerks. I'll...."

RICKY SLAPPED again. He leaned into it a bit this time. Log Kazan, all the way over by the door, winced at the impact. John half-drew the gun, but Log didn't make a move.

Buggy Rutkin collapsed. His head came forward and slapped on the low table behind which he sat. He lay there, unconscious. Rickey said, "I wouldn't of broke his neck I suppose. I just ain't born lucky."

John said, "Come on, pal. We have suckers to trim. These small fry are a-wastin' our time."

He went ahead, straight towards Log Kazan. He recognized the danger in the still, evil figure of the gunman and knife thrower. As he came abreast of the lounging figure, he said, "I'd forget this if I were you. Someone'll get killed if he bothers Rickey too much."

Log Kazan said, "I ain't talkin', Wade."

"Buggy Rutkin's gettin' big for his pants," John went on. "Since when did he have three bodyguards?"

"You better get on your way," said Log Kazan. His eyes were steady, the pupils narrowed to pinpoints. "Bug'll be sore when he wakes up."

John said, "Bug ought to stick to pickin' on hayseeds and umpchays in from the sticks. Rickey's out of his class."

"Nobody's outa Bug's class," snapped Log Kazan. "You'll loin about that, too, Wade."

"Maybe," nodded John gravely. "Maybe I will, Log. Well, keep your powder dry!"

He led Rickey out of the Carlton House. There was a special taxicab waiting for them, driven by a trusted member of the Governor's personal organization. It whisked them through the familiar streets in a maze of back-tracking to throw off possible trailers. The underworld was getting restless since Wade and Boles had joined the forces of Law and Order. Too many of their leaders had fallen by the wayside.

Rickey said, "It seems funny, bein' almost a copper. It gives a guy a kick to slap a cheap gamblin' house punk like Buggy Rutkin knowin' you are on the right side when you do it."

Rickey was quite happy about the whole thing. He leaned back in the cab and grinned. John Wade said slowly, his narrow face seamed with concern, "I don't know, pal. Rutkin was away above himself in there. Three hoods around him—that takes heavy sugar. What goes on that we don't know?"

The cab did a quick sneak up a back street, turned into a driveway and spun right on into a garage at the back of a big house. They had come to the private domain of wealthy, conscientious, crimebattling Fortney Castle.

Rickey said comfortably, "The Gov'll know. He knows plenty. He's a right guy."

That, from Rickey, was accolade enough.

CHAPTER TWO
THE MOBS PLAN
TERROR

THE FINE face of the Governor was tautly serious. He said, "There is, as you probably know, a nation-wide organization known as the Five Mobs."

John said, "I thought the Five Mobs was pretty well busted up what with Dewey in New York and Murphy around and about the whole country."

"The Five Mobs has been operating quietly, lying low, consolidating its strength," said Governor Castle. "Now that the war scare is on and the government agents are frantic with spy scare, the Five Mobs crowd is ready to strike. They have organized in Frisco, New Orleans, Chicago, New York—and they want Midburg to complete the cycle."

Rickey said, "I thought we about bumped off the mobs in Midburg. I thought we were gonna clean up the cops and the courts next."

Fortney Castle said, "An outfit like the Five Mobs, rich in money and man power, can always find an agent. They have picked one in Midburg."

John Wade said gloomily, "Wait! Don't tell me! Let me guess. It's Buggy Rutkin."

The Governor's jaw dropped. He said, "I thought it was a great secret. Sam Parsons dug this up only last night."

Rickey chuckled, "But we dug Buggy up this noon."

"Nice work!" said the Governor cordially. "Your—er—former connections with the underworld have been valuable to us many times. I have never been sorry that we met, gentlemen."

He coughed nervously and went on in a more hesitant tone: "Of course, Parsons—and some of the others—I mean, well, John, you've killed a lot of people. We are supposed to be concerned with bringing justice to Midstate. There have been times when… some people have thought you were hasty. Impetuous…."

John Wade said calmly, "Sam Parsons is a sleuth. I'm a direct actionist, Governor. These criminals, these racketeers with whom we have dealt, have been too well wired in with the supposed forces of law. Bringing them to crooked justice would often have been the same as turning them loose. Circumstances forced us to kill, and if we continue to work for you, we will undoubtedly kill again. You see," he added grimly, "we know the underworld. We've been in it. The only cure for recidivism is lead in the guts unless your court is ready to convict!"

Fortney Castle sighed. He said, "I feel that you are correct, John. Yet, well, in this instance Sam Parsons wants a little leeway. He asks that you remain at the hideout on Avery Place while he, with Miss Morrow posing as his wife, investigates Buggy Rutkin. You will act as a sort of rear-guard, you know? Ready to—"

"Pull Sam's chestnuts outa the fire," suggested Rickey. "The little guy's been gettin' beyond himself lately, Gov."

John Wade interjected swiftly, "Governor, we'll be glad to let Sam carry on without us. Miss Morrow is a good assistant for him, and, as you suggested, Rickey and I will be ready to help."

He arose, his lined face devoid of expression—a mask of politeness. Rickey followed him to the door grumbling. The Governor of Midstate looked nonplussed, started to speak, checked himself. John said from the doorway, "Good night, Governor. You know where to find us."

He led the way through the back to where the cab awaited in the closed garage. They were driven swiftly back into Midburg, sitting side by side, saying nothing.

The house on Avery Place was one of a serried row of cottages very much alike. John went through the doors of the attached garage and gave the signal to open the barred, steel door. Rickey, still muttering, went along. The colored woman greeted them inside the comfortable living room.

"COFFEE TIME, Mist' John. Got some special cawn-bread an' some Floridy honey fo' t'day."

John said, "Thanks, Evalina. Put it out. Rickey'll love it."

Evalina cocked a shrewd eye. She said, "Missy Jean been gone all day. Ol' Mist' Sam and she gone out. She say to tell you 'hey!'"

John said, "Thanks, Evalina."

Evalina said, "She play lak she Miz Parsons agin. Got a dime weddin' ring on."

John said irritably, "Okay, Evalina, okay!"

Evalina said, "I just tellin' you, Mist' John. You needn't to get cross wiff me."

She swept out of the room. She had been cooking for John a long while. Since John had dropped the rackets and turned honest she had, he reflected, never been entirely satisfied.

He wondered if he himself were satisfied. The Governor had been cordial, appreciative. Yet there had been the implied criticism that he and Rickey had overstepped the bounds when they killed the men who were enemies of Fortney Castle and of the state.

They had killed, yes. But always they had killed because they were forced to. No private vendetta had caused their guns to speak. John remembered the first man he had ever shot when he first started working for the Governor. The memory still made him ill.

John Wade was dangerous when angry. He would punch an offending person in the jaw quicker than a struck match will ignite, and he could punch hard. But he didn't like guns—he was not a killer.

Rickey Boles was not a trigger man, either. He was a body-guard, true, but when he fired, it was for very good reasons.

But Sam Parsons didn't like the set-up. Parsons had been in the Governor's employ before John. Sam lived next door, at 24 Avery Place, in a house belonging to John Wade. With him lived beauteous Jean Morrow, ex-college phenom, the cleverest girl in Midstate. She handled Governor Castle's private crime lab with precision. Jean merely posed as Sam Parson's wife.

That was one thing, John brooded. She was not anyone's wife. Not that she could ever be John's wife. An ex-crook, an adventurer with his life endangered every moment both by the police and underworld, could not aspire to marry. But at least she was not Sam's wife.

THE GREY little fox-terrier of a man who was Sam Parsons wouldn't even be interested in Jean. He was a human ferret with no other interest but sleuthing. He could find more angles than anyone in the world. He was Governor Castle's right eye.

But he was not pleased with John Wade. For a long time, Sam had been inveighing against John's habit of getting with Rickey into situations which eventually ended with gunfire and dead outlaws.

And now Sam Parsons had taken Jean Morrow and gone forth to gather evidence against Buggy Rutkin. John said, "The only way Sam could proceed would be through Buggy's club. If he could pin a rap for a crooked wheel against the Rutkin Club even the cops would crack down. The police will take dough from a gamblin' house proprietor only so long as the suckers don't squawk too loud and long."

Rickey said flatly, "What the hell do you care what Parsons does? He put the beef in on you with the Gov. Let him stew in his own pineapple juice, the rat."

John said, "He's got Jean with him."

"You cannot do nothing about that," said Rickey. "You have got orders to stay here and wait. If the Gov. and Sam Parsons think they can run this thing without us, then we will be very smart to stay home and listen to the radio."

"That Rutkin is a vain little egotist," ruminated John. "How the Five Mobs could pick out a heel like Rutkin to organize Midburg…."

Rickey said shrewdly, "The big muggs don't want the lil' muggs too smart, pally. They still gotta control things. This Buggy is got enough bats in his belfry t' make a fine punk for the Five Mobs."

"He hired himself tough hoods," admitted John. "Smart ones, too. Smart enough not to make a dumb play today in the Carlton. Those Kazan boys are mean people."

"All hoods is mean people," said Rickey lazily, switching on the large radio. "And pretty soon dead people."

THE RADIO played soft music, then burst into swing. The Milkman's Serenade was on. Evalina stuck her head into the living room, made a face at sleepy Rickey Boles, who was sprawled on the divan. "Why don't you go to bed, Mist' John? Missy Jean gonna be out late wiff ol' Mist' Sam. You don't needa worry."

The clock struck three. John Wade, his eyes still lively, his cravat as neatly tied as at midday, said, "Coffee, Evalina."

The girl retired, grumbling. John shrugged into a dark coat of loose fit; his shoulder holster did not make a bulge. He reached out and kicked Rickey on the ankle. The big man opened an eye and said, "Huh?"

"We're goin' out," said John.

Rickey yawned and stretched. Evaline brought coffee. John silently handed it to Rickey.

The big man swallowed mightily and said, "They ain't back yet?"

"No," said John.

Rickey said, "Lemme get upholstered, pal."

He slung one gun under his arm. He tucked one into his waistband. He hesitated over a short belly gun, finally tucked it into his coat pocket. He said, "Guess I'm ready."

They got the big coupé out of the garage. Rickey drove through town, down into the boarding house district off Elm Street. He stopped before a brownstone, three-story house inside of which signs indicated that people were up and about. Rickey said, "John, there's people in there don't like us."

"Yeah," said John drily.

"The Gov don't like for us to go about shooting people," said Rickey doubtfully.

"Supposing," said John, "supposing Jean is in there—and can't get out?"

Rickey scratched his head. The blonde, beautiful Jean Morrow was his particular goddess. He said, "This Five Mobs. They ain't only got gamblin'. They have got vice an' white slave dives. They ship gals all over the world. It would not be nice if they should—"

"No," said John. "It wouldn't."

Rickey said, "I guess we got to go in. But the Governor is not gonna like it."

They went up the steps side by side. They rang. A peephole slid open. An eye surveyed them, and Rickey growled, "Open up, Cactus-Puss, or I'll have to bust it down an' bang your head off."

The eye was withdrawn. There was a sound of chains being undone. The door opened. A man whose almost bald head bristled like a desert plant said, "Yer nuts, youse guys. The heat's on youse."

Rickey said, "I ain't even perspirin', Cactus-Puss."

John followed the big bodyguard, his nerves tingling with anticipation. This was the Rutkin Club. This was the gambling house from which the numbers racket, the bolita and the "bond" were all conducted. There was a bookie joint upstairs which was the biggest in Midburg. This was headquarters for the man who had been publicly humiliated by Rickey Boles in the very prominent Carlton House.

CHAPTER THREE
IN THE THIEVES' DEN

RICKY HAD no nerves. He actually swaggered as he walked into the large room which had been thrown open to blackjack tables, roulette wheels, crap and chuck-a-luck tables, all operated by Buggy Rutkin. He was as happy as an ant at a picnic.

John cased the room at a glance. Chipmunk Daley was running the crap table. Borsch Kazan was operating the roulette wheel against the far wall. Log Kazan sat on a high stool overlooking the play. There was no sign of Buggy Rutkin.

Rickey spoke to various underworld acquaintances who were liberally sprinkled among the butchers, bakers and entirely legitimate candlestick makers who were tilting at Buggy Rutkin's games of chance. John speculated grimly on the take and wondered what part of the billion dollars a year waged in this manner by Americans would be collected by the Five Mobs.

There was money going around in the Rutkin Club. Every person present seemed to be preoccupied with the gambling. John stood apart and had plenty of time to search with his eyes for the personable and blonde Miss Morrow. She was not in the room.

John said, "Keep those hoods in here, Rick. I'll have a look around the joint."

Rickey said, "They got a gimmick on that wheel. Look at Borsch movin' his right foot. They ain't even got a magnet—they're usin' the steel gaff."

Rickey knew gambling joints. He had worked in them before coming with John Wade. He took one glance at the crap table and grunted, "Two house men throwin' for the uckersays. Tops an' slicks whenever they need 'em. This Buggy is a crook, pal!"

John murmured, "No!" in mock surprise.

Rickey said, "I was in this joint a month ago, pal. The games was strickly on the level."

John thought about that for a moment. Then he said, "You think Buggy's joined up?"

"He must of," said Rickey positively. "The bulls would not stand for a local gee runnin' a phoney joint. The Five Mobs got dough to buy honester cops 'n this town has got. The payoff must be terrific, pal. This is crude stuff."

The Kazan brothers had caught sight of the two invaders. Log Kazan, on the high stool, reached back and pressed a button. Borsch spun the roulette wheel absently, his eye broodingly upon Rickey.

A door opened. John Wade moved swiftly across the room, his hand lingering near his lapel. For a moment the portal was empty, like a vacant, staring eye.

Rickey had the belly gun aimed through the cloth of his pocket. There were no words spoken; the habitues of the Rutkin Club knew nothing of the drama. Log Kazan stared at the door. Borsch swung the roulette wheel. Chipmunk Daley handled the little rake at the craps table with his left hand.

John Wade kept moving to the open door. It led, he knew, to the office of Buggy Rutkin. There was a corridor and then an ante chamber and beyond that the den in which the little egotistic gambler crouched behind ornate mahogany.

A figure passed through the doorway and into the gambling room. John stared in disbelief. It was a slight, graceful figure in a blue evening dress which contrasted sharply with the fluffy blonde hair. It was Jean Morrow.

In her hand she held a smoking gun. Her blue eyes, lighter than the dress, blending into the picture, were wide and staring. Her mouth was twisted to one side in horror and fear.

Rickey Boles bellowed, "Hold it, everybody. Don't move!"

John gathered speed, going towards the girl. Somehow he knew that he must keep an eye upon Log Kazan, somehow he managed it as he moved. He saw Log's hand streak downward and foresaw the conclusion.

He reached Jean just in time. He swept her off her feet. He heard Rickey's heavy footsteps coming close behind. He plunged for the door through which the girl had appeared.

The lights went out.

THERE WERE no shots behind him. The people in the gambling room were milling and crying out. John thought of Log Kazan's ability with a knife. He clutched Jean closer. He carried her through the door to the office of the Rutkin Club.

The portal behind him closed automatically. It slammed heavily with a sickening thud.

Buggy Rutkin sat behind his huge desk, his oily, smug face alight with satisfaction. In his hand was a large automatic. It was pointed unerringly at John Wade. But John

Wade was staring not at Buggy Rutkin, but at the figure upon the floor.

It was a slight figure, with greying hair. It was crumpled in a heap alongside a large chair. The right side of the skull was bloody and broken. John dropped to one knee and peered closely. Gore oozed evenly and steadily from the fatal wound.

Sam Parsons was dead.

The little ferret, the wire-haired fox terrier of the Governor's undercover staff had been shot to death in the office of the Rutkin Club.

John got to his feet, his face pale. He had not always agreed with Sam Parsons. But they had worked together. No one knew better the faithfulness, the bulldog courage, the tenacity and acumen of the little investigator. John stared at Jean Morrow. She still held the gun clutched in her right hand.

Buggy Rutkin said, "The police are on their way. Stand still and don't make bad moves, Wade!"

John ignored the gambler. He said, "Jean! How did this thing happen?"

Rutkin snapped, "This old gee and his dumb blonde wife come in here and started an argument about gamblin'. She dint want the umpchay t' bet any more dough. He had a snootful and wanted t' gamble. The dame come to me t' stop him. I was givin' him advice t' lay off when she outs with the roscoe and lets him have it."

John said, "Jean! Tell me, quick!"

Heavy footsteps were approaching down the corridor. The Midburg police were here! John Wade knew what to expect from the constabulary. Neither Jean nor any of the Governor's secret agents were known as such to the corrupt law forces of Midburg.

He begged, "Jean! Please talk. Quick, before it's too late!"

She said, "I—there's nothing—it's so confused. I had a drink at the bar… I don't remember, John. Is—is Sam really—dead?"

Her voice was faraway, indistinct. She held John with her cloudy, dimly terrified gaze. He said, "Jean! I—we—don't talk, baby. Don't say a word to anyone. Wait until I get a lawyer before you say a word. Can you remember that?"

Jean said vaguely, "Yes. I—I guess so…."

The police came into the room. Captain Mose Belfry of Homicide was first. He was a beefy, fierce man with a grudge against the world in general and John Wade in particular.

He said, "Wade again, eh? What's the story, Bug? Can we make it stick?"

Buggy Rutkin glibly repeated his story. He added, "This gee, Wade, seems t' be palsy-walsy with the old guy's wife. You know how them things are, Cap. The well-dressed con guy and the old gee's wife!" John did not bother to resent the implication. He said to Belfry, "I came in after this thing happened. I brought the girl back here after Buggy let her wander around with the gun in her hand. You want to pinch me, Belfry?"

"Pinch you? You're a material witness, ain'cha?" smirked the Homicide Captain. "You ain't pinched, Wade. You're just detained. Now ain't that cute?"

A RED-FACED cop named Boffo Cassidy was twisting steel bracelets on the slender wrists of Jean Morrow. John Wade clenched his fists as Cassidy gave a jerk and dragged the girl across the room. Belfry knelt beside the corpse, callously going through Sam's pockets. Something clicked and red chips fell on the floor. There were several of the red chips. One of them fell into the small pool which was Sam Parson's red blood.

John Wade stared at the chips, concentrating on their smooth round surfaces. He wondered if he could mesmerize himself sufficiently to go through with this. He wondered if he could watch the brutal treatment of the girl without cracking loose, giving Belfry the chance to put a beef on him.

They could hold him indefinitely as a material witness. They could keep him incommunicado in a cell while they tortured Jean Morrow, while they framed a perfect case upon her, sent her along the path to the electric chair.

The Governor could do little. There were too many high officials, too many of the judiciary still in the hands of the underworld, still accepting crooked money.

Belfry had Jean by the shoulder, was twisting her, bending her forward so that her face was close to that of the dead man upon the floor. He snarled, "Yuh killed him, didn'tcha? Yuh shot him becuz he was gamblin' a few red chips. Just a few lousy, two-dollar red chips! He was an old guy an' you wuz tired of him. Yuh had yer eye on this slicker, this Wade, didn'tcha? Tell the truth, you lousy lil murderin' twist!"

Jean's face was stark with horror and disbelief. She struggled, fighting to get away from the bloodied head of the corpse. She was returning to consciousness, John saw, regaining complete use of her outraged senses.

John said sharply, "That girl's been drugged. You can see it. Get a doctor in here and examine her. She's been drugged and framed, I tell you!"

Belfry straightened, throwing Jean violently back into the hands of Boffo Cassidy. He sneered, "Every moll that ever gunned her guy has been framed. Save that for the witness stand, sucker. You'll look good up there—a con guy!"

Buggy Rutkin said, "It's goin' to ruin my business, Captain. I'm terrible sorry it should happen here. I couldn't do a thing, Captain."

"Cert'nly, you couldn't," said Belfry cordially. "Don't I know it? It'll be bad, Bug. But you'll come out okay."

John Wade relapsed into silence. Buggy Rutkin would come out fine. Buggy Rutkin had the Five Mobs behind him, John reflected bitterly.

He felt the serpentine eyes of the gambler upon him. He stared back, and the full force of the catastrophe struck him.

Rutkin knew. The gambler, henchman of the all-powerful nation-wide organization, somehow knew of the connection between Sam Parsons, Jean Morrow and John Wade. He had known it before the murder of Parsons. It was all clear now.

Jean had been framed from the start. The Five Mobs was out to get the Governor's undercover crew. Parsons was only the first. They were all marked for extinction. As he was prodded down the hall by Boffo Cassidy and two other giant detectives, his helpless rage congealed to bitterness.

CHAPTER FOUR
HELD FOR MURDER

MIDBURG HAD a city jail which was ancient as the hills upon which the town rested. In the large detention room was a motley collection of petty criminals and witnesses, watched over by a large cop with buck teeth. John Wade paced the floor endlessly, back and forth, back and forth.

They had Jean Morrow somewhere in a filthy cell. They had browbeaten her in the room known as Coney Island until she had fainted. When she recovered they would return her to the third degree until she collapsed again or admitted her crime. It was late afternoon and they had been at it all day.

Haggard, sleepless, John Wade walked like a prowling cat among the silent, uncaring chaff of the police's gleanings. He had to get out. He had to get to a lawyer. He had to see the Governor.

He came near the door. The large policeman stared suspiciously at him. The cops had been warned against John Wade.

Outside the door a voice said gruffly, "I got to see this rat, Wade. Open up, officer. I want Wade for larceny."

Another voice protested, "No outa town copper can get that guy. The Chief wants him in there."

The first voice said, "Open up an' lemme identify him, you cluck. I ain't gonna kidnap him."

A key rattled reluctantly. The door opened. John stepped to one side. The large policeman inside said, "Now what kinda foolishness is this?"

A fist like a boulder reached out and clopped the large policeman alongside the ear. He went down like a felled ox. John stepped out in the corridor. The turnkey was lying on his face, the keys dangling in his limp hand.

Rickey Boles said, "Let's crush Jean outa here and go on the lam."

"How you goin' to do that?" demanded John. "Let's get to Mink Levine and the Governor."

"Where the hell you think I been?" demanded the big man violently. "Playin' Chinese checkers with Evalina? They can't do nothin' yet without spoilin' the whole deal. Mink's got a *habeas corpus* over at Judge Minling's right now—but they ain't turnin' Jean loose. The Five Mobs dough has brought up everybody in office around this burg."

Rickey's eyes were red from fatigue and anxiety. He closed the door against the clamoring of less fortunate prisoners in the detention pen. He said, "They'll be comin' down on us, pal. Let's go."

John said, "But we have to get Jean cleared of this thing by law. If the Governor says so, we must remain under-cover."

"They'll beat hell outa her," said Rickey. "They'll—you know what these muggs'll do to a pretty kid like her, when they find out she ain't got a relative nor nothin'."

The cords stood out on John's neck. He said slowly, "I joined up for the duration of this racket-bustin' business. I suppose I oughta get the hell out of here and work on this thing undercover. I suppose I oughta do what they call 'my duty.' I oughta let Jean take it while we do our 'duty'."

Rickey said, "But you ain't."

John said, "You got ideas?"

"I crushed outa better jails 'n this when I was twenty. I am a bigger boy now. Let's go," said Rickey happily.

They walked boldly down the corridor. They were familiar enough with the building. They went across to the women's department. Jean would be in the far cell, the dirty little horror cell which was used to frighten criminals.

There were a cluster of men outside the door. John and Rickey dropped back around a corner out of sight. John peered cautiously out. They were bringing the girl out of the cell, supporting her on either side. She was pale and weak and her eyes were again clouded by doubt.

Rickey drew in his breath and reached into his pocket. John said, "There are Belfry and Cassidy and the two detectives. You don't need a gat, Rickey. Take Cassidy and as many others as you can reach."

Rickey said doubtfully, "What about the matron?"

John peeked at the formidable, sour-faced woman who trailed along, saw her shove Jean violently. He said, "I'll take her, too."

THE TWO flattened themselves against the wall. Belfry was blatting all the way down the corridor, throwing his weight about, reiterating that he would get a confession or kill Jean in the trying.

They all came around the corner in a heap. John let them get one step by. Rickey blocked out in front. Belfry bellowed, "A break! Get the riot guns! Kill 'em!"

John hit Belfry with a terrific right. He threw the punch from his heels and belted it behind the captain's jaw. Belfry stopped yelling and began to sag. John deliberately threw four lightning blows at the falling cop. Each landed on an ear. The captain would be wearing cauliflowers that year.

The matron started to yap. John mercifully hit her on her thick jaw. She went down, dragging Jean with her.

Rickey had Boffo Cassidy by the neck. He was using the cop as a weapon. He flipped and Boffo's heels came up and knocked one of the detectives colder than a haddock. He flipped again and Boffo, released suddenly, barged into the second detective. Heads collided and suddenly everyone but Rickey and John were on the floor.

Rickey thoughtfully kicked Boffo in the teeth, necessitating quite a chunk of dental work. John plucked Jean loose from the matron and stood her up. He said anxiously, "Can you make it, baby? Can you navigate?"

Jean said, "I guess—I hope so. Is—are we doing right, John? Should we do this?"

Rickey said, "Don't ask! This way."

John seized the swaying girl in his arms. She clung to him, whispering, "John—oh, John. It's a dream, isn't it, John?"

"Sure, baby," he gritted, "a bad dream. Hold everything. Papa's goin' downstairs."

Rickey was opening the side door. They were going down the stairs. Behind them distant noises told the story of an aroused police force. Rickey went ahead, sliding out into the street, glancing right and left, his gun drawn and ready now. They were too close to freedom to take further chances.

John stared unbelievingly. At the curb was his own big, convertible coupé. Rickey said, "I hadda idea we might need it at this spot."

The side entrance was on a little-used street. Rickey climbed behind the wheel. John placed Jean tenderly in the middle. A cop came dashing down the stairs and out onto the sidewalk, a shot-gun in his hands. John leaped and swung.

The cop bowled over. John picked up the shot-gun, and jumped into the car. Rickey, the most skillful of drivers, coaxed the motor to a roar and slid the gear into second. They went away from the curbing like the hammers of all hell, just as a dozen policemen appeared on the sidewalk.

THEY TURNED the corner. They turned three other corners with a screaming of tires that made John wonder why they didn't upset. He said, "We can't go back to Avery Place because Buggy is wise. No use going to the Governor—he can't help us without showing his hand and ruining the whole setup. The radio cops will be combin' every street for us. It looks like we will have to disappear in thin air, pal."

Rickey said, "I got a place. Just hold tight."

He shot down a narrow road. He drove between a rail-road siding and a lumber yard. He tooled the big coupé behind a stack of piled boards and braked. He said triumphantly, "Pal o' mine owns this joint. He owes me a favor."

They were in the lumber yard. There was enough concealment for the present, at any rate. It lacked two hours of growing dark.

John said, "Can you remember about last night, Jean?"

The girl straightened, looked at him dully. She said slowly, "It—was bad, John. Sam insisted on going to that place—the Rutkin Club. He wanted to make sure the wheels were crooked. He thought he could work through the District Attorney to close it up, throw Rutkin into disfavor, make him do something which would give us reasons to convict him and send him to jail."

"That was Sam's way," nodded John.

"We had a drink at the bar," said Jean. "Sam was pretending to have too much. Rutkin was in the game room, wandering about, watching things. After I took the drink, things got hazy. I—dimly remember a shot… Sam falling… the gun in my hand… John! Could I have shot him while under the influence of the drug?"

"If you did," said John grimly, "they fixed you good. They fixed it so you wouldn't be able to prove you were drugged. Belfry refused to get a doctor. That gun must be lousy with your fingerprints. Rutkin's testimony as an eyewitness will be accepted so long as it is coupled with the evidence of the gun."

She said, "But Sam—I couldn't kill Sam. Why should I kill Sam? He was my friend."

John looked at the girl sharply. Her eyes were staring, glassy. Her mouth was slack, the corners drooping. She was on the verge of complete hysteria.

"Jean," he said quietly, "You've got to keep calm. You must keep your head clear, so we can plan."

"Little Sam," she moaned. "Poor little old man. He was good to me. I didn't kill him. I know I didn't!"

Rickey said, "Batty as a bed-bug. What the hell do we do now, pal?"

John said, "The Governor won't like it, Rickey."

"No," said Rickey. "I s'pose he will not like it. And with a historical woman on my hands I don't know if I like it very much."

CHAPTER FIVE
PAY-OFF IN RED CHIPS

IT WAS dark now. The big coupé rolled to a stop on a side street. Jean Morrow was quieter, but there was no coherence in her speech. John got her out of the car and walked her to the corner. She seemed able to handle herself.

A cab came cruising. Rickey hailed it. They got in and John said, "The Rutkin Club."

The driver said scornfully, "Closed tight as a drum. Don't youse read the papers?"

John said, "Okay, then take us down to where the Rutkin Club used to be."

The driver scanned them shrewdly. He said, "I don't think I wanta take youse anywhere, cull."

Rickey said, "But you're gonna."

The driver looked at Rickey. He said, "Well—but the cops'll getcha anyways. The evenin' papers is full of pitchers of youse."

John said, "That's nice. Drive on, chum!"

They stopped down the street from the darkened Rutkin Club. John took a green bill from his pocket, tore it in half. He said to the driver, "Go to Mink Levine with this envelope. If you deliver it faithfully, I'll give you the other half of the bill."

The driver squinted at it. The bill was a fifty. The driver said, "I hope you live through this, Mister Wade. I c'd use this dough."

"If I don't," said John, "see Mink."

The driver said, "Good luck, cull. Buggy Rutkin's got plenty heat around him."

John said, "So long. I got plenty heat on me, too. Only it's agin me, not with me."

Rickey said, "I don't see how we're gonna...."

John said, "Neither do I. Let's just go ahead."

They put Jean Morrow between them and walked down the street. There was a basement entrance to the brownstone house which housed the Rutkin Club. Rickey swung down a couple of steps and tried the door. It was locked, so he put his shoulder against it and pushed.

The door gave way. John said, "Jean, you must keep quiet. I can't leave you. This might be tough but you'll have to go through with it. Can you keep quiet?"

She said docilely, like a child, "Yes, John. I didn't kill Sam, did I, John?"

"No," said John. "You didn't kill Sam."

Rickey went up a short flight of steps. There was another door, but it was unlatched. They found themselves in a small chamber. It led to the large gambling room of the Rutkin Club. John looked in upon the stripped premises and said, "They moved fast. They've taken out everything. I wonder...."

He led the way across the room to the door through which Jean had come with the smoking gun in her hand. The corridor was clear, but the door to Rutkin's office was closed. From behind it came the mutter of voices.

John said, "I'm going in there alone, Rickey."

"Like hell you are," said the big man promptly.

"Yes, I am," insisted John. "You cover out here. Stay by Jean and use your judgment. If you hear me call, come a-running."

Rickey looked at the sawed-off shotgun which John had taken from the policeman and was still holding under his arm. He said, "You gonna take that in there?"

"Yeah," said John. "I thought it was a good idea."

Rickey said, "Well. All right. But I don't like it."

John went swiftly and silently down the corridor, not looking at the tragic face of Jean Morrow. He was desperate, and he did not want her to know. He was taking the longest of chances, based upon a slight observation of the night before. It was far too slim a chance. Too many things had to click into place. It might not work and he did not want Jean to know.

The way into Rutkin's office was easy. He turned a knob, opened the door, closed it behind him as he stepped through. They were not expecting him.

THE KAZANS were there, and Chipmunk Daley, and a strange man in expensive clothes, a sleek haircomb and a hooked nose. Buggy Rutkin was preening himself behind his huge desk, looking over-pleased. When he saw John he did not look so pleased.

John said pleasantly, "Nice weapon, a shot-gun. Blow several of you all to bits if I turned both barrels loose."

The hook-nosed man said, "Is this punk Wade?"

John said, "Yes, Gus. I'm Wade. How are the boys in Chi? I heard you had things nice and easy again."

Gus said, "I don't know you, Wade."

"You will," nodded John. "I'm movin' in. This Rutkin won't do, Gus. The Five Mobs can't use a clumsy crook like Rutkin."

The diminutive gambler said hoarsely, "Log! Borsch! Take this guy."

Borsch Kazan said, "Take him yourself. You tole us he was lammin'. You tole us there wasn't no need for a look-out. You tole us—"

"He told you he was a big shot," nodded John. "He always tells people that. He tried to frame my pals out of his way because he knew we were too hot for him."

Buggy Rutkin said, "Don't listen t' this con guy, Gus!"

"You hear about the lousy frame, Gus?" asked John casually. His eyes were tired from loss of sleep, but he kept all the muggs within his range. He was walking on eggs now. He had to give out in his best confidence-man patter. He had to sell a bill of green goods to the representative of the Five Mobs.

The hooked-nose man said, "Spill it, Wade."

"This stupid little goniff shot my man Parsons last night," said John coolly. "He slipped a Micky Finn to my moll and planted a gat on her. He called the cops and had me rapped as a material. And he slipped in four places. The cops turned me loose, turned my gal loose."

"It's a lie," screamed Buggy. "The cops are on his tail right now. It's a good beef, I tell you—"

John reached out a hand. Buggy shut up, fear in his eyes. John said, "I only wanted one of your cigarettes, Buggy. You're pretty nervous, aren't you?"

He helped himself to a cigarette out of a pack which was near a mahogany box. He reached out his little finger as he picked up the matches and flipped a button.

He drawled, "You used a gat with filed numbers. It was a bum job, Buggy. They used acid on it. You know whose gun it was, Gus?"

He lit the cigarette with one hand, without relaxing vigilance. His eyes circled the men in the room. He saw Borsch Kazan wince, draw in his breath. He went on casually, "Sure. Ask Borsch. You can't file gun numbers any more, Buggy. The police lab will getcha every time. Belfry isn't in the police lab, you know. There's still an honest cop or two. Funny, ain't it? John Wade usin' honest cops to spring his moll."

Buggy Rutkin stared at the hooked-nose man. He begged, "Gus, you don't fall for this guy's guff, do you? He's a con guy. He dishes it out for a livin'!"

"Sure I'm a con guy," laughed John. "I'm enough of a con guy to be smart. You planted red chips on Sam Parsons. I happen to know Sam was superstitious about red chips. He wouldn't bet a dime on 'em. He'd use two whites every time.

"I found three people—respectable citizens—who'll swear Sam never made a bet. You rapped him too soon, Buggy."

Gus of the Five Mobs demanded, "Is this on the level, Bug?"

"I hadda knock him off," moaned the gambler. "He was stickin' his nose inta the joint. I heard he was copper. I dint know Wade had a mob. I figgered Wade was a stool pigeon. I hadda cool this guy before he got hep to the wheels."

"Yeah," scoffed Wade, "that's right. A kid could pipe those gaffed wheels. Those dice were so phoney they rattled queer. Of all the stupid, puny little racketeers, you win the buttons."

Gus said interestedly, "He didn't use magnets on the wheels?"

"This cheap fake is a petty larceny punk," said John. "He wouldn't spend the scratch for magnets. He gimmicked 'em with steel, I tell you. He's small time, Gus. Why don't you big timers get wise?"

Buggy Rutkin was choking behind his desk, tugging at his collar. He squawked, "You can't do this t' me, Wade. I'll have you boiled on oil. I'll have your guts cut out—"

John said, "You bore me, pal. You killed Parsons, usin' Borsch's gun, which was in your drawer... right?"

"Cert'ny, I bumped him," screamed Bug Rutkin. "I hadda, I tell ya. He was rubberin' around—"

The hooked-nose man said suddenly, "Hey! That button. He flipped that button!"

THEY ALL stared at the mahogany box. The button was plainly marked in white letters: *On*.

Bug Rutkin said excitedly, "My loudspeakers system! It's a frame. He's a copper, I tell ya!"

He was exultant, the little gambler. If John Wade was a stoolie or a policeman, the Five Mobs would not snatch his profitable, power-holding connection from him. He repeated, "A lousy John Law! I'll—

The ego of the little man burned like a leaping flame! He dove behind the desk with the celerity of a muskrat into a stream, scrabbling at the drawer of his desk.

Log Kazan reached behind his neck for the knife slung in the lanyard. Borsch Kazan went for a rod at his hip. Chipmunk Daley hit the floor, reaching inside his coat. The man named Gus produced a derringer from his sleeve in the twinkling of an eye.

John Wade turned loose the shot gun. It roared and reverberated in the room. Slugs filled the air as guns spoke in reply.

John sidestepped and went around the desk. Something tore at his impeccable sports jacket. He caught Buggy Rutkin with the swinging barrel of the shotgun. The little man dropped. John flung himself forward, coming around the far side of the desk. Borsch Kazan was crouching, gun poised. His brother lay mangled beside him.

John said, "Borsch! Hold it."

The gun came down. Kazan was noted for his fast, accurate shooting, John remembered. The shotgun let loose with the other barrel. Borsh Kazan spattered against the walls.

From afar came Rickey's bellow, "I'm a-comin', pal!"

John stood up slowly. There was a trickle of blood running down his left arm. He leaned over and picked up Buggy Rutkin's gun. The gambler was breathing but there was a nice lump over his ear.

The man named Gus had taken the first charge along with Log Kazan. He was quite dead. Log had lost most of his face. Chipmunk Daley lay very still under the remains of Log. John said, "Chipmunk! I'm coverin' you right on."

Chipmunk Daley said calmly, "I'm no sucker, Wade. I'm in the clear on this. I ain't fired a shot."

Rickey came into the room. He had two guns in his hands. He said, "Migawd, John! It's a slaughterhouse!"

John said, "Mink? Did he get here?" There were more voices coming down the hall. Rickey said, "Yeah, he got here in time."

Mink Levine came into the room. The dapper criminal lawyer surveyed the fallen men solemnly. He said, "You'll do all right, John. We got every word of the confession."

John hauled the unconscious Rutkin into full view. He said, "Buggy'll sign it. He's alive."

Captain Mose Belfry of Homicide came slowly into the room. His ears were bandaged and his eye was partly closed. He glared balefully at John and spat, "There's charges against this guy right on."

Rickey said innocently, "I don't see our pal, Boffo Cassidy. Where is he at now?"

"In the hospital," said Belfry. "Where you'll be."

Rickey said, "I didn't get any action outa this thing. I could start now. I could put you up there with Boffo. Then you wouldn't be around to prefer charges."

John said, "It doesn't make any difference. I'll stand charges. I just had to prove who killed Sam Parsons."

"You put a crimp in the Five Mobs," said Mink Levine. He stepped close and whispered in John's ear, "The Governor will be delighted, John. Go down to Headquarters with this bunch. I'll have you all sprung in half an hour. They all think you're a confidence man with a mob. How did you ever dig up all that evidence in such a short time? How did you know about the gun, the—"

John said wearily, "I didn't. I guessed it. It had to be that way. I knew about Sam and red chips because I played poker with him. Rickey tipped me off to the wheels. I made the rest up to fit the occasion. I—I gotta go, Mink."

HE WENT out the door. He went down the corridor. He was terribly tired. He found the big room jammed full of cops.

The deep blue dress was almost indistinguishable among the uniforms. But he found it at last. He pushed a cop out of the way. He came close to Jean Morrow and looked into her eyes.

They were clear, blue eyes now. She said, "I heard it over the loud speaker. I'm all right now, John. Just hearing that I didn't kill poor Sam was enough."

He said, "Sam—we'll miss old Sam. It breaks up the combination, Jean. I—I'm worried. You can't live there, posing as a widow. There'll be some publicity. We—it's all going to change. We'll have to—think up something new,"

She soothed him with her soft voice. "We'll work it out, John. We'll always work it out, won't we?"

He said, "Together? You mean we'll work it out together? You and me?"

"And the Governor and Rickey."

He said, "Oh." He pulled himself together. He could have bitten off his tongue. He would never have gone so far, implied so much, had he not been so near to complete exhaustion.

He had forgotten for the moment. Forgotten that he was an ex-crook, a con guy.

He thought sleepily, still holding her hand, that it had been a good demonstration. He had conned the Five Mobs out of Midburg—that was pretty good.

Jean Morrow said breathlessly, "You're hurt! There's blood! Oh, John!"

That was good, too. The concern in her voice, the tears in her eyes. Oh yes, that was good enough for John Wade.

THE BRASS-BUTTON MURDERS

WHEN THE GUNSMOKE LIFTED,
FOUR BLOOD-SMEARED
BODIES LAY IN THE LOBBY
OF MIDBURG'S SMARTEST
HOTEL. SO THIS TIME, JOHN
ACTUALLY HAD TO HIT
THE CRIMSON TRAIL WITH
VENGEANCE IN HIS HEART
AND A TOMMY-GUN IN HIS
ARMS.... AT THE END OF THE
TRAIL WERE BOTH SUCCESS
AND FAILURE—AND POLICE
HEADQUARTERS!

CHAPTER ONE
SWIFT KICKS FOR
COPPERS

JOHN WADE sat in the lobby of the Ritzmore Hotel in the City of Midburg, watching a big copper and idly toying with a sheet of fine rice paper so that it crinkled in his strong hands. The cop's name was Jake "Pickle-Puss" Cram. John Wade wondered how many lushes Pickle Puss would shake down that Saturday night.

John Wade was clad in a dinner coat which fitted him so well that he was easily the best-dressed man in the lobby. His black tie was a careless masterpiece, his brown hair, greying at the temples, curled tightly to his scalp. His had been the best front in the racket—in the old days when a front meant easy dough.

John Wade was no longer a confidence man. The rice paper crumpled in his hands was a confidential report from the office of Governor Fortney Castle, Chief Executive of Midstate, of which Midburg was the capital. It had come to John secretly that night, at the house in Avery Place where respectable suburbanism cloaked his activities on the side of law and order.

Law and Order, John thought cynically, watching the beefy uniformed cop in the lobby of Midburg's finest hotel. Law and Order exemplified by Pickle Puss, who watched the gay people in the Continental room, avid to catch someone overindulging in liquor so that he might shake

them down for a dollar or two, threatening to catch them driving their cars away under the influence.

Law and Order as administered in the police courts, according to the report on the thin paper in his hands, thusly:

> 1: John Manning, 19, Carbondale, in line at football game Saturday with ticket he had purchased last month, was approached by Detective Joe Byrne and asked to sell ticket. Manning refused. Byrne persisted, asking price, Manning said jokingly, "Twenty bucks." Byrne arrested Manning for scalping.

None lived more than a few seconds after the final shot... No witness could remember even so simple a thing as... whence came the gunfire!

Ten hours later J. Manning, Sr., provided bail. J. Manning, Sr., is up-state leader of Reform Party.

2: Izzy Krantz, convicted of running "numbers" was sentenced this morning by Judge Gordon Minting. The Judge pronounced, "It is the sentence of this court that you remain upon probation for one year—and let this be a lesson to you!" Krantz is well-known in police circles as a stool pigeon and petty gangster. He was arrested by county officers.

3: Joel Parker and Miss Mary Martin were arrested and charged with a statutory offense last night when Motorcycle

Policeman Cave Wilkey found them in parked car on side street in front of Miss Martin's residence. The couple are engaged to be married and are leaders in the Young Reform Group.

4: Munroe Dreher, who was charged with drunken driving and manslaughter in connection with the death of Morris Levy on Main Street last year, was dismissed in Judge Minling's court because of insufficient evidence. Dreher and his father are heavy contributors to Police Benevolent Society.

There was more, but John had read enough. The police of Midburg were cracking down on Governor Castle's newly formed and steadily growing Reform Party.

The handsome, brave Governor had been elected by the Conservatives. Neither the Independent Party nor the Conservatives had expected any trouble from the wealthy, retired Castle. Midstate had continued its crooked ways without cessation after the Governor's inauguration. Castle had been unable to do anything about it through legal methods. Corruption had stultified every arm of the law.

The energetic Castle had therefore taken steps. He had hired Sam Parsons, a ferret in human guise. He had hired Jean Morrow, that beauteous blonde who was as capable in a criminal laboratory as she was shapely.

He had hired John Wade, the slickest con guy in the country, and with John he had acquired big Rickey Boles whose fists and guns were a by-word in the underworld.

They had all worked undercover to eliminate the tie-up between crime and politics. Sam Parsons had lost his life fighting, shot down by a murdering crooked gambler. The police had hampered the solution of Sam's murder. The police had abused Jean Morrow.

JOHN WADE'S glance fell upon a couple advancing across the lobby. The man was huge and his winged collar was obviously uncomfortable. He was Rickey Boles.

The girl was clad in a long, black skirt which swirled when she walked. Her bodice was a tight-fitting blue knit jacket, a soft, gorgeous blue sweater with dull gold tracings which outlined her firm, high breasts. She was startlingly blonde and her eyes were the color of a noonday sky. She was Jean Morrow.

Pickle Puss Cram was dreaming of wealthy drunks who could be intimidated. His back was to the oncoming couple. Rickey Boles, all two hundred and ten pounds of him, was irking at his collar. Jean seemed to be staring only at John Wade.

Pickle Puss stepped backwards without looking. His big, flat foot came down on Rickey Boles' patent-leather instep. John Wade sighed resignedly.

The cops were cracking down. Pickle Puss, with no idea of cracking anybody but a flush drunk, was firing the shot which would begin the war. John grimaced apologetically at Jean Morrow and moved swiftly forward.

Rickey had Pickle Puss by the elbow. Rickey was saying, very loudly, "Cops ain't got a right in lobbies of nice hotels. Cops ain't got a right to be with nice people nohow, practically. Cops got less right to step on my foot!"

He was squeezing on the elbow. Pickle Puss was getting very red. Rickey said, "Down on your knees, cop. I don't like cops!" Rickey's huge hand was an iron claw, digging painfully into his flesh. Pickle Puss snarled thickly, "You dirty hood—leggo me! I'll kill you fer this!"

Rickey let go of him, suddenly. Pickle Puss staggered, reaching for his gun. Rickey stepped in with a short left. It banged on the cop's jaw.

Pickle Puss hit the tiled floor of the lobby and skidded into a potted palm. The palm toppled reluctantly and fell on Pickle Puss's middle. The hotel detective came running, his revolver out.

John Wade's foot caught the hotel dick's instep. The man flattened out in mid air, sprawling. Rickey, warmed up now, reached out and cuffed—sent him reeling into a far corner, out cold.

A man in full evening dress said admiringly, "Fine work! I've been waiting for that since they placed that man in here to spy on decent people!"

John recognized Foley Mastervelt, the local banker. He said quickly, "Thank you, sir. Cover our retreat, will you?"

He had Rickey by one arm and Jean by the other. He said, "Out the side door and through the alley. This tears it. We got work to do."

Rickey expostulated, "Now wait a minute. I didn't get dressed up like Mrs. Astor's pet horse for nothin'. I—"

John said, "Outside, bum. Get going!"

They went out the alley and into the street. John's coupé was waiting and they piled into the wide seat. Rickey grumbled, but drove expertly through the streets of Midburg, out to the little, white house on Avery Place, into the garage, where steel doors fell into place behind them.

IN THE comfortably furnished living room Jean Morrow said regretfully, "I agree with Rickey, John."

John said, "You're beautiful, baby. But read this report."

He gave her the rice paper. After she had finished he said, "The police are almost sure that we are Governor Castle's people. Since Sam's death you have been seen with Rickey and me too often. We have records which make us fairly safe as underworld characters. You are—Jean

Morrow, cleverest student ever at Women's College—but, unfortunately, almost respectable."

He grinned at her, his face breaking into a hundred tiny wrinkles. She said, "Too respectable, John. Must I rob a bank?"

John said, "The Governor says the time has come. We must crack the crooked police ring. We must get Chief Joey Watson out of office. We must break every crooked cop on the Midburg force."

Rickey growled, "Swell. I'll break their damn necks."

"Not that way," cautioned John. "We've got to think a bit."

Rickey said, "I on'y know one way. Beat hell outa them."

John said, "It won't last long enough. Jean?"

"We must think," nodded Jean Morrow, wrinkling her lovely brows.

John shouted, "Evalina! Coffee for three thinkers."

They sat and thought. After a while Evalina, black and dour, brought in the tray. She looked at John, sprawled in a chair, at Jean, slouched in another chair, at Rickey, somnolent on the divan.

She said acidly, "Three thinkers? Pooh! You all makes me laugh out'n my mouf!"

Rickey snored gently.

CHAPTER TWO
THE CORPSES
IN THE LOBBY

IT WAS midnight in the lobby of the Ritzmore Hotel. Pickle Puss Cram said to the house dick, "We'll have them guys in Coney Island t'morra. Boy, when I get me a piece of hose and go t'work on 'at Rickey Boles, I'll make hamberger out'a him. I'll mash him t'jelly. I'll...."

The house detective mumbled, holding his sore jaw. Pickle Puss turned his one good eye towards the check room. Two fashionably gowned women were reaching for their wraps.

One was a striking brunette, a tall girl with long, straight limbs and mascaraed eyes which glowed with some emotion indiscernible to Pickle Puss. The other was small, red-headed, pert-featured. Pickle Puss sauntered forward, trying to keep the bruised portions of his physiognomy turned away.

The house dick loitered a few steps in the background. Two men were visible through the door of the Continental Room, arguing amiably over the check. Both were obviously not sober. Pickle Puss surveyed the scene expertly.

The girls turned and came towards the exit. Pickle Puss drifted between them and the door to the Continental Room. The hotel detective puttered in the offing. The two men were matching for the check, laughing boisterously.

The noise of the shots was startlingly close. Two guns banged, the pattern of the sound rattling and echoing in the lobby like a Fourth of July in a tin can factory.

Pickle Puss made a stab at his holstered revolver but missed it. His hand was numb, his co-ordination destroyed. He gazed down at his blue uniform, horrified. Over his left breast was a black hole. Blood did not come at once. He was dead in a moment or two.

The house dick caught one in the head and went down like a ten-pin, his brains scattering on the tile. The thunder of the guns did not cease.

The tall girl with the dark hair stumbled, fell forward, reaching for support, finding none. Her bright eyes glazed, she clutched at her heart and toppled full length.

The red-headed one tried to run. She pulled up her skirts and got to the revolving door, had it spinning, was just about to step in. The last bullet beat into her skull and drove her to her knees. She jammed the whirling door.

People disappeared in all directions. For a full minute the silence, coming on the heels of the thunder of gunfire, was deafening. Then cautious heads reappeared, and when no further winged murder greeted them, pandemonium ensued.

Scattered about, the four bodies lay disjointedly where they had fallen. None had lived more than a few seconds after the final shot. Irate police stumbled about vainly seeking evidence from witnesses too confused, too frightened to remember even so simple a thing as whence came the gun-fire.

JOHN WADE took Jean Morrow home at one o'clock. They were silent, riding in the big coupé to the modest back street house which held the Governor's crime laboratory and where, since Sam Parson's death, Jean had made her sleeping quarters. John said, "Baby, this is the toughest thing yet. If we only had something to go on."

"We can't manufacture evidence," sighed Jean. "If the police aren't checked, we will be eventually whipped. They'll harass the Reform Group into oblivion."

John said, "We've got to make a start. I'll drift down to Pete's Place tonight. Maybe the mob'll know something."

"Be careful, John," she said quickly. "Some of the mob are getting suspicious of you. There have been too many of them killed, sent to jail—after doings with you and Rickey. You can't stay undercover forever."

John said, "Don't worry about me, baby. A crook is safe among crooks."

She sensed the hurt in him, the everpresent feeling that he was inferior to her, that his past was a barrier between them. She hesitated a long moment. Then she said softly, "Please, John, be careful. You know how I depend on you. I couldn't go on with this work—if anything happened."

He drew a deep breath. He said, "I—thanks, baby. I'll be as careful as possible. I—good-night, baby."

He left her quickly, seeing her into the house. He drove recklessly around corners, heading for the Down Neck district where one-eyed Pete ran his dive. He was running away, running away from his thoughts of Jean Morrow— of her soft beauty, her bright eyes, the lift of her breasts beneath the soft knitted jersey of her evening costume.

He was always running away from it, he thought bitterly. What else could he do? He was John Wade, ex-confidence man. No expiation could wipe out the past.

He parked the car down the street and walked up to Pete's darkened door. He knocked, using the crook's signal.

The police did not bother Pete after closing hours. The police needed the stoolies who hung out in Pete's place.

The paunchy, one-eyed proprietor opened the door a crack, recognized John. With amazing celerity he slipped out through the portal, pushing John backwards with a strong, urgent thrust. John said, "What the hell?"

Pete said, "You damn fool, why ain't you lammin'?"

"It isn't that bad, is it?" asked Wade. "We just pushed a cop around a bit."

"Pushed him full o' lead," said Pete. "They got warrants for first degree agin' you and Rickey, an' every patrol heap in town is on the prowl. Ain't you got no sense at all, John?"

John said, "I'm ignorant, pal. Give it to me."

Pete said, "Pickle Puss and the house dick an' two women who got in the way were gunned an hour ago in the Ritz-more. You an' Rickey are it."

"Two women?" asked John. "Give, pal. Who were they?"

"I dunno," said Pete perplexedly. "They just got in the way of lead, I guess. A couple broads out with a couple guys. The guys are bein' held. Name of Smith an' Jones. Couple outa town men, seems like."

John said, "You got anything on it?"

"The stoolies say you an' Rickey had that fight an' the cops think Rickey came back. It was a two-gun thing. Everybody knows Rickey carries two rods when he's gunnin'."

John said, "Does Rickey shoot women who happen to be in the way?"

"Naw," said Pete disgustedly. "But the cops gotta have somebody, ain't they? They'd like t' get you an' Rickey down there for some reason. Maybe they're wise."

John said stonily, "Wise to what, Pete?"

Pete's one eye rolled wildly. He said, "All I know is that you always been right with me. Anybody you an' Rickey ever took care of was a louse. But the Avery Place joint might get turned up by cops, John. You better lam."

John said, "Thanks, Pete. You're a pal."

HE GOT into the coupé and drove it to a downtown garage. He left it with a sleepy attendent and mailed the parking check at the nearest post box, addressing it hastily to Governor Castle.

He walked silently in the shadows through the quiet streets. Prowl cars passed him, but each time he managed to slip into a doorway and escape notice. The city was humming with police. He had to get across town to Avery Place and warn Rickey.

He got to the cab rank near the railroad station. He waited for ten minutes until the cab he wanted came along and nosed to a parking place.

He said quietly, "Avery Place, Red."

The driver almost jumped out from behind the wheel. He jerked around, reaching under his armpit in an unmistakable gesture. John said soothingly, "It's Wade. Let's go, Red."

The cabbie said, "Geez, pal. You scared me t' hell an' gone. The coppers want you, pal."

John said, "Those wrongoes always want somebody. Why not me?"

Red said, "What you wanta go away out Avery Place for?"

"It's respectable," said John smoothly. "They wouldn't look for me there. I got a dame out there'll hide me out."

Red said admiringly, "You're a slicker, pal."

They went cautiously across town. Red Madden was a crook, a roller of drunks, a gunman by avocation. He drove a cab to cover more nefarious activities and owned two apartment houses. He was, however, a square mugg and once Rickey Boles had saved his life in a gun fray. John knew that Red could be useful in this emergency.

He got off at the corner. He said, "Where can I get you, Red?"

The cabbie said, "With the heat you got on you, I shouldn't play ball at all."

John peeled a hundred dollar bill from a roll. He said, "I'll call Pete's. You keep in touch and earn another C note. And keep your nose clean, Red."

The cabby pocketed the bill. He said, "You know me, John. Pickle Puss shoulda got his long ago. It was tough about the broads. But they was a couple hookers anyhow."

He put the car in first. John said sharply, "Wait a minute, Red! You knew those girls?"

"Mitzi and Fitzi?" grinned Red. "A couple badgeroos from Philly. Worked with Izzy Krantz. I know 'em good."

"Strictly crooked, eh?" asked John thoughtfully.

"Took them outa town Johns inta the Bardsley House. Izzy made the play they was his sister an' wife. It was a doublebarrel," said Red admiringly. "That Izzy's cute."

John said, "Red, you're a big help."

HE WENT hastily down the street. He ducked around behind the white house and used his key on the almost invisible back door of the garage, knowing the other doors would be barred by the cautious Evalina. He went in and found Rickey still sleeping on the divan.

The big man rolled beneath Wade's prodding hand, protesting sleepily, "I'll bat that copper's ears down around his bleedin' ankles."

John said pleasantly, "No fun hittin' dead cops."

Rickey came awake with startling completeness. He said, "Dead? I didn't kill that punk. I saw 'im breathe...."

John said, "Somebody killed him. And other interesting people. Smiling Joey Watson has his little men hunting you and me. We are now a couple of lammisters."

Rickey said, "Lemme get upholstered," and came to his feet. John went to the telephone and called the Governor's private extension.

While John talked, Rickey was busy at a chest of drawers. He struggled into a complicated double harness which draped a big gun under each arm. He found a flat automatic to go inside his belt, against his iron-muscled stomach. He stuffed his pockets with fresh ammunition.

John said, into the phone, "That's how it is, Governor. Put a guard over Jean. They'll be after her, too. They had her down there once. If they try it on her again, I won't be responsible for what happens."

He hung up the instrument and said to Rickey, "One gun is all I can handle. Get out the jaloppy and let's go."

"Go where?" queried the big man dubiously.

John said, "The Bardsley House."

"Why, *Mister* Wade," said Rickey in shocked accents.

CHAPTER THREE
HIDEOUT IN HELL

THE BARDSLEY House was discreetly lighted, discreetly located, bore a sign which discreetly said, "Family Hotel." It was the toughest and vilest hostelry in Midstate.

"The bulls are looking for you and me," said John grimly. "They might be here. Cover me, pal."

He was gone before Rickey could protest. He slid through the plate glass door of the hotel and in two strides gained a column. Rickey grumbled, hefting a large gun in each hand, peering through the glass.

There was a door marked, "Manager's Office." John looked for the night clerk, saw him sleeping in a chair behind the desk. The lobby was deserted.

He went across the faded carpet. He opened the door marked "Office", went inside and closed it behind him.

Izzy Krantz was alone. He was counting a sheaf of green bills. He came up with a cannon half as big as his body and snarled, "Hold it, wise guy."

He was a little man with a hooked nose which twisted to one side. He had myopic brown eyes and kinky black hair. He wore a double-breasted blue suit and a snap-brim, low-crowned green hat which defied description.

John said mildly, "Hi, Izzy. Put up the gat and where in hell did you get that skimmer?"

Izzy said, "The hell with that, Wade. There's con heat on you. You got a lousy nerve comin' here."

John said surprisedly, "You gonna turn me in, Izzy? I never figured you for a stool."

The little man lowered the gun uncertainly. He said, "I got friends on the Force, Wade. I can't have you stached up here."

John said, "Look, Izzy. Just for the night. They'll never know. Just let me have a room—give me a key. I'll let myself in. You won't have any kick-back—and anyway, you're wired in right. You c'n let the clerk take the rap."

Izzy Krantz narrowed his eyes. John could see the dollar sign rising to the foreground of the little vice racketeer's consciousness, so he took out a large wad of bills and said, "Five C's? For one night?"

Izzy said, "Put it on the desk. Take a key off the hook. Take 204; that one's empty."

John said gratefully, "I'll remember this, Izzy. You're a right guy."

Izzy shrugged. "I should worry about coppers? They don't feed me. Sleep good, Wade. Maybe in the morning I c'n figger somethin'."

John said, "Thanks, pal."

He paused at the door. He said, "Oh—Izzy. Those broads—Mitzi and Fritzi. How did they get into it?"

"You oughta know," said Izzy Krantz meaningly.

"I didn't do it," explained John carefully. "Rickey didn't do it."

Izzy jeered, "My aunt didn't do it, neither. So go on upstairs, Wade. Them broads was a dime a dozen t' me. I know where they grow. They were gettin' uppity anyhow."

John said, "Uppity? They didn't pay off?"

"They shorted me," said Izzy viciously. "They were clippin' the uckersays for dollars and payin' me off in dimes. They…" He broke off suddenly. He said sullenly, "That's my business, Wade. G'wan, scram before the bulls get in here."

John went outside and motioned. Rickey came in fast. They went over to the desk. John reached behind the sleeping clerk and snatched the key to Room 204. They went up the stairs side by side, scorning the elevator.

THEY WENT down to the room fourth from the end of the hall. John listened, holding his breath. From somewhere came slightly drunken but muffled feminine giggles. There was no roistering in Izzy Krantz's Bardsley House.

John whispered, "Try two-o-six with your skeleton key."

Rickey tried it cautiously. The door opened. John went in, turned hastily, came out. He said, "The cashier of the First National is in there. Try two-o-two."

Rickey said, "Such people! There ain't no decency."

They tried 202. It was empty. John went in and Rickey closed the door. They blanketed the window and the transom and turned on the light in the bathroom so that they could see by the reflected gleam.

Rickey said, "I don't get it."

"Neither do I," said John honestly. "Izzy seemed to think we wanted to be hidden out, so I followed along."

"He'll sell us out to the cops," said Rickey disgustedly. "We'll have to kill somebody."

John sat on the edge of the bed, thinking hard. After a moment he snapped his fingers. He said, "Wait here a moment. Don't stir out of here."

He went back into the darkened hall. He used Rickey's key on Room 206. He went inside. Three minutes later he was back in 202. He said to Rickey,

"We're movin'—into a safe place. The cashier has promised to go out the back-way, quietly, if we don't phone his wife. Izzy will never let the bulls muscle into two-o-six."

Rickey guffawed, "I bet you scared him silly. Serves him right, the old hypocrite. He was a wrong tomato all his life, that penny pincher."

They gave the cashier time to scuttle away into the night. There was a private back entrance to the Bardsley for just such exits, carefully protected by Izzy Krantz's ingenuity, covered to resemble a blind alley, leading to the next street. John had often heard of that alley.

They went into 206 and settled down on chairs to wait. John nodded a bit. It was three-thirty in the morning. Rickey, thanks to his nap, was wide awake.

At three-thirty-five a key grated almost silently in a door. John came awake under Rickey's prodding finger. A voice in the next room growled, "Stick 'em up in there!"

There was a moment's silence. Men breathed hard and feet trampled. Rickey whispered, "Must be a half dozen of 'em. With sho-sho guns, I'll bet."

The heavy voice said, "Try the next rooms men. Batter down those connectin' doors."

IZZY KRANTZ said furiously, "Not that side, you dopes. You wanta get broke? Not that side, I tell ya."

The heavy voice said hastily. "Okay, Izzy, okay. Not that side. If it's occupied, they wouldn't be there anyway."

Another voice said, "They was here in two-o-two. They had blankets up an' a light on."

Izzy said, "They got out the back way, Mose. They must of got rammy and scrammed."

Captain Mose Belfry of Homicide said viciously, "I oughta beat you t' death, you dumb scum. I been after those two for a year and just when I got a good beef on 'em you put the skids under it. You had 'em, you dumb-lookin'—"

Izzy Krantz said in a cold voice, "Hold it, Mose."

Mose Belfry sucked in his breath. He said, "G'wan, the rest o' you. You couldn't ketch cold, you screwballs. Go chase Wade up a rainpipe an' lose him somewhere in the middle."

There was the sound of departing men. Izzy Krantz said, "I know you don't like Wade an' Boles, Mose. But don't never give me that lip again, you hear?"

Captain Belfry said throatily, "I guess I lost my head, Izzy. I know you wouldn't muff it if you could help it."

There was silence. John strained, heard a match struck as someone lit a cigarette. Then Izzy said, "You think this is a good rap, Mose?"

"Did you knock off them broads?" asked Belfry caustically. "They was your laced mutton."

"I don't knock off nobody—in hotel lobbies," grunted Izzy Krantz. "But Wade said...."

"That smoothie could lie his way outa the chair after he was strapped in," said Belfry. "I'm gonna get him in Coney Island some day an' I'm gonna beat him...."

Izzy said scornfully, "Sure. I know. You're gonna. Tell me somethin', Mose. Who was graftin' on them broads?"

"Mitzi an' Fritzi? You was graftin' on 'em," said Mose.

"Someone was beatin' my time," said Izzy darkly. "Pickle Puss was clippin' 'em for nickels, an' that house dick mighta had his hand out. But someone was hittin' 'em for heavy dough. It smelled like cop to me."

Mose Belfry said indignantly, "You got a hell of a nerve, Izzy. Us cops always treated you right. We take some from you—sure. We gotta live. But we let you operate. The cops have made you rich, you lug."

"Somebody was clippin' them broads," said Izzy. "I dunno anything about the killin'—maybe Boles went gunnin' for Pickle Puss an' got careless. But Rickey never got careless before. There's somethin' about this thing...."

The voices faded. The two men were leaving the room. After a full minute had elapsed, John said, "How do you like that, pal?"

Rickey said, "There's a couple honest guys on the Force. Maybe we oughta check on these smart coppers."

John said slowly, "Smiling Joey Watson is so dumb he can be handled. I wonder if we should go to him."

Rickey said, "Smiling Joey is the crookedest Police Chief in captivity. But he's too dumb to make much. He c'n be had."

"If Belfry was clipping Izzy's gals," said John, "it would be very nice to know. Especially if Mitzi and Fritzi had refused to pay off Saturday night."

"If Belfry rapped off those broads and Pickle Puss," said Rickey excitedly, "we got the whole Force by the tail."

"We ain't missed," said John grimly. "Let's get outa this joint before we are contaminated."

Rickey said, "Just listenin' to Mose Belfry makes me wanta gargle. I hate a crooked copper."

John grinned. "Pal," he said. "You hate all coppers!"

CHAPTER FOUR
RAID POLICE
HEADQUARTERS!

RICKEY DROVE the old jaloppy as though it were a Zephyr. The big man could handle any car, even this crate which John had bought for emergencies and which clattered alarmingly, wheezing on the curves. They pulled up to the rear of Police Headquarters and parked.

Rickey said, "I'm gonna like this."

It was ten o'clock Monday morning. They had slept Sunday night in the flivver, out on the road beyond town limits, taking turns at standing guard. John felt very unhappy about his clothes, which were wrinkled. The habit of being well groomed was so deeply ingrained in him that unpressed garments affected his very fibre.

He said grimly, "I won't hate it, either. Let's go."

They used the side entrance. They walked swiftly by a uniformed man at a desk. The cop didn't even look up from the racing form which absorbed him. They slid into an ante room and a girl gasped at sight of their drawn guns.

Rickey said, "Take it easy, lady, we're huntin' cops."

John went straight through the door lettered "Chief of Police". He held the gun at his hip and said,

"Good morning, Joey. Nice day."

Smiling Joey Watson sat open-mouthed behind his desk. He was a fat, pinkish man with a weak triple chin and pale eyes. His uniform did not fit very well and his wispy, sparse hair literally stood on end. He had a face noted only for its vacuity.

He said, "For Gawsakes, Wade, you can't kill me like this."

John said, "I'm no killer, Joey. I just wanted to tell you something. Captain Mose Belfry is collecting heavy sugar from Izzy Krantz at the Bardsley House. The two gals killed in the Ritzmore last night were Izzy's molls. Could it be possible, Joey, that Mitzi and Fritzi were the real murder victims, that Pickle Puss and the house dick stopped wild lead?"

Chief Watson blinked. He said, "There's warrants charging you and Boles with those murders."

Wade said grimly, "So I've been told. I pity the man who tries to execute those warrants."

"You can't come in here and bully me," said Joey Watson weakly.

"I can wire the F.B.I.," said John Wade. "I can have them check the bullets which killed those people Saturday. If they came out of a service gun...."

Joey Watson blurted, "No F.B.I. is gonna mess in my business. You and that murderin' Boles killed Officer Cram and three other innocent people. You'll pay for it, too."

"Of course you would have done away with the bullets," said John thoughtfully. "I thought of that. Maybe I'll just have to knock you off. You and Belfry and cops like Joe Byrne and Boffo Cassidy are ruining the city."

Joey Watson said shrewdly, "You should worry about the city! You're a con guy yourself."

"Con men are not murderers," said John serenely. "The uckersays'll shun this burg if it gets a bad name. Besides,

I don't like that murder rap you've hung on us. Where's Belfry, Chief?"

Joey Watson whined, "You lay off of Belfry. I don't know where he is. You better get out of this state, Wade. You better get out and never come back. You'll fry if you stay here. I promise you."

John said contemptuously, "You're a fat toad, Joey. You're a weak, fat slug."

Watson said querulously, "I'll show you who's lousy. I'll have you in Coney Island yet. I'll have you beat to death. You'll never go to trial when we get you...."

John said, "Nuts. And carry six."

HE WHEELED and went into the outer office. A detective had come in and was flat against the wall, staring at the big guns in Rickey's hands. John said:

"You shouldn't frighten Boffo like that."

Boffo Cassidy was a member of the strong arm squad. He was a red-faced man. He had a plate in his mouth. Rickey had once kicked out his teeth. He was now obviously afraid Rickey would blow out his brains.

Rickey said gently, "I was just warnin' Boffo about tryin' to put the cuffs on us,"

"He'll have a heart attack," said John. "Let's get outa here before we scare 'em all to death."

They went out through the side door. No one offered to stop them. But when they got in the old car, John saw heads at the windows of Headquarters, peering after them.

He said, "We'll have to ditch this heap. Stop at Pete's Place."

Red Madden's cab was parked around the corner of the gin mill run by Pete. The cabby grinned at them and said,

"I know a guy'll hide your crate. Where you wanta go?"

John pondered, sitting in the taxi. He really had nothing upon which to go. There was a tie-up between the murdered quartette and Mose Belfry, Captain of Homicide. But there was no possible way of proving it.

Belfry's conversation with Krantz had been illuminating, but there hadn't been quite enough light in it. John said, "I've got one more chance. We can see Foley Mastervelt."

"That guy's a big shot," protested Rickey. "He's a damn banker."

"He was at the Ritzmore and saw the shooting," said John. "He's an honest man."

Red Madden said, "How you gonna see a guy like that?"

"The cops'll spot us sure if we hang around town," added Rickey.

John said, "Let's go. First National Bank."

IT WAS amazingly easy. They went through a swinging gate and there was the private office of the president. They went inside without ceremony.

John said, "Just a question, sir. About that shooting."

The grey-haired banker frowned. He said, "Wade, I didn't know who you were when you punched those men. I don't approve—"

"Of con guys," grinned John. "You're a big, safe one yourself, mister. All bankers are. But answer me this before you get indignant: who was shot first in the Ritzmore lobby, the cops or the gals?"

Mastervelt blinked. He said, "Why, let me see. I was in the Continental Room… Why… the policeman was shot first. Then the house detective; and then the girls."

"You sure?" asked John.

"The girls were in flight," said Mastervelt, wrinkling his brows. "The men fell where they stood. I remember that particularly, because I thought the girls might have recognized the killers and—"

"Killers? More than one?"

"Now why did I say that?" said Mastervelt, frowning in thought. "The shots came so close together—sounded like a machine gun. I instinctively thought of more than one gunman—but two guns in one man's hands could have done it."

John said, "Check. Now, one more question: From which direction did the shots come?"

Mastervelt said, "The police surely know that!"

"I am not on very intimate terms with the cops right now," said John. "The papers didn't carry it. Where was the killer when the shots were fired?"

Mastervelt said, "Wade, I'm beginning to think you did not kill those people."

John said, "Thanks. Who did?"

The banker considered. He said, "The shots apparently came from the rear of the lobby. The girl who almost got away was running to the front exit. She would not run towards the guns. They could not have been fired from the side, because the Continental Room is on one side and the check room the other."

"The check room," said John softly. "Now what do you know about that?"

"The check room girl ducked at the first shot and saw nothing."

John said, "You've been a great help, sir. If you'll give us a day or so—not turn us in...."

Mastervelt said shrewdly, "The Reform Group has not fared well at the hands of policemen lately. As you know, I am a member of that party."

John said respectfully, "You're a smart man, Mr. Master-velt. Stick with it awhile."

IN THE back room of Pete's Place it was quiet. John dialed a number and waited. The phone buzzed and buzzed, ringing the party. John frowned, hung up and dialed again. There still was no answer.

Rickey said, "Maybe she went out. You ain't called her today and it's almost noon. She gets nervish."

John's face aged while he sat there, staring. He dialed another number. After a moment someone said, "Yes?"

He said, "Give me F.C., quick."

The voice said, "He is not here. He is out of town."

John said, "Has Miss Morrow been there?"

The voice whispered cautiously, "Wade?"

"Yes, yes," said John impatiently.

"The Governor is out now, looking for Miss Morrow," hissed the voice rapidly. "The lab was entered and vandalized. Miss Morrow has disappeared. The Governor went personally to search for her. He said you would know what to do."

John said in a hard voice, "I do."

He pronged the phone and stared at Rickey. The big man said almost tenderly, "They got her, huh, pal?"

"Yes," said John. "They got her."

Rickey lumbered to his large feet. He said. "I guess I better get old Thomas together."

"The machine gun is in the car. I mailed the ticket to—Say!" John leaped up and started for the door. "The Governor has my car. I know that guy. He's been itchin' to get into this battle with the cops. He's goin' it blind, looking for Jean. But I'll lay four to one I know where he is. Red! Red!"

They were in the street alongside Pete's Place. Red Madden snapped, "Ixnay. Opscay."

There were two of them, burly men in uniform. Rickey and John ran right into their arms. The cops backed off, reaching for holstered guns.

The flaps were buckled down on the guns. Rickey laughed jeeringly as the cops fumbled. John hit the nearest with a right and a left and a right. Rickey slapped the other with a hand like iron.

The cops fell over each other into the gutter. John said, "Let's go, Red."

The cabby whistled. He mumbled, "I heard about it. But I never believed it. You guys is poison."

"Cops," said Rickey severely, "are strickly dumb."

"And muscle bound," agreed John. "Take us down to Headquarters, Red. We need to tangle with a flock of cops."

Red shook his head. He said, "Headquarters! They'll murder you. They'll knock you off an' pin a rap on your corpses."

"If they're able," said John lightly. "Take us down, Red. There's another C note coming your way."

"Blood money," said Red wearily. "Nothin' but blood money."

The cab lurched and leaped going towards Headquarters. John relaxed into a corner and tried not to think about Jean Morrow in the hands of Mose Belfry. Once before the police had third degreed Jean Morrow.

IT WAS too soon, he knew. The thing had come to a head before he could track down the connecting link. If he had one hour more....

The Governor was on the prowl. If the Governor got down there and stalled, maybe Joey Watson and his gang would lay off. They two-wheeled around the corner leading to Headquarters. There was a big car parked at the curb.

John snapped forward and said, "Okay, Red. Go on by fast. Turn around and hit for the Bardsley."

Rickey said, "The Gov's in there givin' 'em hell, all right. That's our car. The Gov's a real guy, pal."

John said. "They're too desperate to give in to him. He has no real jurisdiction over them in this state. The Mayor and his rotten mob hold the strings."

"But we gotta take a chance," nodded Rickey sagely. "We gotta tie it in. If they hurt her again, pal, I ain't sayin' it with fists. I'm sayin' it with lead. I'll kill cops if I burn for it."

John said grimly, "We'll go to that chair together if they hurt her this time."

CHAPTER FIVE
TOMMY-GUN
ARGUMENTS

THE GOVERNOR of Midstate was a tall man. He had wide shoulders and a fighting jaw and a handsome face which held no compromise. He stood in Smiling Joey Watson's office at Police Headquarters and said, "You've got a girl, Jean Morrow. I want her."

Watson said in oily accents, "Now, Governor, you're excited. I already told you we haven't got the girl. We want her for consortin' with known criminals. But we ain't got her yet."

Foley Mastervelt said uncertainly, "Maybe they haven't got her, Fort."

"I asked you here to stand by—not give advice," snapped Fortney Castle. His jaw line was becoming more pronounced by the second. He said, *"I want that girl!"*

Captain Mose Belfry growled under his breath from his place against the wall behind the Chief's desk. Boffo Cassidy's false teeth clicked several times. Detective Joe Byrne, a lowering, narrow-browed two hundred pounder, sneered openly.

Joey Watson's voice was like oil. He said, "Really, Governor, this is very unusual. I question your right to come into the office of a city official and—"

"You question me?" roared Fortney Castle. The cords of his sturdy neck stood out like rope. "You pettifogging, doublecrossing, crooked, lying, hypocritical thief! You dare to question ME?"

Smiling Joey said, "There's a stenographer taking down every word you say, Governor. You'll have to prove your statements. The newspapers will have them immediately."

Governor Castle took a deep breath. Caution had completely deserted him. He said, "Prove them? I'll have you thrown in your own jail, Chief Watson. I'll keep you there so long you'll never see daylight again. You grafting, belly-crawling, sycophant of crooks and racketeers!"

The door behind the Governor crashed open. John Wade said coolly, "That's telling him, Governor."

Smiling Joey Watson cried, "Grab that man! He's wanted for murder!"

"Yeah," said Rickey Boles. "Why don't somebody grab him?"

Rickey was cradling a shiny, well-oiled sub-machine gun in his hands. There had been a day when rival gangsters had fought over that gun, each trying to buy it for their defense. It was Rickey's fondest possession, and he could write his initials with it across a thug's chest.

John gave a quick jerk and Izzy Krantz tumbled into the room. Izzy had a black eye and his nose was bleeding. John reached again and a defiant woman with blondined hair appeared beside Izzy.

John said, "This is Bertha. She's the hat check girl at the Ritzmore. She lives in Krantz's hotel."

Joey Watson said, "You can't get away with this, Wade. You'll never leave this building alive."

"If you make any signal," said John, "Rickey will be forced to turn loose his chopper."

The Chief's pink face turned slightly green, making a horrible color combination. John said, "You look worried, Joey. Where's Miss Morrow?"

Joey Watson said, "I don't know nothin'."

John said, "Rickey. See about this."

THERE WERE noises outside in the hall. Governor Castle said, "The police in the building are getting suspicious about something, Wade."

"You ought to see Rickey and that tommy gun in action," said John confidingly. "It's a joy, Governor. If it starts, you stand behind Rickey. We'll kill all the cops in this room first, of course."

Mose Belfry said quickly, "Stick it out, Joey. The boys are gettin' ready to come in and see what makes."

Rickey reached back and swung his big arm. His knuckles spatted against Belfry's face. The big detective hit the wall and bounced off, his knees sagging.

Rickey said gloomily, "How many times I've wanted to bump you off, Mose. I should of done it years ago."

John was saying to the Governor, "These are the biggest thieves in town. These are your real crooks, the patrons of the underworld. They have corrupted honest policemen, deterred other well-meaning members of the force from performing their duty."

The Governor's fighting face was a mask of fury. He leaned over the Chief's desk. He said tautly, "Have Jean Morrow sent up here immediately. If you fail, I will deputize Boles on the spot and order him to kill you. I can cover him, Watson, and you know it."

Belfry opened his mouth to speak. Rickey, alert, backhanded him again. Belfry went down, sinking slowly to the floor.

Watson's color all faded, leaving him a sunken, pasty white. He mumbled, "Okay, Governor."

He picked up the phone. Rickey's gun was at his belly. He said, "Send up Miss Morrow."

They waited. Izzy Krantz huddled close against the peroxide blonde named Bertha. The girl was defiant but frightened, her back to the wall. Rickey caressed the machine gun.

Those moments were like years to John Wade. He kept repeating to himself, over and over, "If they've harmed her, if they've touched a hair of her head, if they've scared her, even… I'll turn Rickey on them. I'll kill them all."

The door opened slowly. A uniformed man paused in blinking astonishment. John said, "Come right in—without noise."

The uniformed man joined Boffo against the windows. Jean Morrow came into the room and walked directly to John Wade. She said, "They haven't hurt me, John. Don't kill anyone because of me. They just questioned me—about you and Rickey—and the Governor."

Fortney Castle said softly, "Ahhh!"

Foley Mastervelt said, "So that's it!"

John said, "Of course. It was a frame. And a stupid frame that only a cop would try. They found out that we were working with the Governor. Too many wrenches have been thrown into the machinery of corruption in this town— and each time Rickey and Jean and I have been close. So they framed us."

Mastervelt said, "The fight with Pickle Puss Cram gave them their impetus. They worked it out crudely from there."

"The whole thing lay in the tie-up with the two women, Fritzi and Mitzi," nodded John. "Sing a little, Izzy."

Izzy Krantz said dully, "Somebody was clippin' them broads. They was shortin' me. I told Belfry about it."

John said, "Belfry was taking graft from you, wasn't he, Izzy?"

"He wasn't makin' social calls every Friday," said Krantz with sudden spitefulness.

John said, "But someone else was taking money from your women?"

"Yeah, and they was scared to peep," said Izzy. "I begged them to wise me up to who it was, but they stalled me they wasn't gettin' the dough. They was scared of whoever was clippin' 'em, all right."

"But you put the pressure on them, didn't you, Izzy?" asked John softly. "You told them you wanted your full cut Saturday—or else."

Izzy squirmed. Rickey glanced at him coldly. Izzy seemed unable to take his myopic gaze from Rickey's big fists. He gulped and said desperately, "A guy's gotta make a livin', ain't he? Sure, I told 'em. I promised 'em the river if they didn't come through."

"And you had Bertha, here," said John, whirling suddenly and stabbing an accusing finger at the hat check girl, "you had Bertha to check on them."

Izzy said, "Why not? She was in the pot, wasn't she?"

"She was the finger for you at the Ritzmore," agreed John. He turned to Governor Castle. He said, "The way those killings were pulled had me puzzled. You see, the murderer had to have a nice, quick getaway. You know the back of the Ritzmore?"

The Governor thought a moment. He said, "It connects with a garage owned by the hotel, doesn't it."

"Right," said John. "A blank wall."

"Then the only exit was by the side door," said the Governor. "The check room is on the alley side."

"Yes," said John. "The cops covered it up. But those shots were fired from the check room."

Every eye in the room swiveled to the blondined Bertha. She moaned a little, swaying on her feet. She was ghastly pale. John said softly, "So Bertha knows who killed those four people. Bertha alone could cover the getaway, through the side door. Do you want to talk, Bertha?"

The girl opened her mouth but no sound came out. She tried again and gasped, "I—he—we—I was against it. I tried to stop it. I—"

She choked for breath. The tension in the room was terrific.

Behind the desk Joey Watson was a mass of quivering jelly. Mose Belfry still lay on the floor where Rickey had knocked him.

John said, "Tell us about it, Bertha."

The girl pulled herself together. She said, "It was after you had knocked Pickle Puss around. I was takin' a smoke—"

CHAPTER SIX
APPOINTMENT TO
HONOR

THE SHOT seemed to come from nowhere. It spat into Bertha's body. She gave a deep, low moan and sagged against Izzy Krantz, bringing him to the floor with her.

John yelled, "I got him, Rickey. Watch the Chief!"

John had his gun around like lightning. He looked into the muzzle of the murderer's revolver and saw death staring from the round O of the barrel. He squeezed hard on the trigger, squeezed again and again. Lead whistled by his ear, but he fired the third time without flinching.

Mose Belfry rolled over against the wall. The service revolver dropped from his hand. He coughed once, almost apologetically. Then he rattled a bit and died.

Rickey groaned, "I shoulda had him. It's all my fault, John. I shoulda given it to him before."

John said tautly, "Hold that gun ready."

There was hammering on the door, excited voices. John went swiftly to the side of Police Chief Watson, his gun steady in his hand. He said, "Cover the door with that type-writer, Rickey. All right, Governor. Let them in."

There were fifty of them milling about. They paused at the sight of Governor Castle and the sturdy Foley Master-velt. Castle said, "Quiet, men, and listen." They grouped, the foremost just within the threshold. John Wade said clearly, "Joey Watson—what is the last name of that hat check girl?"

The Chief stammered, "How—how should I know?"

"She is Bertha Doyle, isn't she?" demanded John.

"I—I tell ya, I don't know!"

"She is your niece, isn't she?"

Smiling Joey Watson wailed, "Arrest these men! This is murder. The Governor is guilty, too. The stenographer has this all down, in the next room. I got this office wired, I tell you. I'm bein' framed!"

"You're so stupid," said John contemptuously. "You weren't getting enough graft so you thought you'd cut in on the vice racket, too, where defenseless women are the prey of any cop in a uniform. Pickle Puss, that dolt, was getting his. So you thought you'd get yours. You put a double cross on your own stoolie—Izzy Krantz. You moved in on his molls.

"Belfry killed those people. I tell you, it was Belfry," Watson cried.

"And now," said John disgustedly, "you'd even try to pin it on your dead sidekick! You know damn well Mose had too much sense to crack down on Pickle Puss. You went down to the Ritzmore and bullied Bertha into letting you in the side way. Pickle Puss had been nickling the girls and you figured that dough should be yours. Then you had the brilliant idea that because of the fracas Rickey and I had with Cram you could pin the beef on us. So you killed Pickle Puss. The house dick was in the way, so you got him, too. You caught the two women going away and knocked them off because they had turned you down after Izzy warned them."

Watson said, "Lies, all lies."

"You stumbled accidentally upon the fact that we were working for the Governor. So you wanted to tie it all in. You thought you could beat Miss Morrow into confessing to anything you wanted. You got the D.A. tied up, you got Judge Minling, you got the City Hall. You thought you were God Almighty. You're a dead coon now, Joey."

A doctor was bending over the girl on the floor. John said, "It looked to me like Belfry wasn't shootin' straight. He missed me completely."

The doctor said, "This girl will live to testify. She is not badly injured."

THE FAT under Chief Watson's skin seemed to have melted, so that his cheeks sagged over his collar and his hooked nose was a gaunt protuberance.

Governor Castle nodded to the men in the doorway. He said, "Take him away, boys. Put him in a safe place. He's object lesson number one."

They had to carry him out. They took Detective Byrne along with him, on general suspicion. They started to take Boffo Cassidy.

John said, "I can't understand why Belfry missed. He and Joey Watson were the best pistol shots in the Department. That was part of it. I wasn't sure—I couldn't be sure. But the shots came so close together—were so accurately placed—that I couldn't believe any of the murders were accidental. Even the house dick probably had a tie-up with Pickle Puss and was given his dose of lead to keep him quiet."

Boffo Cassidy's teeth chattered. He said, "Maybe it was because I sorta jarred his elbow."

"You what?" demanded John amazedly.

"With my toe," explained Boffo apologetically. "I was scared to make a quick move on account of you guys convinced me when I lost my teeth that you might any minute fill me with lead. So I just stirred his elbow with my toe, sorta, and he missed. I even almost made him miss the broad, but he was too quick for me."

Boffo tongued his plate and added, "I could tell you how Moe and Joey worked it. I could tell you lots of stuff."

The beefy detective goggled hopefully. John said, "Why, Boffo! Little comrade!"

The Governor said succinctly, "You are relieved of arrest, Cassidy. You will remain attached to the Chief's office. I am taking over this department, legally or otherwise. It will fight City Hall and whoever else tries to combat law and order in Midburg. I am appointing a new Chief immediately."

John was working his way nearer to Jean Morrow. He wanted to get out of there. He was exhausted and his clothing was unpressed. He needed a shave and he had worn the same necktie for three days. He felt disheveled, which to John Wade was worse than nakedness.

The Governor said crisply, "We are in the open, now, battling the forces of corruption. One man has stuck with me through this battle from the beginning. I am making him my new Chief of Police, and I am determined that the Mayor will back me up. I will have my new Chief sworn in this day. I want you all to know who he will be."

Everyone listened politely.

Governor Castle said, "He will be John Wade!"

The chorus of gasps was audible all over Headquarters. John Wade reeled, his head spinning. Jean Morrow held onto him tightly, saying, "John! John! Isn't it wonderful?"

Rickey Boles said, "John! A cop!"

Governor Castle said, "No other man knows so well the odds against us. No other man can so successfully cope with those odds."

Everyone began talking at once. John Wade, ex-con man, consort of underworld characters, recognized, though never convicted as a slick crook, stood still, saying nothing, holding onto the blonde girl who was Jean Morrow.

CORPSES ON THE FORCE

WHEN GOVERNOR FORTNEY
CASTLE APPOINTED JOHN
WADE, EX-CON-GUY, CHIEF
OF POLICE, BIG MEN'S TOES
WERE STEPPED ON, AND
MURDER BLEW THE LID!
BEFORE THE GUNFIRE DIED
AWAY, JOHN WADE KNEW
THERE WERE A FEW HONEST
COPPERS ON THE FORCE...
COUNTLESS THIEVING RATS—
AND PLENTY CORPSES!

CHAPTER ONE
SIGN OF REBELLION

IT WAS a resplendent uniform. It was deep blue and it had rows of gold buttons and a shining, gold badge inlaid with baked enamel. John Wade surveyed it with deep disgust.

John Wade was wearing a double-breasted grey suit with flaring lapels. His collar was irreproachable, his cravat an eight-dollar foulard. His silk handkerchief peeped discreetly from his breast pocket, matching the necktie with careless decorum.

Rickey Boles was trying on the coat of the second uniform, a coat only slightly less ornate then the first. Rickey's two hundred-odd pounds filled out the wrinkles in the blue cloth with impressive dignity. The big man's corrugated face shone with mingled emotions.

John Wade said bitterly, "Every hip gee, every mobster and numbers runner, every con guy and stool pigeon, yes—and every crooked cop in Midburg is giving us the Bronx cheer."

Rickey said perplexedly, "I dunno. It would always of seemed to me that I would get a pine box before a cop's overcoat. But ain't it pretty!"

Jean Morrow had blue eyes and fluffy blonde hair. She sat very quietly on a chair next to the vigorous, smiling

man whose secretary she had so recently become. She was intent only upon John Wade and John's portentous frown.

Governor Fortney Castle said, "There is a time for secrecy and a time for open warfare."

His strong face was serene, his demeanor confident. He was up for reelection as Governor of Midstate within six months. Yet he had appointed John Wade Chief of Police of Midburg, the capital. And John Wade had a past.

John said, "The underworld hates a squealer. I have no qualms about going straight. When I was a con guy they

John knew he was in for it now.
He heard the screams of the
leader: "Beat him! Beat hell out
of him!... Let the girl see it!"

clipped me from all angles. I paid the police, I sugared the
mobs. But now they will all consider me a super-stoolie."

"Is the opinion of the underworld important to you?"
queried the Governor.

John looked at Jean Morrow. He said, "The opinion of
the people in this room is all that means anything to me.
It's my efficiency which is the question. Undercover, working for you, Rickey and I were able to do some good. As
a recognized officer of the law, my hand will be tipped off
to the crooks by my own forces—the estimable police of
Midburg. How can I help you from such a spot?"

"John, I have publicly announced that you are the new Chief of Police of Midburg," said the Chief Executive. "You have the district attorney behind you, I am strongly and publicly behind you. It is your job to clean up the dirty politico-crime hook-up. How you do it is something that I am willing to leave entirely to you."

John Wade still held the gaze of the blonde girl. Her eyes did not waver; the blue seemed to deepen until he was swimming in their azure gleam. He said slowly, "All right, Governor."

Fortney Castle said with satisfaction, "This review of the Midburg Police is only a formality incident upon your taking office. I hope the uniform fits, John, a better man couldn't wear it."

John said, "I'm not wearing the uniform, Governor."

Castle frowned. "But you must!"

"You said you didn't care how I did it," said John. "I'm taking over. But I'm not wearing the uniform. I'm not appearing as the commander of a group of policemen. I'll do the job the best I can—and then some. But I'll do it in civvies."

The Governor said, "But why?"

"I'm no cop," said John Wade. "I'm a con guy turned straight, enlisted in the war on crime in Midstate. But I'm no bluecoat. I'll never be one and you can't make me one. Review your police? I'll be in the office at Headquarters, studying the records to find how many of your cops should be fired from the force!"

RICKY BOLES took the deputy chief uniform coat from his large person and deposited it gently over a chair. He said, "Gov, if I could of said that, I would of done it. We ain't cops in our hearts, Gov. We ain't got larceny in our hearts any more. But oil is thicker'n water, if you know what I mean."

John tore himself away from the blue eyes. Governor Castle said resignedly, "I haven't always agreed with you boys. I don't agree with you now. But I have found that you get results. I'll have Joe Gann take charge of the review. Joe is honest."

John nodded, "I guess Joe is honest. I'm counting on it, at any rate. We'll be going now, Governor. I hope the parade is a success."

He winked at Jean Morrow, his good nature restored. He motioned to Rickey Boles and led the way down to the big coupé parked at the curb outside the Governor's mansion.

Rickey hesitated. He said wistfully, "Ain't we even gonna get official plates on the heap?"

John said, "No official plates."

Rickey sighed. "I thought maybe plates and a sireen. It would of been fun to snazz down Main Street an' give the boys the thumb."

John said, "And have one of Stacker's mob shoot your ears off?"

Rickey said, "Yeah. I suppose so."

He climbed behind the wheel and delicately coaxed the big motor to life. Rickey was a born driver. John never touched the wheel when Rickey was available. It relaxed him to sit in the big car and roll along. People couldn't get at him. He could think things out.

He opened the door on the passenger side. He bent his head and started to step into the car. He thought of something he had meant to tell Jean Morrow—something that had slipped his mind. He stood there, holding the door open, hesitating.

Something trickled down on the leather upholstery of the seat where he would have been ensconced. He stared at it. A nauseous odor came to his nostrils. The glove leather of the seat began to burn; it sizzled and turned black under his startled gaze.

He recovered himself and snapped, "Rickey! Out of the car on the other side. Quick!"

Rickey fell out and came lumbering around. In his hand was a large revolver. He said, "Who did what?"

John pointed to the hole in the fine leather. He said, "Ingenious. Somebody planted acid over my side. I was supposed to get hell burned out of me when I opened the door and stepped into the car."

Rickey's horrified eyes fell upon the ruined seat. He yelled, "My car! My red leather job! I'll murder the guy did this! I'll boil 'im in oil. I'll fry his ears and eat 'em for breakfast!"

THEIR HEELS echoed hollowly in the corridors of Police Headquarters. The Force was on parade before the Governor of Midstate. A few scattered guardians of the law held the fort. John saluted them mechanically, ignoring their curious, sometimes mocking glances.

The cards were stacked, of course. From the lowliest rookie to the precinct captains, Midstate's police were against John Wade. Any civilian chief would have been unwelcome to them. John Wade, ex-con man, was a bitter joke.

In the spacious Chief's office a man waited. He was an olive-skinned man with hard eyes. His name was Tony Maretta and he was a member of the prosecutor's staff of detectives. He said, "John, you bit off something."

John said, "Hiya, Tony? You got that list?"

Maretta handed over a foolscap sheet. He said, "This is all our office has been able to get. If you fire all the coppers mentioned in this report you won't have even a skeleton Force."

John said, "They must go. What about Deputy Chief Gann, Tony? He always had the reputation of being square."

"Joe's aces with me," said Tony instantly. "If you can line him up he'll be your big stick."

"If I can line him up," mused John. "That's the bloody point. Even the square cops hate me. If I fire all these crooks without reason I'll be no better off because the papers will go after me. This report is not evidence."

Tony Maretta said, "It's a big bite, pal. If you can chew it, you're a hell of a man."

John said, "I might need you, Tony."

The dark man got up and perched a green felt hat on the side of his head. He showed a row of white teeth and said, "Us Marettas never forget a favor. I'm on your side, John, win or lose."

When the prosecutor's dick had gone, John said, "Rickey, this is a strange business. When we were undercover we used to clip a cop whenever he got in our way. Now we got to educate them."

Rickey said, "You can't learn no cop anything."

John said, "We can try." He pressed a buzzer experimentally. A uniformed policeman appeared in the doorway. He was a young man with an intelligent face. John said, "Are you my clerk?"

"Yes, sir. Officer Fogg," said the young man solemnly.

John said, "You can relax. I'm not going to steal your buttons."

Officer Fogg tried to look haughty but it was not much of a job. John said, "You're Bo Fogg. You were a great half-back on the high school team."

Rickey said, "No! Not Bo Fogg! He wouldn't be no cop!"

John said, "You're a cop, Rickey. Circumstances make strange police officers. Fogg, see that my car is printed from stem to stern. Somebody planted an acid bath in it."

Bo Fogg looked startled. John said, "They'll be trying every little thing they can think up. That's just a starter. Put the lab on it and see if anything comes out."

Fogg saluted and departed with alacrity. Rickey said, "That kid was sure pop for a college athlete's ride. He was All State. He was a great youngster."

"His mother is sick," said John. "Not all cops are lousy, pal. There's a few good ones on this Force."

"I never met none of them," grunted Rickey.

CHAPTER TWO
VIGILANTES OF DEATH

THE PHONE on John's desk rang. He picked it up and a voice said, "Cooky, from the garage. You want that hole in your car mended?"

John said sharply, "I gave orders my car was not to be touched without further word from me."

"Sorry, sir," said the voice indifferently. "The order was phoned in and we washed your car. There's a burned hole—"

John said, "You're telling me!"

He hung the receiver up carefully. His face was hard as stone. There was a tap at the door and Officer Fogg stood on the threshold. John said, "Well? What do you think about it?"

The young man said sturdily, "Something slipped."

"You believe they slipped?" asked John.

Bo Fogg struggled with his dignity. He said, "Well, sir. If they didn't—"

"It was washed on purpose. Do you know Steve Stacker?"

Bo Fogg said, "Everybody knows Steve Stacker."

"Got you your job, didn't he?" asked John.

"I took an exam," said Fogg.

"But Stacker fronted for you. Stacker gives away tons of coal and loaves of bread. He pays doctor bills. He also fixes tickets and things. He is the political boss of Midburg," said John. "Any cop would do Steve Stacker a favor. Steve owns the police force."

Bo Fogg said nothing. His cheeks were pink and his eyes were uncertain. John said, "Like washing my car."

Fogg still said nothing. John went on, "Steve Stacker does not own me. He will fix no more tickets—not even for his drunken, no-good son Charlie. Do you still want to hold down that job as my clerk?"

Bo Fogg said, "Will you give me twenty-four hours to think it over, sir?"

"Yes," said John. "I'd like to have you on my side, Bo. You and every other decent cop who has been knuckling under to Steve Stacker. You took an exam. You don't owe him anything. Think it over hard, son."

The door closed very quietly behind the young officer. Rickey said, "I dunno. Maybe you can get a few of them. But washin' the prints off that car was no slip. And Stacker owns most of them!"

There was a separate sheet in the report which Maretta had left. It said, "Most police corruption in Midburg is attributable to the fact that Steve Stacker's People's Club is so well organized politically that the entire city government is in Stacker's control.

"Steve Stacker, age 49, son of immigrant father and native mother, was a ward heeler for Jim Brown in 1909. He grew slowly but surely into power in Midburg through the People's Party, finally succeeding Brown as the power behind the throne. When Abe Schechtel's INDEPEN-DENT LEAGUE broke up, the People's Party took over the First and Third and Fourth Wards and gained complete mastery of the city elections.

"Stacker has headquarters in the Fourth Ward in the building which houses the notorious People's Club."

John made a little fire in a large ash tray. He fed the dossier of Steve Stacker into it, bit by bit. Deliberately, he added to the flames the list of crooked cops now on the Midburg force.

Rickey protested, "Hey! We oughta crack down on them muggs."

John said, "You think I'll forget one of those names!"

Rickey complained, "I never did see the list."

"I want the thing done right," said John grimly. "I don't want you hauling off and killing a few of them."

The telephone jangled. John listened. An excited voice said, "This is Bo Fogg, sir. Just got a call. Someone threw a bomb at the Governor's box during the review. The riot call is in."

John slapped up the phone and came around the end of the desk. His eyes were blazing, his jaw set. He said, "They've bombed the Governor, pal. Jean was in that box!"

Rickey said, "Meet me in front. I'll have the crate out there in nothing flat."

Bo Fogg looked frightened. He was only a kid, John knew. The new chief paused long enough to say, "Just sit tight and answer no questions. Stall the newspapermen. And Bo—keep your eyes open for further attacks. Right?"

"Right, sir," said Fogg. "This is terrible, sir. I—"

"Sure, I know," said John, hurrying away. "When you get into it, it is not nice. You'll be a real copper yet, son."

RICKY TOOK the big coupé through the police line with a wailing horn and a scowl. Bluecoated men, shined for parade, leaped out of the way as the scarlet car fled through their ranks. The fire engine was a problem, but Rickey skirted it on two wheels.

The Governor's box, a hastily constructed makeshift on the courthouse steps, was in ruins. A stout, giant of a man issued crisp orders to laboring, besmirched volunteers and firemen. John leaped from the coupé while it was still in motion and cried, "The Governor? How bad is he, Gann?"

Deputy Chief Joe Gann turned his round face and said, "They took him to the hospital. But he'll live, all right."

"Was his secretary with him? Was she injured?" demanded John.

A small voice said, "I wasn't in the box. I had to go into the courthouse for something."

He wheeled. Jean Morrow was tear-stained, disheveled. Gann said heavily, "This gal got to the Governor first. She came runnin' outa the courthouse an' dug him up outa the wreck. This gal should get a medal."

John said tightly, "Good work, baby. Go downtown to my office and wait there. Please, baby."

She whispered, "All right, John. I have something for you, I think."

She drifted through the gathering men and was gone. John said, "You get the guy, Gann?"

"It was a time bomb," said Gann. "It was planted. Hell will freeze over before we know who did it."

"That's nice police psychology," snapped John.

A deep voice said, "Ah, Chief! This is bad business." A small, well-dressed man with a sharp face was picking his way towards them. Joe Gann said, "Hiya, Steve?"

Steve Stacker said, "Very well, Chief. Who was killed, Chief?"

John Wade got between Deputy Chief Joe Gann and the little man. The cold grey eyes of Steve Stacker swept up and down John's frame, looked vastly disinterested. John said, "Gann, who is this man?"

Joe Gann gaped. He said, "Why—why that's Steve Stacker, Chief."

"I thought as much," nodded John. "Get him out of here. He's within police lines."

Stacker said, "Er—I didn't recognize you, Wade. Thought you'd be in uniform if you were around."

John said, "Stacker, get out. Get going and stay away. Don't come near any member of the Midburg police force until you hear from me. Those are general orders, going to every man in service."

Steve Stacker raised one eyebrow. He had a Satanic countenance. His nose was sharp and long and his chin was very round and determined. He had a look about him of a man accustomed to having his own way. He said mildly, "Why, Wade, I'm the copper's best friend. You can't do things like that to me."

John said, "I can try. If you're their friend—stay away from them. You'll only get them in trouble while I'm Chief of Police."

Stacker said, "Wade, you're making a big mistake."

"I'm new in office," mocked John. "Are you going to scram now or must I have you escorted away?"

Stacker stood for a long moment. Little devils danced in the back of his deep eyes. His hands trembled with passion. But his voice was smooth as silk. He said, "Always glad to co-operate, Wade. I'll—see you again."

He nodded to Joe Gann. He seemed not one whit disturbed. He walked jauntily away, picking his way over the fire hose and debris with great care.

DEPUTY CHIEF Gann said heavily, "I don't get it, Wade."

"It ain't necessary for you to get it, Joe," said Rickey Boles. "When you talk to John, call him 'Chief'—or you won't get an answer."

Joe Gann's red face turned brick color. He saluted and said, "Yes, Chief. Any orders, sir?"

John said, "How many were killed?"

"Three," said Joe Gann. "One was a woman. The other two were Mason Daniels and Manfred Freize."

"The woman?"

"Mrs. Johnson Joley," said Gann.

John was silent. All three of the dead were firm supporters of Governor Castle's Liberty Group, the allied non-partisan organization which was to lead Midstate out of the morass of chicanery and political corruption.

He said, "It wasn't a big bomb. It had to be shrewdly placed. Who gave out the seating arrangements for the Governor's party, Gann?"

The Deputy Chief said stolidly, "I did, sir."

John said, "Check from that angle. I'm putting you in charge of the Homicide Squad. Pick your own men. I have only one stipulation: No one shall be connected in any way with Steve Stacker."

Gann protested, "That's almost impossible, Chief."

John said, "Did you say 'almost'?"

Gann saluted again. He said, "Okay. I'll try it."

His round face was a picture of puzzled wonder. John walked away, towards the wreck of the stand. He poked around with a piece of charred stick. He asked a few questions of the fire chief.

He rejoined Rickey at the coupé. Rickey said, "Hey. Gann is in a hell of a pickle. He just left. Asked me to work on his Homicide Squad. Said he reckoned he couldn't get anybody else. I told him to go it alone."

"Was he angry?" asked John.

"Naw," said Rickey. "He seemed kinda pleased. Funny guy, ain't he?"

"He wanted Homicide for years. They wouldn't let him have it because he was on the level," grinned John. "He wants to hate our guts, but it won't be easy now."

Rickey drove back more slowly than he had come. After a few blocks he said, "I dunno. Maybe I'm wrong. Maybe you *can* learn these cops something."

JEAN MORROW was composed, but John could feel the tension underneath the calm exterior of the beautiful blonde girl. He said, "Baby! I was scared."

"I know, John," she said softly. "I must tell you, John, quickly. I—I'm afraid, even yet."

"You're in police headquarters," said John lightly. "Nothing to be scared of here."

"I don't know," she said uncertainly. "I have a premonition—there seems to be need of haste. John, I think I saw that bomb being planted!"

John said, "No!"

"We—the Governor's party—were all down in the right front corner of the stand," she said rapidly. "It was an unusual arrangement. The Governor is generally in the center. They said it was easier of access that way. I went into the courthouse for a thermos of cold water for the Governor. As I went, I glanced back."

John said, "Yes, baby?"

The girl's voice grew stronger. She said, "Charlie Stacker, Steve Stacker's son, was fumbling with something under the corner of the stand, beneath the Governor. I thought Charlie was drunk again. I went on inside. When I came out it—it happened. I saw it blow, with my own eyes. Charlie was back in the crowd. He looked—strange. Doped, maybe. Exultant; crazy."

John muttered, "He may be on the junk. But a crazy scheme like that… I don't know. It's possible. I don't like to believe it."

"Those Stackers will do anything against the Governor," said Jean. "I can believe it."

"The Stackers," nodded John. "Oh yes, the Stackers. But—"

He whirled as a door opened softly. It was not the door to the ante chamber, where Bo Fogg was on duty. It was the door to the office next in line to John's. Before he could move two men were in the room. Each held a large revolver.

They were squat, burly men. They held the guns very firmly. One was pointed at John. The other was aimed straight at the breast of Jean Morrow. The men were masked in black tight hoods, with slits for eyes and nose.

A third man slipped through, a slighter man with narrow shoulders. He appeared to be the leader. Behind him John could see several others, all disguised, clustered silently in the next room.

The slim man made his voice high and unnatural. He said, "John Wade, you are a crook. You have no right behind that desk. You have no right to hold office in this city. We are executing judgment upon you, John Wade."

John said, "Steve Stacker works fast."

Jean Morrow was pale as a white tea rose. The slight man said, "Tie up the girl."

Two of the men came from the next room with rolls of adhesive tape. They advanced upon Jean Morrow. John Wade pressed the buzzer and leaped across the desk all in one motion.

The nearest hooded man took a shot to the jaw and went down. John kept throwing punches from the shoulder. If he could keep hitting out straight, hold them off until Bo and Rickey got into it, he might make the grade, he thought. He felt his fists go home and saw men fall. He was a terrible hitter for a lean guy.

The door crashed open from the outer chamber. He redoubled his efforts. The hooded men filled the room now. But if Rickey got into it with his great maulies there would be carnage and desolation among the ranks of the invaders.

He saw Bo Fogg come plunging. But Rickey did not appear. There was astonishment on Fogg's young face, but there was no hesitancy in his actions. He hit the masked men like a fullback tearing a line apart.

John heard the blackjack swish. He tried to get to it, to stop it. As he did, he neglected to punch away a springing opponent. The mace cracked home behind the ear of Bo Fogg. The boy went down as if shot through the heart.

CHAPTER THREE
HOSPITAL FOR THREE

ANOTHER BLACKJACK pounded against John's momentarily unprotected skull. He fought to keep from losing consciousness. He knew he was in for it now, knew that he might never recover from this affair. He wanted, if he lived, to know his assailants.

He was in a coma as they lifted him, threw him across his own desk. He heard the high, strained accents of the thin leader, "Beat him! Beat hell out of him! Break his bones! Let the girl see it. It will be a warning to the fools! Beat him!"

They used a whip, John thought. They held him up when he could no longer use his muscles. He hardly felt the sting of the lash. He was trying too hard to stay conscious. He bent every effort of his steely will to staying conscious, to his attempt to discover something by hearing.

His sight was gone. They belted him over the face with a hard object and his eyes closed tight. He kept trying to get loose, to tear at the hoods of the attackers. There was no sound from Jean.

His last conscious thought was that they might be beating Jean. He threw one man off with a herculean effort. He fastened his fingers in a throat and tore like a mad animal. He dimly heard the scream of his victim and then someone hit him on top of the head and he plunged down into the deep, black well of complete dissolution.

Rickey and Deputy Chief Joe Gann found them. Jean Morrow was unhurt, but in her blue eyes was stark, unmitigated terror and pity. She could scarcely speak, telling them about it while they waited for the ambulance.

John Wade still breathed. His heart beat was almost imperceptible. His ribs were stove in. His face was a misshapen gargoyle, the nose spread into a battered wreck, eyes closed tight under rapidly swelling bruises.

Rickey Boles aged ten years in those moments. He kept saying, "But John sent me to work with Gann. He told me on the phone, right outside here in the ante room. Fogg heard him. Fogg heard me answer him. He sent me away."

Bo Fogg lay in a heap, breathing stertorously with the symptoms of a fractured skull. Jean said apathetically, "They faked you. I was with John all the time. He did not call you, Rickey. Oh, Rickey, his poor face! His poor body! They've killed him!"

Rickey said bewilderedly, "It was his voice. Don't I know John's voice? Ain't he my pal?"

Jean said, "The sound of it! The crunching of his poor bones. He's all broken, Rickey—all broken."

Rickey's heavy face lost its benumbed expression. He said, "They got him all right. I wasn't here and they got him. But I'll get somebody for this. I'll go down and clean out every joint in this burgh. I'll get my gun oiled up and I'll clean out every dive in town. I'll start a small war in this burgh...."

Jean said, "No. John's alive. Wait until John can talk. He must be able to talk again."

Deputy Chief Joe Gann's red face was twisted. He mumbled, "That's my office they come through. They got at him through my office."

"We'll comb both rooms for prints," said Jean. "Get the photographers up here, Chief. This must be done right. We've got to use John's brains. Rickey! Call the lab. Get started!"

She was coming alive. She had been the cleverest student ever to attend Midstate's Womens College. The nimble brain which was hers was functioning again. It spurred the big hard-hitting body guard.

Rickey said, "Okay, baby. Okay. We'll start small. But it'll be a big war when I get around to it!"

JOHN'S EYES opened and his mind functioned weakly, but he was not alive. He was an intellect encased in strict plaster casts, in miles of bandages. The pain was not clear to him. It was something very bad, very far off, something which must be endured in order that it should not drive his mind back to blankness.

His tongue explored his teeth. How had they missed knocking out his teeth? One was rough, splintered a bit, but none were missing. He was, he congratulated himself, very fortunate to have his teeth.

He grinned and a voice above him said, "Live? He'll live to bury us all! He's grinning!"

He knew that voice. He whispered, "Hi, Governor— how's Jean?"

Jean Morrow leaned forward. Her eyes seemed very large and very close. She said firmly, "I'm all right, John. They didn't beat me. They thought I would learn my lesson. That's what they thought!"

John said, "Good."

That was all for a few days. Then it was sunny in the room and the Governor was within view. They had raised his head a little. He saw another bed, a wheelchair, the broad frame and handsome face of the Chief Executive.

Castle said conversationally,

"I had them fix us a double room. It's nicer this way!"

John said, "You mean you were taking no chances."

Fortney Castle smiled. He said, "I wanted you to have the best."

John said, "You're a right guy, Governor."

The next day he felt surprisingly strong. He talked for an hour. When they had finished, he was exhausted, but he had many things to occupy his thoughts. He lay there and pondered.

Rickey came. Rickey said, "I told them you'd laugh it off. What the hell, pal?"

But there were tears in Rickey's eyes. The big man kept crumpling his hat and his feet shifted on the floor. He explained painfully, "I been lookin' for a guy that talks like you. I bet I been every place in town. The guy on the phone had you down perfect, John."

John said, "Wait until I get up, pal."

Rickey said, "I'm just waitin'. There's some things. Joe Gann's been doin' a wonderful job, pal. Him and me have rapped off all the gamblin' joints and half the hot spots in town. That Joe put Jake Klem on the vice squad and then we went to town."

John said, "That's great, pal."

Rickey said, "We hung a fifty buck fine on Charlie Stacker for drunken drivin'. But he was hopped to the eyes. He wasn't drunk at all. On'y we couldn't prove it. So we hung a bum beef on him."

John said, "Good goin', pal."

Jean came every day. It was good to see Jean. She was working too hard, of course, trying to get something out of the dust in the Chief's Office, the scratches on the furniture. There had been no prints. She complained, "They didn't all wear gloves. Some did, but not all. Why are there no prints?"

"Fingerprints are not always reliable," soothed Governor Castle.

But Jean was not satisfied. John warned her about over-working, about the danger of an attack upon her should her activities become known. But it seemed that Rickey, in addition to his other duties, was body-guarding Jean. As body-guarding a long list of folks was Rickey's vocation, and as he had never lost a client until John Wade had turned cop, there were few fears for Jean's safety.

Governor Castle's injuries had been painful but not serious. John felt that the Chief Executive could have left long before he showed any signs of going. They had wonderful talks. John related his experiences as a con guy at great length.

The Governor's sole remark was, "People who are taken by con men have larceny in their hearts—or they would not be inveigled."

BO FOGG came in at last. His round face had grown thin and there was a hard, reckless look in his young eyes. He said, "I can't stand the thoughts of a mob. I'll see this through, Chief. You can count on me for any orders you care to give."

So John gave him some orders. The kid goggled at him for a moment, but finally agreed that John might be right.

The days went along swiftly after Fogg's visit. John was mending with great speed.

He was in a wheel-chair alongside the Governor when two visitors were announced one afternoon. The Governor looked at the names and said, "Send them in."

Two men entered. They were Steve Stacker and his son, Charlie Stacker. John gazed at Charlie Stacker long and avidly. The son of the political czar was as short as his father, but thinner, dissipated. His face was hatchet-shaped, cruel, mean. He was a weak carbon of his strong-visaged elder.

Stacker said solemnly, "I want you gentlemen to know that the People's Party feels as strongly as you do about the events of last month. We are here to offer our full co-operation in apprehending the guilty parties."

The Governor said blandly, "Thank you, Mr. Stacker."

The short man said vigorously, "Wade, can you describe any of your assailants?"

John stared at Charlie Stacker. He said, "The leader was about your son's build. He had a high voice, obviously disguised. It reminded me of something. I don't know what."

Charlie Stacker smirked. John went on, "He was taller than your son. Three inches, maybe. Maybe two inches. How tall are you, Charlie?"

The younger Stacker's voice was husky, the voice of a hard-living weakling. He said, "Five-six."

John nodded. "This man was about five-eight. I noticed particularly, of course."

Stacker said, "They were masked, I understand."

John said, "I couldn't identify one of them."

Stacker said devoutly, "A pity! A great pity. Governor have you appointed a successor to Wade?"

Governor Castle said, "Oh, John will be back on the job in a week or so."

Stacker said, "What? Wade is going back? Why—the man will get killed! Wade—you must be aware of the feeling.... Surely, Governor, you wouldn't ask this man to risk his life—"

Governor Castle said, "Why should there be all this terror because John Wade is Chief of Police of Midburg? Can the underworld be so terrified that they must resort to murder? Is that the message you are bringing, Stacker?"

Steve Stacker said smoothly, "I bring no message, Governor. I know little of the underworld—no more than any other politician. I merely came to bring my condolences. We will leave now. We have no wish to excite you."

Father and son beat an orderly retreat. Governor Castle said, "What do you make of it, John?"

"Nothing," said John. He tried to hide his disappointment. "The hooded leader was taller, there is no question of it."

Governor Castle said, "We'll get them, John. When we are on our feet again, we'll get them."

CHAPTER FOUR
THE SECRET JOHN
KEPT

JOHN HAD been on his feet for a month. He had a ridge of cartilage over one eye. He had a twist to his nose that he would carry to his grave. His ribs were tender and his muscles sadly out of trim. But he was able to get around.

The police department seemed to have adopted a highly non-commital attitude. Official routine went along smoothly. Indeed, under the continued raids of Deputy Gann and Rickey Boles, the city seemed in a fair way to run fresh out of criminals.

Meantime, John learned nothing about his attackers. Jean reported no success from the Governor's private crime laboratory, where she labored over microscopes and test tubes. John was with her as much as possible. Life was running very smoothly on the surface.

Then the First National Bank was robbed. It was close to three o'clock when three masked men coolly held up the cashier and made the usual escape in a high-powered car driven by a fourth confederate. The bank guard tried to shoot it out. They chopped him down with a machine gun.

Joe Gann came into John's office. He said, "I got the squad over at the bank. I came back here. They really cut that guard to hell."

John said, "You got anything?"

"The usual dopey witnesses," shrugged Gann. "The men were tall, they were short, they were dark, they were foreigners, they were not foreigners. The radio squad should be reportin' now."

The police mills ground. The bandits deserted their getaway car, got away in another, unidentified vehicle. The newspapers opened up—and the target was John Wade, Chief of Police.

Gann and Rickey raided a vice resort that night. They were looking for a suspect in a recent killing. One of the girls put up a fight. She got shot in the shoulder, accidentally, when a detective named Jake Klem fired to warn her. The newspapers took that up, too.

One of the holdover policeman from the recent regime got caught red-handed taking a bribe from a little merchant who was violating a building ordinance. It was a matter of two dollars, but the papers piled it on the other charges.

John called in the reporters. He got them all lined up and waited for silence. He said, "You think I ought to resign?"

They agreed that it would be for the best. John said, "I resign."

He walked out of the room. He walked out of Headquarters. When last seen he got into a car driven by Rickey Boles and was driven somewhere out towards the southern city limits.

Governor Castle made a statement. He was "sorry things had gone wrong." It was a weak statement.

The city officials appointed Joe Gann Chief of Police. Joe said that he, for one, thought John Wade had done the best he could. That he had helped in every way. But that of course he—Joe Gann—had his own interests to look out for and would accept the job. He would work hard for the people.

Bo Fogg was not asked any questions, so said nothing. He was removed from duty at Headquarters and assigned to a beat in the suburbs, where nothing ever happened.

AVERY PLACE was on Bo Fogg's beat. It was a respectable, quiet neighborhood with unelaborate houses in a row behind neat lawns. Bo slipped around the back, through a fence and into the rear of Number 20.

A colored woman squinted suspiciously at his blue uniform and said, "I reckon it's all right. Mist' John say so. But Mist' John out o' he own haid, playin' policeman!"

Bo said, "Okay, Evalina."

He went into the comfortable, moderate-sized living room. John Wade lay stretched on a divan. He was wearing a mandarin robe of many hues over a new pajama-slack suit.

Rickey was playing with a well-oiled, vicious-looking sub-machine gun, whistling under his breath as he plied a soft cloth with loving hands. Jean Morrow was sitting in a low chair, looking at John through half-closed eyes.

Bo Fogg said, "You look peaceful. Even Rickey."

John sat up and said, "Everything set?"

"I hope so," said Fogg worriedly. "I got the key. I got six men who'll play ball. It took a long while to find six I could trust."

"At twelve o'clock," said John.

Bo said wistfully, "Couldn't I get in it?"

"Your job is here," said John kindly. "Both your official job and the one you're doing for me. They might grab at Jean if they knew she's here."

Bo Fogg said, "But you'll call me—before it's over?"

"You and Jean must be there," nodded John.

The kid cop said, "Okay, Chief."

He went out the way he had come. John looked at Rickey... Rickey said, "I can't hardly wait."

Jean said, "Are you sure, John?"

"Bo Fogg did the ground work," answered John. "While I was still in the hospital the kid was working. I wasn't sure myself until after the bank robbery. That stuff was too pat. It convinced me. Tonight is the night. Bo heard the tip-off today through a pal at headquarters."

Jean said, "You're not strong, John."

"No" said John Wade. "I'm not strong. I'll never be strong until that beating is receipted. It's a canker gnawing at my guts."

She had never seen his face so twisted. John Wade was not a vindictive man, not a violent man. His services in the cause of Governor Castle had resulted in many deaths, but he had never planned to kill a man. She said:

"John, try to be cool. Keep your head. It's better to play it out with a clear mind."

He made a gesture. He said, "Of course you're right, baby. I—it gets me sometimes."

"It was horrible," she whispered. "I'll never forget the way you fought them, John."

He laughed shortly. "I didn't get far." He was grinning again. She felt better about it. The clock struck the half hour. Rickey patted the gun once more, then took it out into the red coupé.

John said, "I'll see you, baby."

She gripped his hand, holding it tight. She said, "John— you've paid your debt to society. Honest you have."

She was not the clever girl graduate, the physicist, the able stenographer and accountant in that moment. She was a fluffy-haired blonde girl, her blue eyes appealing. John steeled himself and said, "Not yet, baby. I'm still an ex-con guy."

She dropped his hand and murmured, "All right, John. Go to it your way."

"I must," he said. "It's the only way I know."

HE WENT out and got into the red coupé. It was a dark night, he saw gratefully. They could park the car in an alley and it would not be noticed. Rickey nuzzled through the late theatre traffic. No one seemed to recognize them as they turned off and got into the *cul de sac* behind Police Headquarters.

They went in a back door which was seldom used. A detective in plain clothes was waiting for them. He had a machine gun in his hands. It was exactly midnight.

The detective said in strained accents, "It's set."

John said, "You got every corridor under control?"

The man said grimly, "Bo says you'll straighten us out. We got every copper in the building under lock and key."

John said, "Every man must stay at his post. Under no condition must you leave. Don't let anyone in this building except those agreed upon. Right?"

"All six of us took our orders from Bo," said the detective.

John said, "Okay, pal."

Rickey fondled the machine gun he carried. He called the weapon "Tough Thomas". It was a relic of his days among the hi-jackers of another era. He could write his name with it.

They went quietly upstairs. They passed the office lettered:

CHIEF OF POLICE, JOSEPH GANN

They went to another door and John produced the key which Bo had brought to him. The lock worked easily. They entered the room.

It was another office. Its side door was a square of reflected light, shining beyond the pebble-glassed upper half of the portal. Men's voices sounded dimly to the two who crept silently to listen.

There were ear phones in a drawer. Bo Fogg's pal in the Electrical Repair Division had not failed them. John slipped one receiver loose and beckoned Rickey closer. They crouched, each with an ear glued to a black earpiece.

They heard John Wade's own voice say from the next room, "I am the Chief of Police of this town! You will show me respect or I will chop off your head!"

There was laughter, deep throated and defiant. Another husky voice said, "What a laugh! That guy is sunk so far he'll never come up for air."

A full-throated bass said, "Let's get some order here. Let's cut this thing up and decide what's next on the docket."

There was a tiny silence. Then Steve Stacker's accents came plainly, "Yes. Let's get organized. And I'll run the meeting, Joe."

Rickey almost dropped the machine gun. He said, hoarsely, "You dint never tell me, John!"

John said, "That Joe Gann was one of them? You'd have rubbed him out, pal."

He could feel Rickey straining at the leash. He said, "They're all in there. Let's take them, pal."

He placed the ear phones carefully back in their hiding place. He covered the telephone on the desk with his hat and dialed a number. After it had rung twice on the other end he replaced the receiver without talking. His signal, he knew, would be recognized eagerly, promptly.

CHAPTER FIVE
THE BLOODY PURGE

RICKY SAID, "Stand back, pal."

John backed to one side. He had an automatic in his hand. Rickey raised the muzzle of the machine gun in his great hands. He nodded to John and brought the steel down hard at the same moment.

Glass crashed. Rickey steadied the murderous gun, holding it on the group of astounded men. John said, "Take it easy, everybody. We're coming to the party."

He was careful opening the door. He covered them with the flat gun while Rickey came around. A big man in the back of the room made a movement.

John fired from the hip, recklessly. The big man stumbled forward, blood pouring from his face. He was Jake Klem, John saw. He had been in charge of the Vice Squad. He was dead before he hit the floor.

Charlie Stacker stammered, "My God, he's kill-nutty."

John came into the full light. His snap brim hat was down to shade his eyes. He was very pale and his teeth glittered a little between parted lips. Rickey took up a position near the ruined door, blocking view into the office he and John had just quitted.

There were a dozen men in the room. Three of them John recognized as common strong-arm men from the

People's Club, undercover hoods for the Stacker outfit. Six were members of the police force who had been on Tony Maretta's list.

Chief of Police Joe Gann sat like a giant stone image behind the desk which had briefly been John Wade's. Steve Stacker and his son sat across from Gann. The thirteenth man was Jake Klem. He just laid on the floor and bled.

From the room behind them a voice said, "Hands up, Wade!"

John grinned, but it was not a pleasant grin. He said, "No dice, Stacker. When I found out that your father came over here as a ventriloquist, I knew about that. Just a little inherited trick, isn't it?"

Stacker's voice was steady. He said, "All this will only get you in trouble, Wade. You can't get away with it."

"No?" said John mockingly. "Were you ever beaten by a gang? Do you think I care whether I get away with it?"

Charlie Stacker squealed, "He'll kill us all!"

"Got a sore throat, haven't you, Charlie?" asked John "I noticed it when you called upon the Governor at the hospital. You wore a scarf, but I could see the white bandage. You wore lifts in your shoes that day you led this bunch in here, didn't you?"

Charlie Stacker was shaking like a leaf. He said, "The guy ain't human, I tell you. He lived through—"

"Shut up," said Steve Stacker without emotion. He addressed John calmly. "You can kill us. But they'll fry you in the electric chair. You can kill me, but you can't scare me, Wade."

John said, "No? I'm giving you time to think about that. Someone's going to talk. I've got the corridors loaded with my men. I've got plenty of time. I can pick you off just as I please."

He looked at his watch. It was a matter of timing now. He had to take it slow and easy until the stage was completely set. He said, "If any of you have any prayers to say, you can start now."

Charlie Stacker's scarred throat quivered, his eyes bulged. He said, "Can't someone do somethin'? This guy is whacky. Lookit his eyes!"

Steve Stacker said, "Shut up."

The squat politician seemed unafraid. No one else in the room moved. Chief Joe Gann said huskily:

"You're makin' a mistake, John. It's all a mistake."

John said nothing. He held the automatic casually, lifting a cigarette. Rickey's machine gun lolled on his arm. But no one moved or spoke. The moments ticked by.

RICKY MOVED, finally. He got both feet planted and said loudly, "John, I'm gettin' tired of waitin'. If nobody's gonna sing let's clean 'em out and lam."

John said, "Joe? You don't want to talk? Not even about those spectacular raids you and Rickey made to build you up while you were taking graft with both hands to leave certain other places alone?"

Gann said, "You're all wrong, I tell you."

"Joe Gann, the honest cop," jeered John. "How did the prints of Charlie Stacker get washed off my car after the acid missed me? How did the prints get wiped out of this very room after they ganged me? How did they get entry to your office to nail me in the first place?"

Gann made a last attempt. He said, "Stacker—"

"Ah, yes. Stacker," nodded John. "Stacker got Rickey out of the way, Stacker, however, was tooled into it. Stacker's crazy son, Charlie, planted a bomb under the Governor. Then it was necessary to do something. Jean had seen him, almost caught this charming youth placing his dynamite. So they got after me, thinking I would call her off."

"He's nutty," wailed Charlie Stacker as John's hard eyes found him, picked him out.

John said, "Every man has his Achilles' heel. Steve Stacker has his."

The short politician got slowly to his feet as Rickey watched carefully. Steve Stacker said, "You are entirely out of order, Wade. This is ridiculous...."

John brushed him aside. The satanic glitter appeared for a dangerous second, then Steve Stacker sat down again. John fastened his hand in Charlie's collar, firmly dragged him away from the desk.

He shook the youth as a terrier shakes a rat. He said, "You hop yourself up, then you play with people's lives. You drive your car like a maniac all over town, you try to kill people, you play God because your father is Steve Stacker. You played once too often when you played horse with me, rat."

Charlie screamed, "No! Don't let him! Stop him, father."

John backed the Stacker boy around until he could glimpse Steve's face. He deliberately slapped Charlie across the mouth. He said in an ugly growl, "You gave it to me. Now I'm going to give it to you. I'm going to pistol whip you to death, you rat!"

He raised the automatic, holding it by the butt. He brought down the muzzle, slicing at Charlie Stacker's face.

Out of the corner of one eye he saw Steve Stacker reach the breaking point, snap. He pivoted away from the son. He hit the father on the jaw with a right hand which dropped the politician where he stood. He dropped the babbling, screaming offspring atop his sire.

Rickey said, "Hold it, gents. Specially you, Joe. You tossed me once, copper. I'd love to give it to you."

Steve Stacker clambered to his feet, striving for the shreds of his dignity. He said, "All right, Wade. I can't see you do it to my son."

"Talk," said John. "I want to hear it before I kill all of you."

Stacker said, "Charlie planted the bomb. He gets—notions. He thought it would help. He knew I was disturbed about the Fourth Ward graft when you were made chief. So he figured out that acid business. He planted that during the night, of course."

THE POLITICIAN'S voice was steady. He went on, "No court would convict Charlie. He is not entirely sane. After I knew what he had done, I tried to get him in the clear. Joe Gann was always crooked. He made things look good, but he was on the make from birth."

Joe Gann roared, "You lie!"

Stacker said contemptuously, "You fool, you're caught. Wade is smart. He's had certain members of the force working for him since he was in the hospital. I was goin' to tell you that tonight."

Rickey said admiringly, "The coot is pretty wise himself."

John said, "I want the name of every man in that lovely party we had in this office—the guys that mobbed me."

"They are all here this minute," said Stacker coolly. "You shot them. I was not here, of course. I got Boles away. Gann was not here. But the others—my men and the cops—were your attackers."

John looked at the sullen, scared faces of the men. He said, "Charlie had to be there. I got Charlie's throat. The others—anybody want to talk?"

Nobody said anything. John said softly, "Gann?"

The big officer sat silent, glowering like a trapped animal. The others fell away fearfully, inching to leave him alone. John said, "Up, Gann."

Gann weighed all of two hundred and thirty pounds. He came forward, his arms dangling. John said, "You sold out, didn't you, Gann? You sold out to Stacker. Stacker is lousy. He is a foul desecration upon the face of any city. But he is a rat because he cannot help being a rat. Even his spawn is a rodent."

He toed the blubbering Charlie out of the way. He said, "The others beat hell out of me, Gann. They were hired to do it, spurred on by a demented cokey. But without your treachery they couldn't have got me.

"Without your treachery the bank job wouldn't have succeeded. Jake Klem shot that girl on orders from you. The cop that took two bucks from a merchant did so because you and men like you set the example. I'm going to set an example, Gann. I'm not as tough as I was before your thugs got to me. But I'm still tough enough to take on a treacherous murderer."

He tossed the automatic along the floor. It slid to a stop as Rickey blocked it with his toe. Rickey said, "If any of you guys think I ain't watchin', just try somethin'."

John was going forward. Joe Gann lowered his head between his thick shoulders. Through the broken glass of the door to the next office Jean Morrow cried in a small, still voice, "John!"

JOHN NEVER heard her. He stabbed his left. He felt it go home on the big man's face and all the pent-up fury of those weeks of pain, weeks of lying on his back in a hospital bed, weeks of planning and probing with every brain cell he possessed; all those weeks and all that rage took him by the heart and led him.

He threw the right hand. It crashed and smashed and seemed to rumble. It went through Gann's guard and banged against his jaw. The giant trembled from head to foot. His mouth sagged open.

Gann's teeth sprayed on the floor in tiny sounds like the rattling of parchesi dice. He bent in the middle. John hit him relentlessly with a hook. He bent sideway and fell on his bloody face.

The Governor was waiting. Jean stood at his side, notebook in hand. Bo Fogg, another notebook open, was at the desk. The six men with weapons displayed came in from the halls. The prisoners marched, the stretcher bearers took Jake Klem to the morgue and Joe Gann, under special guard to the hospital.

The Governor said, "It will be easy now, John. You've convinced them you can clean up by using their own methods. Bo Fogg's tireless probing, the processes of deduction by which you arrived at your conclusions are police methods."

He coughed, hiding a grin. "The—ah-strong-arm third degree of Steve Stacker was, I understand, also police procedure."

John said, "The job is easy, all right. I've got a man for you, too. Tony Maretta, prosecutor's detective, has investigated the Midburg police force—knows it backwards. Make him your Chief."

The Governor protested, "It's your job, John!"

"I don't want it," said John wearily. "I'm a tired guy, Governor. I need a rest."

Unexpectedly, Jean Morrow said, "John, you're right. You do need a rest."

The Chief Executive threw up his hands. He said, "I know better than to fight the three of you. I suppose Rickey thinks the way John does?"

Rickey said, "Well, Gov. We cleared it up *after* he resigned, dint we? I think we go better undercover, sorta. And John won't have no official plates anyhow!"

www.ingramcontent.com/pod-product-compliance
Lightning Source LLC
Chambersburg PA
CBHW031339020726
47499CB00005B/1327